DANGEROUS FLOTILLA

JONATHAN DIACK

ABOUT THE AUTHOR

Jonathan Diack is an international freelance journalist, editor and author who for many years was based in Southeast Asia and the Middle East. He recently returned to England, to the magnificent dales of Yorkshire. Now editor and associate author for the Old English Press, he is closely involved in the publication of works that reflect the humour and style of great English literature.

ABOUT THIS BOOK

Published in 2021 by Old English Press
ISBN 9781838423452

Every character, place and institution in this book is entirely fictitious and no reference is intended to any living person.

PART 1 THE CONVOYS

Woolwich Arsenal

Near the end of the small tree-shaded canal linking the River Thames with Woolwich Arsenal was a reinforced concrete overhang which provided shelter for munitions barges waiting to unload at the depot. Swallows built their nests in the overhang from which they swooped to collect insects hovering on the surface of the water. A heron stood on the opposite bank unperturbed by the passage of boats watching for ripples that betrayed the location of perch and carp. Beyond the old towpath the barrels of anti-aircraft guns pointed upwards from their bunkers.

There were washrooms and WCs built into the concrete wall for the use of the barge crews. Fresh water and diesel fuel pumping stations had been installed next to the tunnel where the canal flowed into the arsenal. During daylight hours members of the Women's Voluntary Service dispensed mugs of tea and home-made cakes from a mobile canteen on the narrow wharf. Hanging from hooks at the back of the canteen were steel helmets which the WVS staff were supposed to wear during air raids but which in the opinion of the staff were not much good when munitions barges were exploding around their feet.

Pinned to the noticeboard on the concrete wall were details of local church services and dances, advertisements for accommodation and second-hand clothing, tidal and blackout schedules, information on how to grow vegetables in window boxes, official warnings about the hazard of discussing military matters with strangers, and the following notice:

VOLUNTEERS WANTED

Crews required for munitions transport operations in the Grand Union Canal

Previous barge experience essential

Apply to Weedon Narrowboats via your Supervisor or Liaison Officer

From the discussions that took place in front of the canteen, it was plain to the WVS staff that the vacancies at Weedon Narrowboats were not going to be filled promptly. Right now the munitions barges for Woolwich Arsenal originated at Waltham Abbey gunpowder mill linked to the Thames by the comparatively short Lee Navigation Canal. If the Grand Union Canal was going to be employed for munitions convoys the distances would be much greater and the barges more exposed to German bombing raids. Most of the crews shook their heads at the notice, observed the WVS staff.

North Sea Escort Destroyer

'How extremely . . .' said the sub-lieutenant doubling up and clasping his right knee. Transported on a stretcher by the wardroom stewards to the operating table in the sickbay he finished his complaint. '. . . inconvenient.'

'Bad luck,' said the medical officer removing the right leg of the sub-lieutenant's trousers and applying a tourniquet above the knee which had sustained multiple traumatic articular perforations and was gushing blood.

'No rugby for a while,' said the medical officer cheerfully, steadying himself as the destroyer heeled over. The ship must have abandoned the chase of the E-boats which had attacked the convoy and impudently sprayed the destroyer with machine gun fire while escaping.

‘What about dances?’ said the sub-lieutenant.

‘No problem with slow foxtrots. You'll need some support from your partner though, for a while,’ said the medical officer. He removed the needle from the sub-lieutenant's arm, returned the box of morphine capsules to the cabinet and reached for the swabs.

‘Girls are good at that,’ said the sub-lieutenant drifting off into the mists of sedation.

'I've stabilised the wound but he needs surgery,' reported the medical officer to the captain on the bridge. A moderate swell was running. Seawater swilled over the focsle as the bows of the destroyer dipped into the waves. Half a mile to starboard the merchant ships dispersed by the E-boats were resuming their positions. A flock of gulls swooping at the wake of the foremost tanker indicated that the convoy was approaching land.

'We'll be in harbour tonight,' said the captain. 'Send a signal to the port authorities requesting transport to hospital. How are the others? Anyone else hurt?'

The medical officer shook his head. 'Only Lindsey.'

Town Hall, Aylesbury

Chickens squawked from the wake of the motorbike as it sped through the countryside. Crouched over the handlebars, leather helmet strapped under his chin with goggles over his eyes the head of Buckingham's civil defence service, Brigadier Smythe, represented a fearsome sight to the children momentarily submerged in clouds of dust from the machine's powerful wheels as they searched for blackbird's eggs in the hedgerows on their way to school. Clinging to the pillion seat at the back of the motorbike was the brigadier's batman Lance Corporal Barker whose duty was to guard the machine while his superior officer attended meetings, inspected his troops and quenched his thirst in taverns on the way home.

The motorbike halted outside Aylesbury town hall and the brigadier bounded up the stone steps.

'Of all the damned stupid things,' he said to the members of the defence service assembled in rows of old wooden chairs in the main hall. 'What is the point of jeopardising a major industrial artery between the midlands and the south? One bomb and the whole lot comes to a halt. Ridiculous, in my opinion. Anyway, we're not here to criticize. Our job is to prevent damage arising from damned fool decisions.'

'These convoys, brigadier, what exactly will they be carrying?' said a voice from the hall.

'Munitions.'

'Yes, but what kind?'

'CFZ.'

'What does CFZ mean?'

'I don't know. It's a new development.'

'The army must have provided some details?'

'Just that CFZ is significantly more powerful than cordite.'

'Why can't it be transported by road?'

'It's too unstable.'

'In which case, there's not much option but to transport it by water.'

'Of course there is,' said the brigadier. 'Munitions should be manufactured in industrial zones near the point of use, not in rural areas. This damned fool idea simply invites the Germans to bomb the Grand Union Canal.'

Those in the audience who disagreed with the brigadier's assessment of the situation remained silent. There was no point in discussing the validity of government decisions. The brigadier was an excellent man and good leader, well-connected, who got things done but sometimes went off at a tangent. The transport of munitions was always a problem. Whether by road or inland waterway the consequences of a major explosion were inevitably devastating. The answer was to be properly prepared, which they were in Buckinghamshire, thanks largely to the brigadier's energy and efficiency. Patiently they waited for him to focus on the emergency response measures for a breach of the canal.

'So this is what we've got to do,' said the brigadier, hands clasped behind his back while he outlined his strategy.

At night the munitions barges would moor equidistant from locks and never closer than one hundred yards from lock gates or buildings. They would moor opposite the towpath to minimise access by unauthorised personnel. The mooring position would be signalled every night to the air raid precaution (ARP) control room. The control room would arrange for the perimeter of the site to be patrolled to negate the possibility of saboteurs sneaking across country and lobbing hand grenades into the cargo bays. A copy of the safety procedures for the barges would be demanded from the ministry, and reviewed. Appropriate liaison would be maintained with civil defence services in adjacent counties bordering the canal.

Calculations showed that the volume of water released from the breach of a canal was directly proportional to the distance between locks and, where fitted, stop gates. Lockkeepers would be reminded to minimise volumes by closing the appropriate upstream or downstream gates at night, and ARP wardens would check that lockkeepers were complying with the directive. Repair gang locations and callout procedures would be reviewed. Subject to rainfall levels, residential areas should not be unduly affected by flooding. Fields adjacent to the canal would be affected, however, and farmers would be reminded to keep valuable livestock on higher ground or at a safe distance from the water's edge.

Search and rescue teams would be deployed to residential areas where the usual requirement to turn off gas, electricity and water supplies and repair or pull down damaged buildings would apply. Fire and medical services would confine their activities to the perimeter of the explosion and attend affected residential areas and canal-side business areas such as boatyards and warehouses. There was no point, for example, in the fire services wasting water and effort at the scene of the blast where the conflagration should be allowed to burn itself out. ARP wardens would patrol the towpaths as usual, messengers and welfare would be mobilised in the customary manner. Gas decontamination teams would not be required.

'Any questions?' said the brigadier.

It was the police superintendent attached to the team who came up with the most pertinent of the enquiries. 'To what extent has information on the forthcoming CFZ convoys been publicised?' he asked.

West End Central Police Station, London

'Whitehall on the phone, sergeant,' said the duty constable at the front desk of the police station serving London's most fashionable residential area.

'Mayfair transmission again?'

'Yes, sergeant.'

'Get on with it then, send them out.'

To the sound of screeching tyres the constable recorded in the station logbook that a patrol car search had been initiated for the source of an unauthorised radio transmission in Mayfair district, as notified by Whitehall at 0920 hours. Not that there was much chance of success, reflected the constable. They could be anywhere in all that traffic, hidden in a truck, or the back of a delivery van, or the floor of a saloon car.

Bletchley Park

The head of the signals intelligence and traffic analysis section at Bletchley Park walked through Hut 15 towards a desk which, on the surface, contained a mechanical device for sharpening pencils, a calendar and three filing trays labelled *Difficult*, *Too Difficult* and *Impossible.*

'Late night?' he said to the bespectacled figure wearing a tweed jacket and grey flannel trousers sprawled in the chair at the desk. The young man, Rupert Maynard, had been recruited from Cambridge as a communications analyst. Fond of beer, slow to start but, on his day, brilliant by lunchtime, was the assessment of his college. The section head would have preferred someone brilliant after breakfast but beggars couldn't be choosers.

'Frankly I can't remember,' said the communications analyst.

'But you remember where you are now, Rupert?' said the section head anxiously.

'Oh absolutely, clear as a bell.'

The communications analyst removed his spectacles and stared at the section head with a pair of bloodshot but intelligent eyes.

'In which case, Rupert, I would appreciate a summary of the Mayfair radio transmissions case.'

'What aspect in particular, chief?' said the communications analyst reaching for a file in the *Too Difficult* tray.

'Progress, Rupert.'

'Not much there, I'm afraid.

'But you've started?'

'Oh absolutely, knee deep.'

'But not deep enough for a conclusion?'

The communications analyst shook his head. 'Nothing sensible yet, I'm afraid.'

'Some rather important people are pressing for answers on this one, Rupert. So, if you were forced . . ?"

'Right, well, it's perfectly simple, in principle. You locate a police patrol car at the junction of every street in Mayfair and wait for someone to start transmitting. For that you need - I've got the number somewhere - hang on a minute, here it is - thirty thousand police cars.'

'Rupert . . . '

'Approximately, to the nearest thousand.'

'Rupert . . . '

'Hang on - there's another way. Why didn't I think of it before?' The communications analyst pretended to cuff his head in annoyance. 'Don't bother with police cars - simply find a nightingale in Berkeley Square and strap a camera to its legs.'

'Rupert . . . '

The young man removed his spectacles and cleaned them slowly with his college tie.

'There's no pattern to the transmissions, chief, that's the problem,' he said. 'They occur at random intervals, at random times, in random places. 'It haven't given up, but it would help if our friends next door deciphered the associated intercepts.'

'They're trying,' sighed the section head.

Ambassador Club, Park Lane

There was nothing much to like about Fingleton Kelly the floor manager of the exclusive casino in Park Lane where the upper classes disposed of their incomes and inheritances. Smiles of greeting from the members were not returned, save for the faint elevation of an eyebrow which passed for recognition. He did not indulge in small talk. Attempts by members to engage him in conversation were dismissed curtly with a nod and the swift turn of his back. The proprietors of the Ambassador Club employed him to oversee the profitable operation of the casino. There was nothing in his contract that said he had to be on terms of familiarity with the members, any one of whom regardless of wealth, rank or title might during the course a visit drink too much or lose too much and have to be dealt with.

The dinner jacket, black tie and gleaming patent leather shoes did nothing to alleviate the air of cold efficiency that accompanied him across the thick carpet of the casino, eyes darting right and left at the croupiers and roulette wheels and blackjack tables, his fingers snapping at the waiters dispensing drinks or at the hostesses in long white gowns with jewels around their necks stalking their prey.

There was more than a hint of menace about Kelly. The scar on his face contributed to the impression of an unsavoury past. According to one of the hostesses there were scars on his body too, information conveyed at the time in undertones to the other girls with advice to keep clear of the floor manager's apartment in Bermondsey at all costs. The casino staff were under no illusions about his ruthlessness. Croupiers attempting unofficial pay rises were known to have ended up on crutches selling apples from Covent Garden barrows.

This evening, noted the croupiers, Kelly was circling the roulette table nearest the archway leading to the bar. He appeared to be watching a middle-aged army officer in dress uniform wearing a patch over his right eye. The officer, a recent member of the club, was losing heavily and had already cashed a large cheque. The mountain of chips in front of him had almost disappeared and with each unsuccessful spin of the roulette wheel he became more restless, fumbling in the pockets of his jacket as if searching for additional funds.

Slowly the officer reached forward and placed the last of his chips on number eighteen. When the ball in the roulette wheel stopped bobbing up and down and the wheel slowed sufficiently to reveal that the ball had settled over number thirty three he slumped back in his chair. He remained like that for a few minutes staring at the roulette wheel then stood up, swallowed the remains of the whisky, collected his gloves and cap from the cloakroom and disappeared into the blacked-out streets of Mayfair.

Later, at the reception desk, Kelly examined the membership register and entered the officer's home address and telephone number in his notebook.

General Hospital, Ipswich

The cleaning lady in the main corridor of Ipswich general hospital propped her mop against the wall and wiped her face. It was always like this, on inspection days. Anyone would think the royal family was visiting what with all the fuss. Grumbling she retrieved the mop and continued down the corridor to the Officers Surgical ward where she stopped and peered through the partition windows. Such nice young gentlemen. Always laughing and joking, unlike the patients in the medical wards silent in their beds or the poor little wide-eyed mites in the children's wards. Brave too, the patients in Officers Surgical, covered in bandages and plaster. It was a downright disgrace the way Hitler was causing so much pain and injury. He should be strung up and no mistake.

'Nearly finished, Gladys?' said a figure hurrying past in a starched uniform.

'Yes, sister.'

'He'll be here in a minute,' said the figure over her shoulder.

Inside the Officers Surgical ward the patients with beds at the window stared out at the line of cars rolling importantly along the driveway. The pennant flying from the large black saloon at the front of the motorcade heralded the presence of a senior general.

'He's here,' the patients at the window called out.

Two minutes later came the sound of feet trampling along the corridor.

'Lie to attention everybody,' instructed the senior officer in the ward, an artillery captain with legs elevated at forty five degrees by an arrangement of wires and pulleys.

The partition doors swung open and the imperious figure of a full general gleaming with red insignia strode into the room followed by a procession of military and hospital staff. Hands clasped behind his back, moustache neatly trimmed, brass buttons burnished, eyebrows jet black and jaw jutting forward the general advanced from bed to bed addressing in the clipped drawl of a cavalry officer each of the patients lying ramrod-stiff amidst starched white sheets.

'Lindsey,' said the general arriving at a bed in the centre of the room and reaching for the board attached to the rail. 'Naval contingent, eh. What's the matter with you?'

'Injured leg, sir,' said the sub-lieutenant.

'Treating you all right here, food up to scratch?' said the general. 'Anxious to get back to your ship and into action again, no doubt?'

'Not if they blow my other knee off,' said the sub-lieutenant pleasantly.

'That's the spirit. Very good. Nothing wrong with chaps who can joke about their wounds. Carry on, Lindsey,' said the general proceeding to the next bed.

'Pssst,' said the sub-lieutenant to the auburn-haired nurse at the tail of the procession.

'What?' she hissed back.

The sub-lieutenant beckoned her. 'He's just told me to carry on.'

'So . . . ?'

'So, continuing our conversation, are you going to take your clothes off and jump into my bed, or not?'

'Behave yourself,' hissed the nurse.

'You can wait until the general's finished his inspection, if you like.'

'Stop it. I shall call matron.'

'There's not enough room in the bed for matron as well. It's you I want, not her.'

The muffled explosion of laughter from the vicinity of the sub-lieutenant's bed caused the general to glance back over his shoulder.

'There's nothing we can do about it, of course, but I sometimes wish the Royal Navy would stamp down more on their junior officers,' said the general to his ADC.

Grand Union Canal

Dragonflies skimmed the surface of the water in the early morning sunshine. Harold Tree watched from the cockpit of motor barge *Brunnhilde*. He had finished shaving, a practice uncommon amongst canal boatmen. Towel draped around his neck he emptied the contents of his shaving mug overboard, pouring carefully to avoid splashing the graceful insects skimming below on brilliant-coloured wings.

Misfortune had brought Mr Tree and his young family to the canals fifteen years ago. Once a piano tuner he had sought refuge from the poverty of the 1920s by working and living on the water. The money was poor but at least his wife and children slept with a roof over their heads. Schools were out of the question. The transient life of a boatman saw to that. Few canal children could read or write. Mr Tree possessed the priceless advantage of a good education however and every night of the week except Sundays his two daughters were transported under the glow of a paraffin lamp to the world of literature, art and music.

There was a cost. His eldest daughter, nineteen years old now, pretty as a picture with her mother's pert nose, had just left home. Suitcase in her hand, her favourite hat pulled down over her hazel eyes, she had set off along the towpath towards the bus station while they stood waving from the deck of the barge with tears in their eyes.

Well, he reflected, there was no point in educating a girl and expecting her to stay at home and marry the illiterate offspring of a fellow boatman. It was right and proper she should want to advance herself, but the pain was intense nonetheless.

'Don't worry about me, daddy,' she had said, arms around his neck. 'I'm a big girl now.'

Fortunately for Mr Tree as he prepared to descend the steps to the barge's small cabin for a breakfast of porridge, eggs and cream obtained from a farm with meadows along the banks of the canal he was unaware of the method by which his golden-haired daughter intended to advance her prospects.

Special Air Operations, Berlin

The smell of furniture polish pervaded the conference room on the third floor of the Abwehr special air operations building in Berlin. Groups of smartly dressed Luftwaffe officers stood drinking coffee and discussing the latest news from airfields in France and Russia while awaiting the arrival of the Abwehr representative on the air intelligence committee. Mingled with the aroma of coffee, the lavender smell from the polished surfaces of the table and chairs hearkened back to the days of pre-war Teutonic elegance when the building had been a luxury hotel and the conference room a bedroom suite draped with damask fabric.

The Luftwaffe officers stood to attention as the Abwehr colonel entered the room. Waving at them to sit down he took his place at the head of the table.

'So, why am I here?' he said.

The Luftwaffe captain, who had remained standing, clicked his heels and walked to the large-scale map on the panelled wall.

'The main source of ammunition for British troops and ships in southern England is the gunpowder mill at Waltham Abbey here,' said the Luftwaffe captain pointing at the map. 'The ammunition, mostly cordite, is transported by barge down the Lee Navigation Canal here, across the River Thames to Woolwich Arsenal here. The British employ the canal to avoid damage to the road network if we hit one of their ammunition lorries. Both Waltham Abbey and Woolwich Arsenal are protected by barrage balloons and heavy concentrations of anti-aircraft guns. The canal runs within the greater London area and the convoys of munitions barges are thus similarly protected. We have been unsuccessful in targeting the barges so far.'

'We have learned that an alternative supply route to Woolwich Arsenal is being opened, from the ammunition depot at Weedon Barracks here via the Grand Union Canal here. It is possible that the British are merely trying to divert us away from the London area. On the other hand there are reports that the Weedon barges will be transporting a different type of ammunition, possibly more powerful. The arsenal is surrounded by anti-aircraft guns but you will note that, unlike the Lee Navigation Canal, the Grand Union Canal passes through extensive areas of unprotected open countryside. The purpose of this meeting is to seek your authority for tactical bombing operations in this zone of southern England, here.'

With his cane the Luftwaffe captain drew a circle on the map.

'Reckless of the British, this new route, isn't it?' said the Abwehr colonel.

'The Grand Union Canal is a busy waterway, sir, with large numbers of barges carrying coal and construction materials. We anticipate the British will be relying on the difficulty of differentiating munitions barges from ordinary barges, from the air.'

'You can overcome the difficulty?'

'Yes, sir.'

'Do you want to tell me how?'

'Appropriate arrangements are being made on the ground, sir.'

The Abwehr colonel raised his eyebrows but made no comment.

An orderly hurried into the room with a signal pad. Clicking his heels he tore the front sheet from the pad and passed it to the captain who, after studying the contents, showed it to the table.

'Now then,' said the Abwehr colonel leaning back in his chair, 'that complicates your operation.'

The Admiralty, London

The flower vase in the oak-panelled room awarded to the head of the Admiralty appointments division displayed an assortment of roses. Yesterday it had overflowed with gladioli. The arrangement was changed each morning by a WREN secretary who bought the flowers from a stall outside Trafalgar underground tube station with petty cash from the divisional 'Miscellaneous Disbursements' account.

The role of the appointments division was important. The wrong officer in the wrong ship might seriously impair the efficiency of the vessel. An officer promoted too early might flounder, promoted too late and perhaps over-compensate for lost time. The wrong commander in terms of character or qualifications appointed to a capital ship or shore establishment could jeopardise the effectiveness of the entire war effort. 'Never take risks' was the motto of the appointments division. Rear Admiral Haldenby, the square-jawed officer currently in charge of the division, whose career had flourished from successful practical applications of risk taking, had modified his outlook accordingly.

'Senior instructor, Whale Island, sir?' said the lieutenant standing in front of the rear admiral's desk reading from the official schedule of vacant and soon-to-be-vacant positions.

'Who is available?' said the rear admiral referring to the list of names in front of him.

'Phipps, sir.'

'Very well. Approved.'

The lieutenant ticked the schedule, and moved to the next vacancy.

'Assistant Naval Attaché, British Embassy, Washington?'

The rear admiral thumbed through the schedule.

'No names submitted yet. Who have we got?' said the rear admiral.

'Sub-Lieutenant Lindsey, sir. Recently discharged from hospital.'

'Why him?'

'Available, and good breeding. sir.'

The rear-admiral stood and walked to the window. He looked across the parade ground to the trees in St James's Park.

'I dare say it would suit a young officer like him very well, cocktail parties every night, attractive young American females fluttering their eyelashes at him. However, he should be returned to active service as soon as possible, for his own good.'

'His knee, sir. He's not fully mobile.'

'He can walk?'

'Yes, sir, with a stick.'

'Weedon.'

'Excuse me, sir?'

'CFZ convoys,' said the rear admiral.

'But . . . barges, sir?'

'There's more to that operation than meets the eye. Lindsey can recuperate his knee on the Grand Union Canal.'

Grand Union Canal

Mr Browning the managing director of Weedon Narrowboats was not surprised that the applications for CFZ convoy positions had come exclusively from women, and that only three of the applicants were appropriately qualified.

The final interview took place in his office. Mrs Meredith, the personnel manager, sat beside him, the applicants sat on the bench by the window. The papers on his desk included a report from the yard manager to the effect that all three candidates had passed the boat handling test and demonstrated proficiency in the operation and maintenance of canal barges. Separately Mrs Meredith had provided him with typewritten details of the girls' families and background.

Mr Browning adjusted his spectacles. Completely bald and outwardly severe he looked like a bank manager or tax official although the austerity of his manner masked a generous disposition and, as his matronly personnel manager often remarked, he liked a bit of a joke. You always knew when he was that way inclined, she would say, because of the way he leant back in his chair and examined the ceiling while he was talking.

'Miss April Tree, you are from a boating family, have traversed the Grand Union Canal frequently and are familiar with the sequence of locks. You applied for this position voluntarily and are aware that the work involves the transport of hazardous materials from Weedon Bec Depot to Woolwich Arsenal. Is that correct?'

'Yes,' said the youngest of the girls on the wooden bench. She wore a cotton dress, blue hat and solid black shoes. Her legs and arms were bare. Her skin was golden brown from sunshine and fresh air. Her hazel eyes were alert and bright. She possessed a sweet pert nose set amidst an oval face. Her hair was blonde and bob-cut beneath her hat. Remarkably attractive, Mr Browning reflected, for a canal girl.

'Miss Megan Leigh-Harvey, your father is a clergyman. You have interrupted your studies at Cambridge University to assist with the carriage of munitions on our waterways. You recently served on the Lee Navigation Canal as a boatman, and have volunteered for transfer to munitions barges on the Grand Union Canal. You are aware that the work here involves the transport of hazardous materials from Weedon Bec Depot to Woolwich Arsenal. Is that correct?'

The largest of the three girls smiled cheerfully. She was dressed in dungarees, open-necked shirt and boots and conveyed to Mr Browning the impression of a well-fed farmer's daughter more than the academic offspring of a clergyman. Her brown hair was brushed, but not with much care. One of her boot laces was undone. Despite the casualness, however, Mr Browning detected flecks of steel in her eyes.

'Miss Pippa Howland, your parents are artists. You too interrupted your studies at Cambridge University to assist the war effort. You are a friend of Miss Leigh-Harvey and worked on the Lee Navigation Canal as a boatman or perhaps we should say,' said Mr Browning leaning back in his chair and examining the ceiling 'boatmaid. You have volunteered to join the team here and are aware that the work involves the transport of hazardous materials from Weedon Bec Depot to Woolwich Arsenal. You suffered an injury at your previous posting, bruises to your right arm and shoulder it says here, but have now fully recovered and are completely fit. Is that correct?'

The dark-haired girl at the end of the bench, who was dying for a cigarette and had rolled her eyes at Mr Browning's quip about being a boatmaid, nodded. She too wore dungarees and an open-necked shirt but with greater effect than her friend Megan. The silk scarf at her throat converted the shirt and dungarees into an altogether more feminine ensemble. Wiggling her toes inside her expensive shoes she stared impassively at Mr Browning waiting for the bit about danger money.

'On behalf of Weedon Narrowboats and our clients the War Office I would like to thank you for applying to join the CFZ convoy team. All three of you meet our criteria for employment but before proceeding I must acquaint you with the current situation. The flotilla will consist of four barges with a total crew of five persons, two from the Royal Navy, three from Weedon Narrowboats. Unfortunately the naval contingent doesn't arrive until the end of next week. Meanwhile the first two barges are ready for operation and the War Office is anxious to proceed. So we have decided on a trial run. The two available barges will be loaded with empty munitions boxes on Monday and despatched to Woolwich Arsenal to determine the likely average transit time, familiarise the lockkeepers with the processing of munitions barges and sort out any teething troubles along the route. Regrettably we cannot spare any of our boatmen so we would like to invite you to crew the barges for us, for the trial run, as a prelude to becoming full employees of this company.'

Mr Browning looked enquiringly at the girls. The girls looked at each other and nodded.

'Excellent,' beamed Mr Browning. 'In which case I am delighted to welcome you formally to Weedon Narrowboats. Mrs Meredith will give you the appropriate papers to sign after this meeting. Meanwhile I expect you would like to know that on completion of the trial run you will be transporting a new type of explosive called CFZ which we are told is similar to cordite in terms of handling characteristics though more powerful when detonated. From the point of view of safety there's so much traffic on the Grand Union Canal these days that you should be able to slip through without any trouble. Your barges are each painted with the usual red warning band around the hull plus an irregular yellow band to indicate the CFZ nature of the cargo. The purpose of the markings is to allow the appropriate authorities to track your progress, and warn commercial craft to keep clear. The markings are not, of course, visible from the air.

'During the trial run we must ask you to act as if your barges are loaded. For familiarisation purposes we want everyone on the canal to respond appropriately during your passage. If commercial barges, for example, learned that you were transporting empty boxes they wouldn't get out of the way and we wouldn't achieve an accurate estimate of transit times. Miss Leigh-Harvey, as the senior person in terms of years, I'd like you to take charge until the naval contingent arrives. You will be responsible for issuing the daily convoy reports and ensuring full compliance with onboard safety procedures. You will be briefed on these functions in detail before departure.'

'Mrs Meredith will bring you up to date on our battle with the War Office regarding special reimbursements for hazardous work. The rate being suggested is too low in our opinion. Leave that to us. Good luck. I'm sorry we can't release any of our boatmen but they're all allocated to other duties. However, I am confident you three young ladies are experienced and competent enough to see the trial through successfully on your own without support.'

'What he means, my dears,' said Mrs Meredith to the girls later, 'is that our boatmen are too bloody scared.'

Aylesbury Central Police Station

Briefed by his superintendent on matters relating to the recent civil defence service meeting at the town hall, Detective Chief Inspector Standish in charge of criminal investigations in Buckinghamshire summoned Detective Sergeant Quinn.

'How's the family, Sam?' he said waving the sergeant into a chair.

'Doing grand, sir.'

'And your wife?'

'Grand too, sir.'

'Children alright?'

'Yes, sir' said the sergeant wondering what he'd done wrong.

'Good, because you'll be away for a while,' said the chief inspector.

The sergeant's new assignment, explained the chief inspector, was to travel the length of the Grand Union Canal on bicycle, along the towpath from Weedon Bec to London, calling at public houses, boatyards and all occupied waterfront premises to determine the extent to which the initials CFZ initiated a response and, in the event of a response, to ascertain the particulars of the person in question and the circumstances in which he or she had encountered the initials.

'I'll arrange for you to have clearance through adjoining counties. I'm sorry about the bicycle,' said the chief inspector, 'but cars are in short supply. Anyway I expect you'd like the exercise.'

Well-built and affable, a rugby player in his time, Detective Sergeant Quinn conceded with a broad smile that jobs involving fresh air and public houses were not unwelcome. He was also smart enough to continue the sequence of pertinent questions relating to the forthcoming munitions convoys.

'Why not just ask Whitehall, sir?'

'We have,' said the chief inspector. 'They won't comment.'

Grand Union Canal

They called them *Daisy* and *Buttercup*. The official names on the hulls were GUC/WO/W1 and GUC/WO/W2 but the girls decided they would prefer to be blown up in something more friendly.

Daisy was the diesel-driven powered vessel (motor boat) and *Buttercup* was the unpowered towed vessel (butty). Apart from the engine and configuration of towing bollards the barges were identical. The cabins were the same size (7 feet wide and 10 feet long). Each contained a stove on the port (left hand) side which was kept permanently alight for cooking and boiling water for tea and, in winter, for warmth. Next to the stove was a large cupboard for domestic implements with a door hinged at the bottom to form a table. On the starboard (right hand) side of the cabin was a sofa-bed with storage space underneath. At the forward end was a double bed formed by a mattress on a wooden flap which was folded up during the day to provide additional seating space on a bench. The double bed was divided off from the rest of the cabin by curtains at night.

For the first time in her life April enjoyed the privacy of a single cabin. By virtue of greater experience in boat handling she was appointed to *Daisy.* Megan and Pippa slept on *Buttercup*, sharing the double bed which was more comfortable than the sofa. The three girls took turns to cook and dined together in whichever cabin the meal had been prepared.

The most complicated manoeuvre for a pair of working narrowboats is to change from line astern towing, in which the motor boat pulls the butty behind her (singled-out), to parallel towing, in which the two barges proceed through the water side-by-side (abreast), and vice versa. Laughing and cursing at the tow ropes which were arranged differently from the configuration they were used to in the Lee Navigation Canal, Megan and Pippa rehearsed the changeovers under April's direction.

'They'll be more difficult to handle when loaded,' said Megan slumping onto the sofa in *Daisy's* cabin at the end of the first day.

'Thank heavens for shade,' said Pippa following her down from the cockpit. 'April, darling, could you spare a plaster from your first aid box?' She held out her left hand which was bruised and bleeding slightly after a mistimed attempt at securing a tow rope. 'Don't worry, nothing's broken,' she said.

'She's always doing that,' said Megan.

Greenbrook Toll Point

Under the blue summer sky the youth temporarily assigned to Greenbrook toll point to assist Bert Simkins, the toll collector whose lumbago confined him to the chair inside the small octagonal building on the banks of the Grand Union Canal, completed the gauging of the scrap iron barge drawn up alongside.

'Thirty two tons,' he shouted to the skipper.

Belching smoke from its old diesel engine the barge chugged off from the stone quay. The youth waved at it and returned to the toll building.

'Thirty two tons, Mr Simkins,' he said leaning the gauging rod against the wall behind the iron stove which kept the building warm in winter.

'Thanks, lad,' said the toll collector. He withdrew the pen from the inkpot on the walnut bureau, waited for the blobs on the nib to drop back into the pot and having minimised the possibility of blotching the ledger entered the figure thirty two in the right hand column of the page.

'What's next, Mr Simkins?' said the youth.

'Coal barges all day, lad. And before I forget, telephone notification from the Ministry. Munitions barges next week, with new markings. Must be something special. They don't stop, remember. I wouldn't like that kind of work myself, but there's good money for those bold enough. How about you, lad? They're looking for recruits at Weedon Narrowboats.'

'Munitions?' said the youth. 'No fear.'

Weedon Bec Barracks

April had not been to a dance before. Not a proper one. Jigs on the banks of the canal to the music of an accordion with drunken boatmen lurching over the grass did not count as dancing, very definitely did not.

She wore a clean dress. Pippa wore a dress too, of emerald green cotton which suited her dark hair and smouldering eyes. Megan wore slacks and a blouse. Bicycling along the towpath to the barracks the girls agreed to share the proceeds of the evening in terms of cigarettes and alcohol and, they giggled, cash and diamonds from any impressionable dance partners. April was to pretend she smoked and accept cigarettes if offered. Megan, who carried an empty vodka bottle in the voluminous handbag which swung from the handlebars of her bicycle, was to flirt with the bar stewards. Pippa was to pretend she had lost her purse at the railway station.

Strands of music from the band reached them as they parked and padlocked their bicycles. They joined the stream of soldiers and village girls making for the hall, paid a shilling each at the door which entitled them to a free drink and pushed their way through the throng of khaki uniforms towards the bar. Dazed at the noise from the band and the thump of army boots on the dance floor, April lagged behind and was swept into the arms of a soldier who pirouetted her through the haze of cigarette smoke to the centre of the hall.

She stumbled at first, she didn't know any of the steps but during the course of the evening, by virtue of the unrelenting demand for her as a partner, she learned the basics of the most popular wartime dances - the foxtrot, quickstep and waltz.

'Where do you work?' enquired a handsome young corporal, arm around her waist.

'On the barges.'

'No, you're joking, a girl like you.'

'I'm not joking.'

'That's hard work, that is.'

Not once during the course of the evening did April sit down. Each time the music stopped she was surrounded by soldiers wanting to dance with her and offering her cigarettes which she placed in her purse, for future use she explained smiling prettily. The attention of the soldiers was very flattering but she would have liked to sit down to catch her breath.

At midnight when the lights dimmed and the bandmaster announced the last waltz she selected the handsome young corporal from the throng of soldiers clamouring for her attention.

'I fancy you, you know,' he said tightening his grip around her waist.

'Thank you,' she said politely.

'We've got a lot in common.'

'Like what?' said April.

'Things, you know.'

'You mean like feet?' suggested April.

'You're funny, you are. How about I see you home afterwards, if you know what I mean?'

'Unfortunately my father and three older brothers will be waiting outside,' she said knowing exactly what the corporal meant.

Later on the barges the girls shared their spoils. From her handbag Megan produced the vodka bottle which now contained a colourful mixture of vermouth, gin, brandy and green chartreuse. April emptied the cigarettes from her purse onto the table and Pippa waved a ten shilling note in the air.

'From an adorable old major with an eyepatch,' she said. 'I'll share it out tomorrow, when we get to the pub.'

Megan and Pippa, who had spent the evening accepting expensive cocktails in the section of the hall reserved for officers, demanded to know how April had got on, who she had danced with and whether she had encountered anyone interesting.

'Well, there was this rather good looking corporal . . .' said April.

The stillness of the night on the canal was shattered by shrieks of 'Corporal!'

'Listen, darling,' cried the older girls. 'It's a good thing we're here to look after you. No more corporals, do you understand? With your looks you can capture a general.'

St James's, London

Expressing approval of the brown Windsor soup at luncheon, which in itself indicated a privileged background because nobody in their right mind except those who had suffered the privations of a public school education would regard the insipid concoction in question as edible let alone praiseworthy, two elegantly dressed men collected their hats and umbrellas from the vestibule of their club and headed down St James's Street. Faces shaded from the summer sun by the brims of their hats they commented on the shortage of taxicabs but agreed the exercise would do them good and that the display of roses in St James's Park was worth a detour.

'Excellent meal, I thought.'

'You can't beat brown Windsor.'

'In a class of its own.'

They crossed The Mall saluting with their umbrellas the motor cars that slowed down to allow their leisurely passage.

'I hear Buckinghamshire CID has taken the bait.'

'Apparently.'

'That's very good news.'

'So much easier.'

'They're better equipped than us, and zealous too, that's the important thing. Hell hath no fury like policemen scorned.'

The two men strolled through the gates of St James's Park, admired the roses at the entrance and turned left towards Whitehall.

Weedon Bec Depot

The branch of the Grand Union Canal feeding the depot at Weedon Barracks was referred to on maps as the ordnance canal. Wide enough for two barges it ran under a portcullis and continued past the storehouses to the loading quay outside the CFZ compound. At 1400 hours in accordance with their instructions the girls moored *Daisy* and *Buttercup* alongside the quay. The loading operation, carried out by soldiers who filled the racks inside the barges with wooden boxes and battened down the tarpaulins over the holds when they had finished, was completed by 1600 hours. By the time boat traffic stopped for the night (locks closed at 1900 hours in the Grand Union Canal in compliance with wartime regulations) the barges were a few miles south of Grafton Regis moored alongside a grassy bank on the opposite side of the canal from the towpath, as required by the safety procedures for munitions barges. Bicycles were no use here. The girls raced across the field, over the stile, along the farm track and over the lock gates into the smoke-filled saloon bar of the Horseshoe Inn.

'Three beers and keep them coming, bartender,' said Pippa in a low-pitched voice to the squint-eyed innkeeper.

The girls raised their glasses, gulped the contents and reviewed the soldiers' attempts that afternoon at the barracks to flirt with them while carrying the empty boxes onto the barges, attempts that had been constantly thwarted by the loud red-faced sergeant major in charge of the loading operation.

'Did you see the little fat one being marched off for blowing kisses at Pippa?' said Megan.

'I wonder what happened to him?' said April.

'Castration,' said Pippa.

'No!' cried April.

Megan shook her head. 'They only get castrated if they blow kisses at each other.'

From behind the bar counter, under the medieval oak beams which travelled the length of the sixteenth century hostelry, the squint-eyed innkeeper wiped empty glasses and listened to the girls chattering.

'More beer, please,' said Pippa. 'Can you change a ten shilling note?'

Plucking the banknote from Pippa's hand the squint-eyed innkeeper nodded in April's direction. 'She from the munitions barges too?' he said, which April thought was a strange remark.

'Leave her alone,' cried Megan and Pippa. 'She's reserved for senior military personnel only.'

From a chair at the inglenook fireplace hung with brass fittings and sepia prints of horse-drawn barges Detective Sergeant Quinn watched the girls too, but more discreetly. His brown overalls bearing a Ministry of War Transport badge on the front supplemented his cover as a surveyor assigned to inspect the banks of the Grand Union Canal for erosion. A map lay open on the small table beside him, together with a notepad, pencil and pint of beer, chargeable to the government. The notepad already contained a description of the girls. He was surprised at their youth and attractiveness. Somehow he had assumed that the CFZ convoys would be crewed by stout stern-faced older females in bullet-proof vests. The ten shilling note puzzled him. There was an expensive look about the girl called Pippa. Debutante type, he mused, though well-bred girls didn't normally flourish large sums of money in saloon bars. A question mark terminated the associated entry in his notepad.

The girls paid no attention to the man in overalls. At closing time they tripped gaily out of the Horseshoe Inn back across the field to the barges where tired and full of beer they turned in immediately. Silence descended over the canal as they fell asleep, Megan and Pippa cuddled together in one double bed, April's arms around a pillow in the other, each bunk separated from the cargo bay by a thin metal bulkhead.

West End Central Police Station, London

'The cars are back, sergeant,' said the duty constable at the front desk of West End Central Police Station in London.

'No luck?'

'I'm afraid not, sergeant.'

'Write it up then.'

The duty constable reached for the station logbook.

'I've been thinking,' he said.

'That's twice this week,' said the sergeant.

'It occurs to me that these Mayfair radio transmissions always occur when the weather's fine - you know, clear skies.'

'Do you know what I think?'

'No, sergeant.'

'That the biscuit tin in the tea room needs replenishing.'

The duty constable waited until the sergeant's back was turned before making a rude gesture in his direction.

Bletchley Park

The head of the signals intelligence and traffic analysis section at Bletchley Park replaced the telephone receiver and walked along the corridor to the desk with the nest of whimsically-labelled filing trays.

'Good afternoon, Rupert, bearing up?' he said to the communications analyst who was scribbling mathematical equations on his blotter.

'If only one wasn't so thirsty.'

'Never mind, it's nearly opening time. Meanwhile the police in London have forwarded a memorandum to the effect that the Mayfair radio transmissions always coincide with fine weather.'

The communications analyst read the memorandum and jumped from his desk. Shielding his eyes theatrically with his arms as if to protect himself from dazzling rays of celestial inspiration he cried out, 'Of course, so obvious, why didn't I think of it! When will I learn to address complex issues of serious importance with greater thoroughness and perception. Gadzooks, I am undone!'

'Rupert . . .

'To think that a policeman has solved the mystery that has afflicted me night and day for so long,' cried the young man leaning dramatically against his desk as if the forces of inspiration were simply too great to bear. 'To think I have been outwitted, by a mere copper!'

'Rupert . . .

The young man sat down again and retrieved a grey folder from the *Too Difficult* filing tray. 'As a matter of fact,' he said in his normal voice, opening the folder and flicking through the pages, 'according to meteorological data there is no correlation between weather conditions and the Mayfair transmissions.'

'Oh,' said the head of signals intelligence and traffic analysis.

Weedon Bec Barracks

The subaltern attached to the CFZ unit at Weedon Barracks would not have described his superior officer Major Alasdair Macleod as adorable. A more appropriate adjective would have been piratical in view of the major's black eyepatch, although piratical conveyed an impression of ebullience. Major Macleod was not ebullient. The word that came to the subaltern's mind most prominently was taciturn.

On the other hand it was said that the major had been something of a lad in his time. What's more, rumours were circulating that he had drunk too much at last Saturday's dance and been observed giving handing to an attractive girl half his age. It was really very awkward, and frightfully difficult to know how to handle oneself in his presence.

'Excuse me, sir,' he said knocking on the major's door. 'You wanted to see me?'

'Come in.'

Major Macleod was sitting at his desk - jet black hair, tidily brushed, greying at the temples, clean shaven face, firm chin, neatly pressed uniform - in every respect a typical example of a smart and efficient army officer and evidently, by virtue of the eyepatch, a gallant one.

'The loading went well?'

'According to plan, sir.'

'In every detail?'

'Yes, sir. Sergeant-Major Anstruther followed the plan exactly and reported the boxes all fitted in their designated positions without difficulty.'

'Ventilation shafts and stacks?'

'Arranged as instructed, sir.'

'Good show. Any problems?'

'None, sir. . . .'

The subaltern shuffled his feet.

'. . . except that the crew were all female, sir.'

'So I hear,' said the major. 'Why not? It's normal these days.'

'For munitions barges, sir?'

'There's no choice at the moment. I don't like that sort of thing myself but Mr Browning says the women are highly experienced. It's a sign of the times, I'm afraid.'

'Couldn't we lend a hand, sir?'

'Out of the question. We're short of men ourselves, without sending them on boating jaunts. You'll be glad to know however,' said the major reaching for a sheaf of signals, 'that once the shipments start in earnest the navy are sending a detachment.' He thumbed through the signals. 'Sub-Lieutenant Lindsey and Chief Petty Officer Jones,' he read out.

'That's a relief, sir.'

Major Macleod sat back in his chair.

'Security. Add the following to my standing orders.'

'Yes, sir,' said the subaltern reaching for his notebook.

'Sentry to be posted at the gate to the CFZ compound during working hours.'

'Yes, sir.'

'Nobody allowed in the compound without a pass, signed by me.'

'Yes, sir.'

'Gate and doors within the compound to be padlocked out of hours. Two sets of keys, one in the guardroom, one in my office.'

'Yes, sir.'

'In event of fire, for whatever reason, no heroics from the emergency response team. If any of the buildings are threatened by fire the entire area is to be evacuated immediately. Is that absolutely clear?'

Delphinium Cottage

Twenty miles away in a picturesque cottage with a striped green lawn the major's slim and amiable wife Alice dusted furniture. Housekeeping in the absence of maidservants was one of those important duties by which army wives accomplished the wellbeing of their husbands. Other duties included maintaining silence at breakfast while newspapers were being read, making sure that soda syphons were promptly recharged, not blubbing unduly when offspring were killed in action, looking after the garden, gushing politely while conversing with senior officers' wives and, most important, ensuring that male clothes were meticulously preserved, socks darned, shoes polished, uniforms cleaned and pressed.

After dusting the furniture Alice removed her apron and, mindful of her most important duty, climbed the wooden staircase. Alasdair had been to London recently. She had better check the condition of his dress uniform. Opening the wardrobe door she removed the garments and inspected them. Heaven knows what they got up to at those mess dinners and subsequent jollifications. Why, not so long ago, after what had obviously been a riotous party she had found a complete set of Dover sole fish bones in his jacket pocket!

She searched the trouser and jacket. No fish bones, just a handkerchief, and his cheque book which she placed on the dressing table before heading for the door with the jacket which needed pressing. Half way down the stairs she stopped, retraced her steps and opened the cheque book. Except for the stubs, it was empty. Descending the stairs slowly a few minutes later the major's wife looked concerned.

Transit to Weedon Bec

Sub-Lieutenant Lindsey shared a railway carriage with half a dozen children supervised by an elderly lady in a tartan shawl. The children stared wide-eyed alternately at the walking stick resting on Lindsey's outstretched leg and at the cows in the fields visible between puffs of steam from the engine.

'Them's cows?' said the children pointing to the fields.

'That's correct, my dears,' said the elderly lady. 'Do you know what they provide us with?'

'Milk?'

'Quite right.'

The children switched their gaze back to Lindsey's walking stick.

'I've got a stiff knee,' he explained to them.

'Does it hurt, mister?'

'Only when I do cartwheels.'

The children's wide-eyed stares were slowly replaced by toothy smiles.

'Where are you all going?' enquired Lindsey.

'To the country.'

'We're being excavated.'

'Away from the bombs.'

'Evacuated, my dear,' said the elderly lady.

'I'm sure you'll enjoy the countryside,' said Lindsey.

The children edged towards him along the seat, on both sides of the carriage, clutching their teddy bears and toys.

'Where are you going, mister?'

'I'm going to be taking charge of some boats. I'm in the navy, you see,' he said indicating the single gold ring on his sleeves.

'I'd like to be in the navy,' said one of the girls.

'You can't, you're only six!' scoffed the boys.

'I'll be nine next year,' said the girl defiantly.

'As a matter of fact, there are some girls in my crew, and I'm not entirely sure how to handle them. Perhaps you can advise me,' he said to the six year old, whose little pigtails were tied with pink ribbons. 'You see, I don't know what to do if they disobey my orders or misbehave onboard the boats. If they were men I could punish them according to naval regulations, but they're not. Do you see what I mean?'

The little girl considered the matter gravely.

'If they're naughty, I think you should send them to bed without any supper,' she said.

'Excellent advice,' said Lindsey.

Grand Union Canal

By nightfall on Tuesday the barges had reached Marsworth. They were averaging approximately three miles an hour which was faster than anticipated. At the current rate they would reach Woolwich Arsenal on Friday morning, calculated Megan. They had expected to be held up by regular traffic but the sight of the red and yellow danger markings on the hulls as *Daisy* and *Buttercup* bore down on them was enough to scatter the commercial barges to the sides of the canal. *Daisy* and *Buttercup* passed through the locks alone. None of the vessels carrying coal, iron, aluminium and other wartime cargoes to London wanted to berth near munitions barges.

April had never experienced such speed through the Grand Union Canal. She was used to the queues that built up in the approaches to the locks and the jostlings for position which often involved bad tempered protests and shouts and fist waving. Her father had once been knocked overboard by an irate skipper, a large redheaded man who claimed that *Brunnhilde* had manoeuvred unfairly in front of his boat. She remembered her father thrashing about in the water. He couldn't swim. She remembered screaming as her mother reached out with a boathook and dragged him to safety.

The ARP wardens along the route of the canal contributed most to the swift passage. Notified in advance by the ARP control centre of the barges' arrival time they hoisted red flags at the lock gates to warn regular traffic of the approaching hazard. The wardens opened the upstream gates for the girls, cranked up the paddles that lowered the level of water in the lock and opened the downstream gates on behalf of the lockkeepers who pretended to be engaged in important administrative tasks as far away as possible from *Daisy* and *Buttercup.* In exchange for the wardens' help the girls passed them mugs of tea and chatted to them while the water level dropped, enquiring about their families and smiling at them, not exactly flirtatiously but with enough warmth in their eyes to gladden the elderly men's hearts and ensure a reciprocal service on the return voyage.

At a lock near Leighton Buzzard the warden had a familiar face. April dived into the cabin but too late. 'April, is that you? God bless my soul, so it is,' he said when she re-appeared sheepishly. The warden had worked in the boatyard where *Brunnhilde* docked for annual maintenance. 'What on earth are you doing in one of these?' he asked tipping his helmet back and scratching his head. April talked to him quietly and made him promise that when he next met up with her parents he would not disclose the nature of their daughter's current employment.

Delphinium Cottage

Major Macleod's wife, Alice, was on her way to the kitchen to prepare dinner when the phone rang.

'May I speak to the major?' said a male voice.

'Of course. Who's calling?' said Alice.

'Tell him it's Kelly'.

Alice hurried to her husband's study.

'Someone called Kelly on the telephone for you, darling.'

'Kelly?'

From the kitchen she could hear her husband's voice. He was speaking quietly and his words were indistinct. It was highly improper to eavesdrop on a telephone conversation. She normally took appropriate counter-measures when in the kitchen, like running a tap or switching on the radio for the duration of the call. But tonight Alice found herself standing still and listening. There had been something about the man's voice. Cold and, frankly, rather common. Alice was not snobbish but the Macleods moved in circles where King's English was spoken. Tradesmen knew their place and did not normally presume to telephone private houses in the evening.

'Anything important, darling?' she said round the kitchen door when she heard the receiver being replaced.

'Just routine,' said the major returning to his study.

In accordance with the unwritten code of conduct for army officers' wives, Alice did not pursue the enquiry.

Grand Union Canal

Detective Sergeant Quinn trailed the barges from a distance. When they were inside the locks he continued his investigations, recording in his notebook the results of interviews with people who worked in the vicinity of the canal. 'Excuse me, I'm working for the Ministry of War Transport surveying these banks and saw a couple of barges go past with red and yellow markings on the hulls, do you happen to know anything about them, my office didn't warn me about any special shipments' followed if successful by 'That's most interesting, as a matter of fact how did you know they were carrying CFZ munitions, perhaps you're registered on some kind of official communications loop? I do wish my people would keep me informed.'

The drawback with this line of questioning was the possibility of being reported for suspicious activities. However it was a productive line. Quinn was so affable and convincing that people who should have known better, sometimes standing or sitting directly beneath WALLS HAVE EARS notices, responded openly to his enquiries. All the same, just in case, Quinn made sure his police identification papers were safely secured inside his MoWT overalls before setting off on his bicycle each morning.

On Wednesday he booked into a guest house near the junction with the Regent's Canal. He assumed the girls would take the direct route to the Thames via Brentford but the task of trailing the barges in the built-up approaches to the city was becoming more difficult. He didn't want to end up in Brentford to find the girls had chosen the Regent's Canal and were miles away in north London.

Whichever route the girls chose, when they reached the Thames they would cross the river and head east towards Woolwich. To follow them he would have to cross the river too. Studying his map he searched for a likely spot near the entrance to Woolwich Arsenal feeder canal where the girls would moor for the night. Two hundred yards upstream of the arsenal he found what he was looking for. A pub overlooking the river called the 'Smugglers Arms'.

Weedon Narrowboats

'Reporting for duty, sir,' said Chief Petty Officer Jones disembarking from the bus at Weedon and saluting the sub-lieutenant waiting in the shade of an oak tree.

Lindsey returned the salute and shook the petty officer's hand.

'Welcome aboard, chief,' he said.

The two men sized each other up. Lindsey saw a bluff Devonshire face, lined with age and experience, ruddy complexion, twinkling eyes and sturdy shoulders accustomed to the burden of mountainous seas, thunderous gales, cannon shot and gunfire. Jones saw a young officer, inevitably of limited experience, the kind of junior rank he had guided professionally for forty years ashore and afloat, probably without much experience of canal craft and, by the look of the walking stick, temporarily or permanently incapacitated.

'We're not aboard yet, of course,' said Lindsey on the way from the bus station to the boatyard, 'but you know what I mean.'

'Very right and proper, sir.'

'Which would you prefer, bosun or chief?'

'If you please, bosun will do grand, sir.'

'How was your journey?'

'Very comfortable, thank you, sir. Nine hours from Plymouth, not bad these days, all things considered.'

They signed the visitor's register at the gates and walked across the yard towards the office building. Boats in various of stages of completion were resting in the slipways. Bursts of noise from pneumatic hammers and rivet tools scattered the birds from the trees on the other side of the canal. The quay was double-parked with brightly-coloured barges and, in the shade of the fabrication shed, a larger vessel, the size of a coastal minesweeper, was taking shape.

'I don't know which are ours, I'm afraid. I've only just arrived myself,' said Lindsey.

At the reception desk they signed a second register and were led down a corridor to a door marked 'Personnel Manager'.

Mrs Meredith's jaw dropped. She couldn't believe her eyes. The man in the uniform of a chief petty officer standing in the doorway was so like her husband, the late Mr Frank Meredith, that she had to stop herself running across the room and jumping into his arms. The same hair, the same assured expression that made a person feel ever so protected, the same burly chest which, she thought shivering pleasurably at the recollection, would be matted with hair and decorated with an "I love you Mabel" type of tattoo which in appropriate circumstances, she reflected, could be changed and, oh dear, the same twinkling eyes.

She was so captivated by the stalwart chief petty officer that she barely heard the tall sub-lieutenant beside him apologizing for arriving later than expected.

'Not at all, come in, do please sit down,' she said, so flustered that she knocked over the bamboo pen holder on her desk.

Retrieving the pens and collecting herself, Mrs Meredith explained that Mr Browning had gone to Aylesbury. He was the managing director of the Weedon Narrowboats and would be dealing with them personally. He would be back shortly, meanwhile she would be glad to discuss the arrangements for accommodation and victualling. That would be the extent of her involvement because as regulars of the Royal Navy they would have all personnel matters attended to by the appropriate naval department, including pay and allowances. However she would be very glad, indeed would regard it as a privilege, to assist them in the event of any difficulty if required.

Accommodation had been arranged at the Market Hotel until the barges were ready. She had prepared a list of stores for the vessels, she said fumbling through the papers on her desk and knocking over the bamboo holder again. Unfortunately the list appeared to be missing but she would arrange for copies to be made available as soon as possible. The hotel was a family-run establishment and very comfortable. The company would pay for rooms and meals but unfortunately not, she said blushing delicately, alcoholic beverages. There was a cinema in town for entertainment. As members of the armed services they would also of course have access to the facilities at Weedon Barracks, which included a NAAFI store.

'Maggie gets rather carried away with details,' said Mr Browning taking over the induction on his return from Aylesbury and ushering the two men back out into the sunshine. 'But worth her weight in gold. Here we are, this is what you want to see, no doubt.'

He indicated a pair of barges with gleaming green paintwork pulled up in the central slipway.

'GUC/WO/W3 and GUC/WO/W4. Smart looking craft, aren't they? Racing green - an appropriate colour - though not quite as fast as Bentley motor cars, of course,' said Mr Browning.

The boats were identical in specification to the first two barges, which were already in operation and due back from their trial run to Woolwich Arsenal shortly, he explained. The refit had included installation of brand new Lister diesel engines, new steering gear, specially designed racks in the cargo bays for the CFZ munitions boxes, and complete refurbishment of the cabins including new fittings and upholstery. Only the rudders were missing, due within the next forty eight hours, at which time the barges would be re-launched and ready for action. Until then a pair of similar size barges could be made available for boat handling familiarisation purposes on the canal if required although, said Mr Browning, that did not imply any lack of confidence in the seamanship capabilities of the Royal Navy.

'Definitely required for me,' said Lindsey.

'Why not look around while I make some arrangements?' said Mr Browning.

'I mean it, bosun. I've never handled one of these before,' said Lindsey as Mr Browning departed leaving them on the slipway.

'Nothing to it, sir,' said the bosun.

'You have?'

'Yes, sir. Many times, seeing as how I grew up near the Exeter Ship Canal. Heavy old dears, they are, but docile and easy to manouevre. Don't worry, sir, you'll soon get the hang of them.'

'Good. I don't want to make a fool of myself in front of the girls.'

'Girls, sir?'

'The other two barges are crewed by females - volunteers, experienced in canal and munitions convoy operations apparently - but girls, I'm afraid.'

'I see, sir.'

'We'll talk about that particular aspect of the job later. Meanwhile, let's get aboard, bosun.'

The bosun watched thoughtfully as his new commanding officer made three unsuccessful attempts at hoisting his right leg over the gunwale of the nearest barge before eventually managing to hop onboard with the aid of his walking stick.

The Admiralty, London

'How's it going at Weedon?' said Rear Admiral Haldenby rising from his desk on conclusion of the morning meeting and walking to the table in the centre of his oak-panelled office.

'Lindsey has taken up the appointment, sir' said the admiral's assistant from the door.

The assistant consulted his schedule and frowned.

'There's a note here about flags, sir.'

'Flags?'

'Yes, sir, apparently Lindsey has requested permission to fly the white ensign.'

The rear admiral raised his eyebrows.

'From his barge?'

'Yes, sir.'

'A civilian vessel?'

'The flotilla is under the command of a serving naval officer, sir.'

'Yes, but the barges are owned by Weedon Narrowboats and leased by the army.'

'It's complicated, sir.'

'Anyway, Operations will sort it out.'

'Yes, sir.'

The rear admiral leaned over the table and sniffed the arrangement of fresh freesias in the flower vase.

'Lindsey will be asking for a Royal Marine band next.'

Smugglers Arms, Woolwich

The appearance of the Smugglers Arms had not changed for hundreds of years. Spared the great fire of London by the wide expanse of the river at Woolwich the exterior displayed its original Elizabethan timbers and leaded windows. The cavernous dark interior with low ceilings and sawdust floors was still partitioned into sections of rough-hewn stalls dimly illuminated by candlelight. The ceilings were so low that customers were forced to stoop in transit from the bar to the benches with tankards of ale drawn from ancient oak barrels. Carved into the wooden partitions were the initials of countless swashbuckling brigands who in earlier times had feasted in the hostelry with wenches upon their knees before setting sail from Woolwich to plunder and enrich themselves at the expense of innocent seafarers.

Landlubbers were not welcome in the Smugglers Arms. Ignored they waited for service at the end of the bar under the scornful eye of a grey parrot which screeched at them 'Pieces of eight - one, two, three, five, fuck forgot the four - Pieces of eight - one, two, three, five . . .' The hostile stares from the regulars were not conducive to revelry so, when eventually served, the landlubbers gulped their drinks, paid the inflated prices demanded by the proprietor and hurried from the premises.

From the gloom of an inner stall Captain Binbow, the scar-faced owner of a converted trawler which subject to price could be engaged for activities of questionable legitimacy, watched as three girls came through the door and walked gaily to the bar. The crews of the munitions barges were frequent visitors to the inn. They were not subjected like the landlubbers to sullen receptions and overpriced beverages. The wharf downstream of the Smugglers Arms was a popular port of call for barges preparing to unload at nearby Woolwich Arsenal. Binbow recognized two of the girls and could hear them introduce the third, an attractive young female with bobbed hair, to Black Jake, the proprietor of the establishment rumoured to be the great grandson of the infamous Crossbones Hawkins.

Across the room in a distant stall, a stranger sat examining a map in the light of a battery-operated torch. He had been there all afternoon. Unperturbed by the surly greeting from Black Jake the stranger had ordered a sandwich with pickles which he had eaten slowly between sips of ale, replenishing his glass twice and giving no sign of imminent departure. Binbow didn't like the look of the man at all. For a start he was wearing overalls which Binbow, no stranger to the world of covert operations, regarded as suspiciously clean. Then there were the questions he had asked about the different markings of river and canal barges, which Black Jake had deflected, growling that he was an innkeeper not a beeding encyclopedia. And finally the way the man had leaned back in his stall and pretended not to notice the arrival of the girls. Policeman, decided Binbow, reaching for his tobacco pouch.

West End Central Police Station, London

Spattered with rain the windows of West End Central Police Station in London resembled abstract works of art. The layers of dirt and dust from the recent spell of hot weather were etched with rivulets from the summer shower. A bucket in the corner of the reception area collected water from a leak in the roof. The plinking noise irritated the duty police sergeant who was breathing heavily over a confiscated photograph of a nubile young lady wearing remarkably little in the way of underclothes.

'Do something about it, Johnson,' he snapped.

'About what, sergeant?'

'The plinking noise.'

'I've been thinking, ' said the duty constable emptying the bucket out into the street.

'Not again, Johnson.'

'If my theory is right, the radio transmissions will stop during wet weather.'

'Do you know what I think?' said the sergeant.

'That the biscuit tin needs filling, sergeant?'

'That we need more of these photographs. How many did we confiscate? I'd like to see the complete collection, for investigative purposes.'

Bletchley Park

The head of the signals intelligence and traffic analysis section at Bletchley Park hurried along the corridor of Hut 15. In his hand he carried a scathingly critical memorandum from Whitehall mandarins to Scotland Yard, copied to Bletchley, regarding lack of progress on the Mayfair radio transmissions which, they pointed out, were taking place right under their very noses.

'Good morning, Rupert, how are we today?' he said to his communications analyst who was sitting with his feet on his desk staring blearily out of the window, cradling a mug of coffee in his hands.

'Frankly, not as bright as usual,' said the communications analyst, slowly removing his feet from the desk and sitting upright in his chair.

'I hesitate to impose on your recovery, Rupert, but have a look at this.'

The communications analyst squinted at the memorandum.

'It's a piece of paper.'

'Read it, Rupert,' said the section head patiently.

The communications analyst put on his spectacles and read the contents, his lips moving slowly in conjunction with the motion of his eyes.

'Somebody woke up on the wrong side of the bed this morning,' he said.

'Yes,' said the section head.

'Not very polite.'

'No.'

'Quite amusing though, scything through the police like that.'

'They're pleading for our support, Rupert. What can we tell them?"

'I'm afraid we're still stuck, chief.'

'There must be something we can suggest. How about roadblocks at strategic locations.'

'You mean, stop traffic in central London?' said the communications analyst.

'Something like that.'

'Including military vehicles, fire engines and ambulances?'

'No, of course not, Rupert. You'd have to let official vehicles through. You can't bring London to a complete standstill.'

'What if the transmissions are coming from an official vehicle?'

'Oh dear, a fake ambulance - I hadn't thought of that.'

The head of the signals intelligence and traffic analysis section returned along the corridor to his office where he threw open the window, took a deep breath of moist air from the recent thunderstorm and reached into his jacket pocket for the packet of aspirins that helped him endure the challenges of warfare.

Grand Union Canal

In pouring rain Lindsey steered the motor boat towards the butty floating untethered alongside the bank. Water dripped from the sides of his sou'wester. Fifty yards from his target he saw that the motor boat, on loan from the yard together with the butty for the purpose of boat handling practice, was going too fast. He cut the engine and tried to engage reverse gear. There was a loud clanging noise from the engine compartment accompanied by the smell of burning oil.

'Sorry, bosun,' he called out. 'I'll go round again.'

'Take your time, sir,' said the bosun waiting patiently with a towing strap in the bows of the butty.

Lindsey steered the bows of the motor boat into the bank and allowed the stern to swing round. While the stern was moving he stopped the engine and rechecked the gear positions. Back in open water opposite the boatyard he turned the barge using the same bow-into-the-bank manoeuvre and approached the butty again. This time he judged the speed correctly. Adjusting direction to allow for the sideways thrust of the propeller in reverse, he nudged the motor boat alongside the butty, leaned over the gunwale and attached his towing strap to the nearside stern bollard.

'Proper job, sir,' said the bosun as the straps took the strain, binding the barges together in abreast formation.

Grosvenor House Hotel, Mayfair

Seated regally in the lobby of the Grosvenor House Hotel drinking cocktails with quaint colonial names like 'Manhattan' and 'Mombasa Screwdriver' the wives of well-heeled members of London society discussed the latest divorce cases whilst waiting for their husbands to take them into dinner. Without exception they wore long gowns and diamonds. Sophisticated, sharply amusing, they glanced reprovingly at the waiters who flinched when percussion from the bombs falling in the vicinity rattled the windows of Mayfair's favourite watering hole.

Amidst the opulent splendour, Fingleton Kelly, floor manager of the nearby Ambassador Club, sat in an armchair smoking a cigarette. He was wearing his customary dinner jacket and black tie and from a distance looked smart enough to be mistaken for a person of distinction. Closer examination however revealed a pinched countenance and a cigarette held uncouthly between finger and thumb. Fingleton Kelly was not, evidently, a gentleman. Seated beside him, separated by a small table, was a middle-ranking army officer.

'When I think of my days as a street orphan in Dublin, when cabbage leaves were something to be fought over with shards of glass from broken bottles, and I look around me tonight, I feel aggrieved. I mean just look at them,' said Kelly.

The army officer stared silently into his whisky glass.

'The diamonds alone could feed Ireland for a year. I doubt anybody here has ever seen a cabbage, let alone eaten one. Do you know what's on the menu this evening?' said Kelly nodding in the direction of the dining room. 'Lobsters - flown from Scotland courtesy of the RAF.'

'Really,' said the army officer without expression.

'I'm not complaining - I'm not a socialist. As a matter of fact I'm quite comfortably placed these days,' said Kelly drawing on his cigarette. 'They look after their employees, at the Ambassador Club.'

Peals of laughter from the regal throng drowned the sound of a fire engine clanging past the hotel.

'How are things at the barracks?' said Kelly.

'Barracks?' said the army officer.

'Weedon.'

'What makes you think I'm posted there?'

'Your home address. Being so near, I assumed . . .'

'I'm afraid I cannot discuss military matters.'

'Quite right. You never know, I might be a spy,' laughed Kelly.

The army officer did not return the smile.

'Talking about looking after people, in addition to the generous staff remuneration policy the Ambassador Club takes a sympathetic attitude to debt. Which is why, of course, I suggested we have this little chat.'

The army officer waved his hand airily. 'I'll pay it back.'

'Naturally,' said Kelly. 'The club's attitude is that a friend in need becomes a friend indeed. We want everything to be sorted out amicably - normal service to be resumed as soon as possible, so to speak.'

'I'm relieved to hear it.'

'It's slightly more awkward, unfortunately, when the debt is forced on the club.' Kelly drew from his dinner jacket a cheque for fifty pounds marked "Refer To Drawer" in red ink. 'The management prefers indebtedness to be the subject of prior arrangement.'

Unaccustomed to being reproached by persons of subservient status the army officer struggled to control his temper.

'I didn't realise it would bounce,' he said.

'Of course you didn't. Someone in your position would hardly make a habit of passing dud cheques.'

'There were sufficient funds in my account, I thought.'

'Naturally.'

'I'll sort it out.'

'Of course you will. The problem is, when? We must try to avoid complications.'

'Complications?' said the army officer.

'Take the case of the distinguished member of the club from a different part of the country who recently ran into a spot of difficulty like you,' said Kelly. 'To avoid solicitors and publicity and similar inconveniences, he sold some land and, hey presto, everything was back to normal.'

'I don't have any land.'

'You have a salary?'

'Yes.'

'There we are then. All you need is a temporary loan. You can't approach your bank, I suppose?'

'Hardly.'

'Well then,' said Kelly extracting an envelope from his pocket and passing it across the table.

The army officer took the envelope, looked at it thoughtfully then sliced it open with his finger.

'One hundred pounds!' he exclaimed.

'To keep the wolf from the door, so to speak,' said Kelly.

'Where does it come from?' said the army officer.

'A charitable foundation, shall we say. Dedicated to the welfare of people in need. The other item in the envelope is a short form of agreement, for one hundred and fifty pounds. On acceptance of the agreement, the foundation will settle your account with the club, leaving you with one hundred pounds to be repaid at your convenience, at a modest rate of interest. What do you say to that? Next time you visit the club you might even want to consider placing the hundred pounds on a colour and, if it comes up, making yourself a handsome profit.'

'What precisely is your modest rate of interest?' said the army officer.

'Twenty percent,' said Kelly.

'Per year?'

'Per month.'

The army officer gave a hollow laugh. 'You chaps certainly know how to make a living.'

He stared at the banknotes and sheet of paper then slowly reached for the fountain pen in Kelly's outstretched hand.

From his armchair, watching the army officer depart through the swing doors of the hotel, Kelly reflected that war heroes with eyepatches were no different to other people when they ran out of money.

MV 'Sea Snake'

Captain Binbow tapped the barometer in the wheelhouse of his converted trawler *Sea Snake*. The trough of low pressure responsible for the rainstorms over England had passed. The weather was set fair. With luck there would be a moon tonight. The tide was running south-east 230 degrees 5 knots according to the tide tables. At the predicted wind speeds he could hold the trawler steady enough for a transfer.

'Keep your eyes skinned,' he said through the open window to O'Reilly the deckhand.

'That I'm doing, to be sure,' said the deckhand staring intently at the horizon.

'You're looking in the wrong direction, you fool,' snapped Binbow.

The deckhand lowered his hands from his eyes and walked to the window.

'What direction is it that you'll be wanting?'

'Give me strength,' snapped Binbow. 'I've already told you a dozen times. Over there!'

Binbow turned and pointed in the direction of Chatham Dockyard approximately twenty miles southeast of the trawler's position.

'At the first sight of a warship coming from that direction, shout. Is that clear?' he snapped.

Town Hall, Aylesbury

Humming a tune from this morning's 'Music While You Work' radio programme Lance Corporal Barker stood outside Aylesbury town hall guarding Brigadier Smythe's motorbike. The rain clouds had dispersed and the sun beaming down from a blue sky reduced the likelihood that the lance corporal's face would be drenched with muddy water when the brigadier took a corner at high speed. Inside the town hall the brigadier was presiding over a training lesson for new ARP wardens. The lance corporal checked his watch. If the lesson finished soon they should be back in time for lunch. The brigadier's cook had promised him jugged hare with mashed potatoes. Visualising the plate deep in rich dark gravy he observed a dishevelled figure stumbling from the pub across the street towards him.

'Gie us a lift, Jimmy,' said the figure, identified as being of Scottish descent by his speech and the accompanying cloud of whisky fumes.

'On your way now,' said the lance corporal firmly.

'Here's tuppence for the ride,' said the figure fumbling in his trouser pockets and collapsing onto the pavement.

The lance corporal was about to reach for the ankles of the comatose figure and pull him clear of the motorbike when the doors of the town hall flew open.

'Felled him, have you, Barker?' cried the brigadier striding down the steps. 'Good man. Trying to make off with the bike, was he?'

'He's drunk sir.'

'We can't have that. No reason to let standards drop in wartime. We'll inform the police, let them handle it. Come on,' said the brigadier jumping onto the motorbike.

At the central police station a few minutes later the brigadier came face to face with Detective Sergeant Quinn.

'Quinn, isn't it? What are you doing here, in those overalls? Oh, I get it,' he said tapping his nose when the sergeant offered no explanation. 'Not a word to mother.'

Grand Union Canal

"Hands fall in. Clean ship". He must have piped those commands a thousand times in his seafaring career. In a thousand places - Scapa Flow, Trincomalee, Singapore, Hong Kong, Bermuda, Rosyth, Gibraltar. In Malta, on the mighty battlecruiser HMS *Rodney* anchored in Grand Harbour under the ramparts of Valletta. He could still hear the sound of sailors clambering through the hatches with buckets of hot water and the shouts of the petty officers and the cries of seagulls circling overhead and the expletives from the sailors as the seagulls despoiled the white surface of the immense teak decks.

What would his shipmates think of him now, Chief Petty Officer Jones, standing in the cockpit of a canal barge with a mop in his hand?

They would laugh, of course, and talk about it in the mess and recount how CPO Jones had once reprimanded Lord Mountbatten for untidy ropework and perhaps, if they were feeling generous, recall the regattas he had won and the lives he had saved at Jutland and then, with reference to their old shipmate's latest and probably last posting before retirement, shake their heads and murmur 'how the mighty fallen.'

But they would be mistaken. Senior ratings approaching retirement were normally posted to shore establishments to spend their closing years at desks, passing pieces of paper from department to department, or in lecture halls poised in front of blackboards explaining to naval recruits the principles of laying guns or loading torpedoes or marking-up charts. Laugh by all means but at least their old shipmate was afloat, in a vessel of his own, newly painted, smart as belaying pin, on active service contributing to the defence of the nation from a small but nonetheless important front line position.

He removed his jacket and hung it on the tiller. After two days of rain the sky had cleared. The temperature was climbing again. The trees on the banks of the canal provided shade in the early morning but the sun soon escaped the shelter of leaves and burned down on the pair of barges moored upstream of the boatyard. Wiping his brow he continued along the gunwale with his mop. By now he knew every inch of munition barge GUC/WO/W4 and every inch, from the stove in the cabin to the forward rope locker, was as clean and shipshape as a baby's powdered bottom.

'Flotilla vessels in sight, bosun,' he heard the sub-lieutenant call out.

He shaded his eyes and looked in the direction of the lock. The gates were opening. Two green barges, secured abreast, with red and yellow markings above the waterline, were emerging.

He lashed the mop to the bulkhead and returned along the gunwale to the cockpit to collect his jacket. The sound of dance music drifted through the air, growing louder as the pair of barges glided towards them from the lock. He glanced sideways. The sub-lieutenant was standing to attention. The bosun buttoned up his jacket and stood to attention too.

'Better greet them properly, bosun,' the sub-lieutenant called out.

As the barges drew level the girls onboard started waving. How the mighty fallen indeed. His shipmates would have enjoyed this particular scene, CPO Jones standing to attention in the stern of a munitions barge saluting a group of attractive young females swaying to the music of the Glenn Miller orchestra. Controlling his smile the bosun watched, nodding approvingly, as the girl at the helm of the motor boat swung the pair of barges inwards and came alongside the bank without bumping or scraping the timber piles, thirty yards upstream.

He followed the sub-lieutenant along the towpath. During the first bout of introductions and handshakes he stood respectfully to the rear.

'I'm Megan. This is April, our boat handling expert and resident beauty queen, and this one is Pippa, cabin boy,' said the biggest of the girls.

'My name's Lindsey. It's a pleasure to meet you all,' said the sub-lieutenant extending his hand.

The girls were dressed in dungarees, short-sleeved shirts and gym shoes. Not much older than his grandchildren, thought the bosun. Early twenties, perhaps younger. Faces shining from the sun, wind and rain. As healthy and attractive representatives of the gentle sex as one would be privileged to find anywhere in England, he thought. Exceedingly pretty, the one with bobbed hair and hazel eyes. He felt a surge of pride that such attractive carefree young ladies should be risking their lives on a munitions convoy.

Lindsey was beckoning him forward.

'This is Chief Petty Officer Jones,' said the sub-lieutenant. 'He's the flotilla bosun.'

Grinning broadly he shook hands with the girls.

'I hope you didn't mind us waving at you. Should we have saluted first? You won't court martial us?' said Megan relieved at handing over command of the barges so that she could get on with her job and not have to worry about distractions like daily reports.

'Not on your first day,' smiled Lindsey.

Pippa, amused at the contrast between her dirty clothes and the smart naval uniforms, recognised in the bosun's twinkling eyes the promise of spicy yarns to enliven nights on the water after the pubs had closed.

'What exactly does a bosun do?' she asked him.

'Keeps everything shipshape and administers the daily rum ration, miss.'

'Rum ration!' she cried, clapping her hands.

By contrast April remained silent throughout the encounter. In nineteen years of life as a canal boatman's daughter she had never seen anything as handsome and glamorous as the tall sub-lieutenant propped on a walking stick a few feet away smiling down at her. She had fallen immediately and deeply in love.

Market Hotel, Weedon Bec

They dined at the Market Hotel accompanied by the personnel manager Mrs Meredith and managing director Mr Browning.

'Dinner is on us tonight,' said Mr Browning smiling benevolently at the group of nicely dressed young ladies and men in smart uniforms assembled around the oval table in the chintz-furnished dining room hung with hunting prints.

Mrs Meredith had arranged a room for the girls so that they could freshen up after the journey to Woolwich. The had girls rewarded her with grateful hugs, and thanked her again at the table.

'Oh, it was so heavenly, a hot bath! Thank you, thank you, darling Mrs Meredith,' they cried.

'I know what's it like, my dears,' said Mrs Meredith.

'Imagine if there was a bath on one of the barges,' sighed Pippa.

'Unfortunately,' said Mr Browning leaning back in his chair and examining the ceiling, 'the army would be unlikely to approve the installation of bathing receptacles, female, for the use of.'

'Never mind, my dears. We'll book a room for you each time you come back,' said Mrs Meredith.

During the course of the excellent mushroom pie, roast chicken and strawberry trifle feast April asked the handsome sub-lieutenant sitting opposite her about his wounded leg.

'I was standing in the wrong place at the wrong time. Very careless of me, but it's fine now,' said Lindsey.

'Does it hurt?' said April.

'Hardly at all,' said Lindsey.

'Won't it be difficult on the boats, with a walking stick?' said April.

'The answer's perfectly simple,' said Megan. 'Our new skipper stays in the cockpit while we're on the move, and we handle the ropes for him.'

'The ARP wardens do all the work in the locks anyway, thanks to April' said Pippa.

'Not thanks to me!' protested April.

'Thank you for your concern. Actually I can manage the gunwales quite well now,' said Lindsey. 'The bosun can testify to that, and I'm getting better at them every day.'

'That's the ticket, you'll be chasing the girls across the fields soon,' said Mrs Meredith fortified by several large glasses of sherry before dinner.

'Why would I want to do that, Mrs Meredith?' said Lindsey lightly.

'Get on with you!' guffawed Mrs Meredith, winking slyly at the bosun.

'It certainly solves the problem of bombing raids,' said Pippa.

Lindsey raised his eyebrows.

'What problem?' he said.

'The instruction for staying onboard during attacks. We're more likely to be killed running away, the experts say, because bombs rarely hit their intended target, and we'd probably run straight into the blast. Now we've got another reason for remaining on the boats,' said Pippa. 'We can't very well run off and leave our skipper behind.'

'That's very chivalrous of you but, if the instruction from the experts ever changed, I would probably get ashore quicker than most,' smiled Lindsey.

'We would help you,' said April quietly. 'Can you walk well enough to dance?'

Lindsey looked into the pair of radiant eyes examining him across the table.

'It's funny you should say that. Apparently that was my first question after I got shot. Not very heroic, but it seemed important at the time.'

'April loves dancing. She's graduating upwards from her current boyfriend, an army corporal,' said Pippa.

The beautiful eyes flashed.

'He is not my boyfriend!'

'Unfortunately you will all miss Saturday's dance at Weedon Barracks, ' said Mr Browning. 'The boats are scheduled for loading tomorrow - you'll be half way to Woolwich Arsenal by the weekend.'

Aylesbury Central Police Station

Detective Sergeant Quinn reported to the chief inspector's office in Aylesbury central police station and waited while the inspector read his report.

'Everywhere, Sam?' said the chief inspector, looking up halfway through the document.

'Whitehall might just as well have erected notices along the length of the canal announcing that a powerful new type of explosive was about to be transported by barge, sir,' said Quinn.

'A fishing expedition, then,' said the chief inspector finishing the report.

'It looks that way, sir.'

'It doesn't surprise me.'

The chief inspector offered Quinn a cigarette.

'No thanks, sir.'

'Of course you don't smoke. You're looking fit and suntanned, Sam. Lost some weight?'

'Yes, sir,' grinned Quinn.

'Are these your expenses?'

'Yes, sir.'

'Two pints of beer a night? Very modest, after all that bicycling,' said the chief inspector thumbing through the receipts and signing the form.

'It was hot, sir. Most of the time.'

'Two birds with one stone, then,' said the chief inspector leaning back in his chair. 'Divert attention from the Lee Navigation Canal, and flush out any snoopers.'

'Why don't they just tell us, sir, straight out?'

'It's a game, Sam. They're taught it at boarding school.' The chief inspector rose from his chair, tipped an imaginary straw hat over his eyes and, humming the Eton boating song, pretended to punt along the river past Windsor Castle. 'If we work it out for ourselves, we're more likely to respond effectively, that's their strategy. They don't have enough people to tail the CFZ convoys, so they delegate, so to speak.'

'It may be a game, but there are girls on those barges, sir.'

'So I see from your report. I hope they've been properly warned. Anyway, it's back to the Grand Union Canal for you. We need to stop snoopers passing convoy times and locations to Herr Goering. I'll speak to the other counties and tell them Buckinghamshire is taking control, subject to the usual notification in event of arrests. Is your family alright, Sam?'

'Yes, sir.'

'Children?'

'Fine, sir.'

'Good luck. One more thing,' said the chief inspector as Quinn stood up. 'The manufacturing process for CFZ cordite is completed within a special facility at Weedon Barracks. An army major called Alasdair Macleod is in charge of the operation. Special Branch are interested in him - drinking heavily, gambling, that sort of thing. Keep an eye on him, will you?'

'Very good, sir.'

Quinn walked towards the door.

'And stay clear of those barges during air raids,' said the chief inspector.

Grand Union Canal

CPO Smith gently imposed authority over the operation and maintenance of the barges, pointing out to the girls the seemingly unimportant fittings on the vessels which if not cared for properly could result in corrosion, slippery surfaces and accidents. He obtained a small portable pump from the boatyard for hosing down the cargo tarpaulins which delighted the girls who had spent hours during the first voyage trying to keep the tarpaulins clean with brushes and mops. On the motor boats the power supply for the pump was taken from the electrical distribution board, and on the buttys from the small diesel-driven generator sets which supplied electricity to the cabins.

Equally gently, Sub-Lieutenant Lindsey declined the proposal from the girls that the second pair of barges GUC/WO/W3 and GUC/WO/W4 be named *Primrose* and *Tulip* explaining that the alphanumeric designations had to be retained for official reporting purposes. Instead he agreed to a simplified format whereby the boats would be referred to as W1, W2, W3 and W4, and promised the girls that they would not be court-martialled for referring, informally, to the original pair of barges as *Daisy* and *Buttercup*.

Existing vessel and cabin allocations would be retained. April would continue on motor boat W1 (*Daisy*), and Megan and Pippa on butty boat W2 (*Buttercup*). Lindsey would be on motor boat W3 and the bosun on butty boat W4. Existing procedures for the operation of munitions barges on English canals would apply. CFZ convoys would proceed in abreast formation, boats W1 and W2 first, followed by boats W3 and W4 close astern. During air raids the distance would be opened to a minimum of one hundred yards. At night the barges would moor equidistant from locks and never closer than a hundred yards from lock gates or buildings. The minimum distance between the barges at night would also be one hundred yards, which meant a longer walk for the crews of the barges moored furthest from the selected pub.

The naval contingent would wear uniforms on and off duty in accordance with established Admiralty practice. The girls would continue to wear dungarees or overalls on duty and refrain from sartorial displays prejudicial to good order when off duty. This latter regulation was the subject of giggled discussions between members of the female crew and grins from the bosun. Lindsey pointed out that the flotilla had been granted the privilege of flying the white ensign. As such it was important that sartorial decorum be maintained by convoy personnel on and off duty. The girls wanted to know if nightdresses were classified as decorous, at which point Lindsey changed the subject and proceeded to stores and victualling.

Arrangements for provisioning the barges had already been established. Stores of basic foodstuffs sufficient for each voyage would continue to be provided by Weedon Narrowboats, chargeable to the army. Within specified limits the cost of fresh produce - eggs, milk, vegetables and bread and so forth - would be reimbursed on return to Weedon, also chargeable to the army. The bosun would administer all victualling activities and maintain a cash box for miscellaneous purchases. As far as certain other stores essential to the wellbeing of personnel were concerned, the good news was that members of the armed services were entitled to purchase cigarettes and alcohol at duty free prices from NAAFI stores. Even better news, said Lindsey to cheers from the girls, was that the bosun would shortly be taking possession of a barrel of rum.

'To be kept under lock and key on my barge,' said the bosun.

'Shame!' cried the girls.

'The contents to be dispensed at appropriate intervals,' said the bosun.

'Yes!' cried the girls.

Agreement was also reached that in exchange for provision of cigarettes and alcohol by the naval contingent the girls would be responsible for meals Breakfast would be prepared at 0700 hours and distributed at the first available lock. When the bosun expressed his opinion that the perfect mariner's breakfast consisted of fried egg sandwiches the girls exclaimed that if they ever ran out of eggs they would roam the countryside, raiding farms if necessary, such was the importance they placed in looking after the person in charge of the rum barrel. Lunch would be prepared at 13:00 hours for distribution at the nearest lock. Dinner would be served in the duty cook's cabin at 1930 hours after the convoy had moored for the night.

Weedon Barracks

While the barges were being loaded alongside the quay in Weedon Barracks, Lindsey requested a meeting with the officer in charge of CFZ operations. He was led into the bleak stone building constructed during the Napoleonic War to a gloomy office overlooking the portcullis which when lowered isolated the barracks from the ordnance canal and depot. An army major with a black eyepatch waved him through the door and invited him to sit down. Hanging on the wall behind the desk was a painting of a field gun battery moving at high speed across a viaduct amidst clouds of dust billowing into the background of purple-peaked mountains.

'Fine picture, sir,' said Lindsey.

'Manoeuvres, India, 1928,' said the major.

'Quite a contrast from Weedon Barracks, sir.'

'That, young man, is an understatement.'

The purpose of his visit, Lindsey explained, was to investigate the characteristics of CFZ explosives. He knew the substance was more powerful than cordite but was looking for detailed information. For example, was CFZ as stable as cordite and how did it react to changes in temperature and humidity?

'CFZ has similar characteristics except in terms of volatility,' said the major.

'I'm not sure what that means, sir.'

'It's less stable than cordite. Which is why it's being transported by barge not road. However I shouldn't worry too much about that. One of our men dropped a box of CFZ a few days ago and nothing happened. He's still in hospital suffering from shock.'

'Very fortunate, sir. Do we know how CFZ will react to the humid conditions on the canal?'

'The ventilation channels in the holds are designed to keep the air moving and maintain humidity and temperature within safe limits. You don't have to worry about toxic fumes.'

'What is required in the way of routine inspections, sir?'

'Nothing. Our men will seal the holds. Just keep the tarpaulins battened down, and the filters on the chimney cowls clean. Report any problems by radio. But you shouldn’t have any trouble.'

'Thank you, sir.'

'You're loading now?'

'Yes, sir.'

'Setting off this afternoon?' said the major.

'Immediately after loading, sir?'

'Which means you should reach the Thames by Monday, assuming you maintain the same progress as the trial convoy, is that right?'

'More or less, sir, assuming we do.'

'Excellent. You should be back by next weekend. There are females in your crew, aren't there? Has that lively dark-haired one found her purse yet?'

'Purse, sir?'

'She lost it at the railway station apparently. I helped her out with ten shillings. Poor things, they don't get paid enough.'

'I didn't know . . .'

'Not that I expect it back. It was a most entertaining evening. Charming young lady,' said the major escorting Lindsey to the door.

Special Air Operations, Berlin

The Abwehr colonel responsible for German air intelligence marched into the conference room on the third floor of the Abwehr special air operations building in Berlin to the sound of clicking heels

'Sorted it out yet?'

The members the air intelligence committee took their seats at the conference table and looked at the Luftwaffe captain standing in front of the large-scale map of England on the panelled wall.

'We think so, sir,' said the captain.

'Good,' said the colonel flicking a speck of dust from the sleeve of his silver-grey jacket.

'Within the limits of the test programme, the equipment functioned perfectly, sir,' said the captain.

'Then, you're ready to try it out?'

'With your permission, sir.'

'When and where? Show me.'

'The barges will be approaching the Thames on Sunday. On the previous trip they moored for the night here,' said the captain pointing at the chart. 'You will observe the open expanse of country. Our aircraft will have a clear run at 200 feet altitude from this point here. Proposed takeoff at 0100 hours, sir.'

'Very good. Go ahead,' said the colonel.

Grand Union Canal

The flotilla moored downstream of the Horseshoe Inn which the girls said was easy to reach though Lindsey might need help over the stile, which he did, leaning on Megan's shoulder while April steadied him with her hands. The bosun remained onboard in compliance with the safety regulation that required munitions barges to be manned at all times, which the girls had ignored on the previous voyage on the basis that, as females, they could neither man nor un-man their boats and anyway they were thirsty.

'This is our skipper,' said Megan introducing Lindsey to Sid Prone, the squint-eyed innkeeper behind the bar.

'Rule Britannia, the Royal Navy's in town,' said the innkeeper. 'In charge of the munitions convoy, then?'

'Something like that,' said Lindsey.

'Hurry up with the beer, Sid, our tongues are hanging out,' said Pippa.

Lindsey moved pointedly away from the bar with his glass. The girls followed.

'I'd rather not discuss our operations in public,' he told them.

'Quite right, skipper,' said Megan.

'Don't worry, Sid's more interested in April than munitions convoys. Who's paying for the next round?' said Pippa.

'That reminds me,' said Lindsey. 'Did you ever find your purse?'

Pippa coloured.

'Oh, dear. You must have been talking to my army major. That's where you went this afternoon while the barges were being loaded, isn't it? How embarrassing. We were rather short of money at the dance, you see, and he was being affectionate, so I rather pretended to have lost my purse and he gave me ten shillings. Is that awful?'

'Yes,' said Lindsey.

'Prejudicial to good order?'

'Yes.'

'Should I pay it back?'

'Absolutely.'

The return journey over the stile was complicated by the happily inebriated condition of CFZ flotilla personnel. Lindsey ended up on top of Megan when she collapsed onto the grass under his weight. Helping him up, April decided she would be the one to offer Lindsey her shoulder next time they visited the Horseshoe Inn.

Delphinium Cottage

Alice Macleod was becoming increasingly concerned about her husband. All those overnight trips to London, and the unconvincing explanation of evening meetings. Meetings were held during the day, surely? And the drinking. The smell of alcohol filled their bedroom on Saturday nights. Then there was the letter from the bank, addressed by hand. She hadn't opened the envelope, of course, but obviously it did not contain the usual monthly statement of account. And that awful vulgar man had telephoned again, and Alasdair had lowered his voice when talking to him.

'Marjory is building a greenhouse this year, dear. It sounds an awfully good idea. We could grow tomatoes. What do you think, dear, can we afford one?' she attempted at dinner.

'What would we do with hundreds of tomatoes?'

'Soup, dear.'

'We'd get sick of them,' said the major.

Changing the subject he described the visit he had received that afternoon from a naval officer and how much the young man had admired the painting of field guns being driven across the plain in the Punjab and, continued the major, demonstrating the skillful process by which officers and gentlemen were able to maintain a continuous flow of conversation at the dinner table when they tried, how the young man's interest had brought back memories of that summer in Simla when they had shared a bungalow in the hills with the Percival-Dunnes and found a tiger asleep in the gunroom.

'Those were the days,' said the major.

'Yes, dear,' said his wife.

Greenbrook Toll Point

The youth temporarily assigned to Greenbrook toll point to assist old Bert Simkins watched the green barges approach.

'Four of them now, Mr Simkins,' he shouted.

'Aye, and a right bang there'd be if Jerry got them,' said the toll collector.

The youth looked nervously into the sky.

'They're flying a flag, Mr Simkins,' he shouted looking back again at the barges.

'Aye, that's the white ensign, right enough.'

'What are they, those men in uniform, Mr Simkins?'

'You see the one on the butty, lad? That's a chief petty officer - backbone of the Royal Navy, my father used to say,' said the toll collector.

West End Central Police Station, London

The duty constable in West End Central Police Station entered details of the missing pearl necklace in the logbook. When the distressed elderly lady had departed he turned to his friend from the squad car division who was visiting the front desk for a chat.

'I was right, you know,' he said.

'About what?' said the friend.

'Those radio transmissions. They started again as soon as the rain stopped, just like I said they would.'

The constable looked round to check that the duty sergeant wasn't in the room.

'Old thunder guts didn't believe me, but I was right.'

'Didn't believe what, Johnson?' said the duty sergeant appearing in the doorway holding a teacup and digestive biscuit.

'I was just observing to my colleague that I didn't believe police sergeants could be so dedicated, efficient and intelligent, sergeant.'

'I'm watching you, Johnson.'

'Yes, sergeant.'

'For your information,' said the sergeant dipping the digestive biscuit into the teacup, 'I have informed Special Branch of all your observations on the radio transmissions, and they assure me your comments have been forwarded to the appropriate authority.'

Bletchley Park

The head of the signals intelligence and traffic analysis section at Bletchley Park walked through Hut 15 accompanied by an earnest young cryptologist called Adrian Dawson from an adjoining hut. They stopped at the desk where the labels on the filing trays had been changed to *Pending, Ridiculous* and *Postponed.*

'Good morning, Rupert. How's progress?' said the section head to the communications analyst sprawled in the chair at the desk.

'Not too good actually. They've run out of pale ale.'

'Bad luck. Never mind, Adrian is here with glad tidings,' said the section head indicating the cryptologist, who was wearing an Oxford college tie. 'As you know, Adrian has been working on the Mayfair intercepts. However, before he imparts his good news, could you spare a minute and talk him through the current status of our countermeasures?'

The communications analyst described to the visitor the network of intercept stations and DF (direction finding) vans monitoring radio traffic in London, and the procedure for responding to intercepts which included mobilisation of squad cars from local police stations, and how the procedure was fundamentally useless when applied to short-duration transmissions from moving vehicles, particularly when the vehicles concealed themselves in rush hour traffic in the vicinity of Hyde Park Corner.

'You've thought of road blocks, presumably?'

'What a brilliant idea,' said Rupert spreading his hands in pretend wonderment.

'Yes, we have thought of that, Adrian,' said the section head hurriedly. 'The problem is the number of military and civil defence vehicles on the roads. Now why don't you forge ahead and tell Rupert about your encryption breakthrough?'

The cryptologist produced an electromechanical-device printout and placed it on Rupert's desk.

'We're not completely there yet, but you can see the pattern. Ignore the letters at the top, concentrate on the numerals in the middle. They look like map references, don't they? Either that, or they've doubled up on the code, which is unlikely, we think. Anyway, the point is - while we're working on it - we thought you might like to participate, seeing you're involved. A different approach, as it were. You might welcome a change of direction, something to refresh the mind, by tackling different images images of . . . '

'Nude WREN officers?' suggested Rupert.

'Not like that at all,' said the cryptologist, shocked. 'Personally, when seeking to refresh my mind, I think of village greens and cricket nets and sunlight on the pavilion clock.'

Luftwaffe Base, Carbon-Dreyville

The domestic staff at Chateau Carbon-Dreyville in northern France were searched before boarding the transport lorry at the end of each shift. Their bags were opened to check that the Luftwaffe officers in residence at the chateau were not being robbed of food or valuables. At random intervals the staff were stripped and searched in the guard house. Possession of items of potential interest to the French resistance movement resulted in the gruesome interrogations for which the Gestapo were renowned.

Set in parkland with magnificent gardens the chateau had been requisitioned by the Germans on account of the spacious accommodation, extensive wine cellar and proximity to the local airfield converted for use by the Luftwaffe's special air operations squadron. A barbed-wire fence protected the estate from unlawful entry through the gardens, and road traffic was controlled by the guards at the gate. Two categories of servant were employed within the chateau, German stewards and French domestic staff. The stewards served at table and acted as valets for the pilots. The domestic servants were recruited from the local village and confined to the kitchen and cellar areas, except for the maids who were allowed into the main body of the chateau for two hours a day to clean and dust the rooms under supervision of the stewards.

The restrictions on the movement of domestic staff were enforced to minimise the possibility of discussions between pilots and other senior Luftwaffe personnel being overheard. The risk was further reduced by testing potential recruits for linguistic aptitude and rejecting candidates for domestic staff positions who responded to questions in German. Confident of the effectiveness of these security measures, discussions of strategic importance were conducted freely within the building and, notwithstanding the linguistics tests, duly recorded by those members of the domestic staff planted by the Maquis who were fluent in both languages and skillful at concealing themselves behind curtains.

Arrangements for transmitting urgent information from the chateau to the resistance cell in the village centred upon the curious lack of attention paid by the security personnel in the guard house to the gardeners' bicycles. The gardeners themselves, pensioners from local farms, were rarely searched on account of their deliberately low standards of personal hygiene. Their bicycles with wobbling wheels and rattling frames were never examined.

On Sunday evening, at approximately the same time as the CFZ munitions flotilla was approaching Hemel Hempstead, a sheet of lavatory paper was concealed deep inside the handlebars of one of the gardeners' bicycles and duly delivered to an address in the village. The paper contained a warning that the Luftwaffe were about to test a new guidance system capable of delivering bombs with sufficient accuracy to blow small strategically-important targets to smithereens (*mille morceaux*) from an altitude of two hundred feet.

Unfortunately the gardeners had departed by the time the order was received from the chief steward to prepare late dinner for three pilots and attendant personnel. Celebratory dinners after midnight were a frequent occurrence at Chateau Carbon-Dreyville. The menu normally included smoked trout, truffles, prime steak and vintage wine from the cellar. Working backwards from the designated time for the celebratory meal the domestic staff calculated that the pilots would be taking off from the airfield at 0100 hours.

Grand Union Canal

The sound of church bells drifted across the field as the CFZ convoy moored alongside the bank a few miles south of Hemel Hempstead. Lindsey pointed at the church steeple beyond the trees in the distance and enquired if anyone wanted to attend evensong and everybody except Megan, whose father was a vicar, agreed that attendance would be a good thing and everybody including Megan decided they would rather visit the Rose & Crown instead.

To April's disappointment Lindsey remained onboard. There were too many hedges to climb, he said, and anyway it was the bosun's turn for a run ashore

The bosun's attitude to the girls had been reserved at first. Miss Megan and Miss Pippa were from a different social class and very sophisticated in behaviour and speech. Miss April was less remote in terms of background but so good looking that he experienced the tongue-tied awkwardness familiar to men of all ages in the presence of beauty. In her sweet way she teased him, however, just as the other two teased him and it was difficult to remain reserved when treated with such open affection. By Sunday evening all vestiges of shyness had gone and he accompanied the girls happily through the long grass on the bank of the canal towards the pub.

Lindsey read for a while in his bunk. He was asleep by the time the party returned from the inn. By midnight the last cabin light was extinguished and the moon cast long shadows on the water.

Bombing Raid 1

The Heinkels from Carbon-Dreyville flew low over the English Channel. They were not picked up by radar until they reached the coast at Rye. Night fighters were immediately scrambled from Biggin Hill but too late. The intruders had gone by the time the RAF planes swooped over the fires burning on the bank of the Grand Union Canal south of Hemel Hempstead.

Grand Union Canal

Awakened by the noise Lindsey's first reaction was that he was back at sea on his destroyer. The ship was rolling in a storm and waves were battering the hull. Overhead, aircraft were roaring past. Night action, he thought jumping out of his bunk, why hadn't the alarm sounded? The pain of his wounded leg landing on the deck jerked him to reality. He groped for the light switch. What the devil was wrong with the barge? Why was it rolling, what was drumming on the bulkheads, and what was raining down on the cabin roof? Overhead, aircraft thundered past again. We're being bombed, he thought, clambering into his uniform, the flotilla's under attack. He hopped to the door still fastening his trousers. The door was stuck. He heaved with his shoulder and tumbled out into the cockpit, to find it full of earth.

April's first thought was for Lindsey. Megan and Pippa were already on deck clinging to the stanchions as *Buttercup* rocked in the water and staring at the lane of fire where the trees had been. April saw Lindsey emerge from his cabin and drop out of sight. She ran along the bank, leapt over the gunwale and found him struggling to pull himself up.

'The commanding officer is supposed to look after his crew, not the other way round,' said Lindsey accepting April's hand.

'If you say so. Are you alright?' said April.

'Never felt better,' said Lindsey brushing down his clothes.

'Have you hurt your leg again?' said April.

'Not much.'

'Liar,' said April seeing him wince.

'How about you?' said Lindsey.

'I'm fine. We've just been bombed, haven't we?'

'I'm afraid so.'

April stared into the sky.

'Will they come back?' she said.

'I think the RAF chased them away, in the second wave.'

Lindsey climbed awkwardly over the gunwale and hopped to the middle of the field. April collected his walking stick from the cabin and followed him. Silhouetted against the flames from the burning trees and bushes they gazed at the line of craters running parallel to the canal approximately fifty yards from the bank.

Megan and Pippa watched from *Buttercup*. 'Where's the bosun?' said Pippa suddenly. They looked around. He wasn't in the field or on the deck of his boat. The girls ran along the bank and clambered over the clumps of soil into the bosun's butty. The door was blocked with earth. They cleared it away with their hands and burst into the cabin. In the light of the moon and flames from the field outside they saw a shape in the bunk. Moving closer to the shape they heard the sound of snoring. The girls looked at each other and burst out laughing.

'Now then, what's going on here?' said the bosun waking up.

He reached for the cabin light.

'I knew it. You're after the rum,' he said sitting up.

The girls were shaking with laughter.

'We've just been bombed, bosun. You slept through it,' they cried.

The bosun looked towards the open door. In the varnished surface he saw the reflection of flames.

'Turn your backs please, ladies,' said the bosun, 'while I get dressed.'

Fire engines had gathered on the road beyond the burning trees. Figures in uniforms and helmets were running across the grass towards the craters. An ambulance swayed along the farm track from the church to the canal.

'Who's in charge here?' shouted an ARP warden shining his torch in Lindsey's face.

Lindsey pointed at the canal and told the warden he was in command of the four munitions barges moored alongside the bank. Nothing appeared to be damaged, he told the warden, except the surface of the meadow and, having noted the bosun moving about on the boat with Megan and Pippa, added that all members of his crew were accounted for.

'Lucky escape,' said the warden swinging his torch at the craters. 'What a mess. Half the field's missing.'

'Into the barges, mostly,' said Lindsey.

'Come with me,' said April taking hold of Lindsey's arm.

She led him protesting towards the ambulance parked on the path. The rear doors were open and white-coated medics were unloading stretchers.

'You won't need those,' she told the medics. 'Nobody's been hit, but can you check this officer's leg, please?'

'It's just bruised,' protested Lindsey.

The medics sat him down on the running board and probed his leg while April watched, arms crossed, wondering what to do if they took him to hospital. The bosun would have to take over his barge, and Pippa would have to transfer to the bosun's boat. The convoy had to keep moving. The skipper would be left behind.

'Nothing broken,' said the medics.

'That's a relief,' said Lindsey.

'Your right knee's swollen though,' said the medics.

'Yes,' said Lindsey.

'You'd better see a doctor when you can,' the medics told him.

'I'll make sure he does,' said April.

Leaning against *Daisy's* hull later, clasping glasses of rum, scarves around the necks of the men and coats around the shoulders of the girls, the officers and crew of the CFZ flotilla watched the flames subside along the hedgerow. The ambulance and fire engines had gone and the ARP wardens were plodding back across the meadow. From above, the moon bathed the scene in silver light. The rims of the craters and the smouldering undergrowth bore testament to the unsuccessful attempt by the Luftwaffe to destroy the barges. The German aircraft had missed by at least fifty yards. The experts were right, it was difficult to hit small targets from the air.

Ironbridge Lock

In view of the attack Detective Sergeant Quinn broke cover next morning. He waited for the second pair of barges to reach Ironbridge lock then approached the naval officer in the stern of the motor boat.

Producing his police badge he asked if he could step aboard. The naval officer, whom he identified as Sub-Lieutenant Edward Lindsey, received him with a cheerful smile which impressed the detective who had been monitoring events from the other side of the canal and knew how tired the crews of the CFZ convoy must have been after working through the night to clear the mounds of earth which the German bombs had deluged onto the vessels.

Quinn was equally impressed by the Lindsey's insistence on offering him tea, hopping up and down from the stove in the cabin, obviously enduring a painful leg. The right kind of temperament for hazardous assignments, thought Quinn, who had been injured often enough on duty as a police officer and, off duty, as a rugby player.

While the level in the lock dropped Quinn explained he had been assigned to investigate the possibility of enemy activity relating to CFZ production and transport. Thanks to the bombing raid, the possibility had become a certainty. The enemy had known exactly where to find the flotilla and could not have obtained the information by aerial reconnaissance because the identification markings on the barges were not visible from the air. Someone was obviously tailing the convoy at ground level, or had access to the confidential mooring location schedules.

The lock gates opened while Quinn was still onboard. Lindsey engaged the engine, steered the two barges through the gates and swung them towards the canal bank downstream of the lock. Before jumping ashore Quinn gave Lindsey a telephone number. The switchboard was manned night and day, said Quinn, waving as munitions barges W3 and W4 swung back to middle of the canal and continued their journey astern of barges W1 and W2 to London.

Main Office, Civil Defence Service, Buckinghamshire

Snorting at the contents of the report on his desk, Brigadier Smythe, head of Buckingham's civil defence service, crumpled the typewritten sheet and tossed it in to the wastepaper basket. He glowered out of the window for a few minutes then retrieved the report, smoothed it with his burly hands and dropped it into a drawer of the filing cabinet beside the desk.

The damn fools in the Hertfordshire civil defence service had done everything wrong. The home guard duty officer had got lost. Nobody had assumed command at the incident site. The ARP wardens had wandered over the field like a herd of lost sheep. The search and rescue team had never arrived. The medics failed to conduct proper checks of personnel exposed to the blast from the attack and had driven too fast across the field given the condition of the farm track, unnecessarily risking lives if the ambulance had turned over with casualties in the back. The fire brigade had wasted precious time trying to extinguish foliage which would have burned out safely anyway, and completely failed to send fire engines to the other side of the canal where they could have shielded the munitions barges from the blaze by creating a wall of water. Nobody had taken statements. Nobody had contacted the farmer of the affected field to initiate the compensation process. Nobody had assessed damage to the local church. The whole thing had been a complete shambles.

Exactly what happens, snorted the brigadier, when you appoint people from the wrong regiment to positions of authority.

Bletchley Park

'Whitehall has suggested there might be a link between the Mayfair transmissions and last night's bombing of the munitions convoy on the Grand Union Canal,' said the head of the signals intelligence and traffic analysis section at Bletchley Park to his communications analyst.

'Why?'

'I'm sure you'll find out, you're the clever one, Rupert,' said the section head placing a package on the communications analyst's desk.

The analyst stared at the sealed envelope with bloodshot eyes, the result of yet another late night at nearby inns.

'I'm not at my best, so early in the morning,' he explained.

'I know that, Rupert. However if you could find time to examine the information and, where appropriate, pronounce upon aspects of mutual interest, everybody, including myself, would be most grateful.'

The communications analyst stirred in his chair.

'Just as soon as my head clears,' he said.

'Adrian Dawson will be along shortly to discuss the dossier with you shortly. He's excited about the map references.'

'You mean the Oxford cryptologist, the one deeply moved by sunlight on pavilion clocks?'

'I know he's a little intense, but they're very impressed with him next door.'

'Intense!' said Rupert reaching for the package. 'He's so wet he left a pool of water behind last time.'

Grand Union Canal

Marine vessels carrying explosives or inflammable cargoes on the Thames within the Greater London area were required, when moored, to cast off and proceed to the middle of the river during air raids to minimise the prospect of damaging the city's infrastructure. On account of this directive, and the safety regulation requiring munitions barges to be under constant supervision when loaded, Lindsey faced an awkward decision. Either he turned a blind eye to the regulation and allowed everyone into the Smugglers Arms for the party they richly deserved or risked a mutiny by insisting that both pair of barges be manned whilst alongside the wharf and that celebrations for surviving the previous night's bombing raid took place in shifts, a most unsatisfactory outcome.

The girls came up with the solution. As soon as the convoy moored they hurried along the wooden planks to the old converted trawler lying near the inn and returned with an elderly man, toothless and grinning, bald under a tattered seaman's cap.

'This is O'Reilly,' said Megan. 'For half a crown he'll stand guard for us.'

'We used him last time,' said Pippa.

'He's a deckhand on the trawler,' said April.

'Top of the day to you, admiral,' said O'Reilly touching his cap.

'I'm not an admiral,' smiled Lindsey.

'But you will be, a grand looking person like yourself, to be sure,' said O'Reilly.

'He'll warn us if anyone comes near the barges,' said Megan.

'That I will,' said O'Reilly.

'If there's an air raid, he'll fetch us from the pub, in case we don't hear the siren,' said Pippa.

'That I will, to be sure,' said O'Reilly.

Lindsey looked down from the cockpit of barge W3 at the line of enquiring faces.

'Can we spare half a crown?' he called out to the bosun who was coiling ropes on barge W4.

'I think we can manage that, sir. Sundry expenses,' said the bosun.

'All ashore then,' said Lindsey.

'Thank you!' cried the girls.

'A fine job I'll be giving you, right enough,' said O'Reilly touching his cap.

The dark interior of the Smugglers Arms was bustling with trade. Two large tugs and a freighter from Jamaica had berthed in the river nearby and discharged their thirsty crews to the inn. Ladies of the night, powdered and scented, blouses full and hems low, circulated the wooden stalls. Amidst the throng were crews from several Waltham Abbey munitions barges, shaking hands with April and hugging Pippa and Megan who had worked with them on the Lee Navigation Canal route. The regulars of the Smugglers Arms watched from the depths of the establishment, their weather-beaten faces dimly illuminated by the flickering flames of the candles on the upturned barrels which served as tables. A scarecrow harridan with cigarette dangling from her lips was playing an accordion and several of the Jamaicans were dancing in the open space between the door and bar counter, their feet splaying to the rhythm of the music.

The bosun propped himself contentedly against the bar. Similar establishments, he reflected, were to be found in all corners of the globe, adjoining jetties and quays, on palm-fringed coasts where the sea lapped white-sand beaches, beneath towering cliffs where the waves hurled themselves at the rocks, and within the deep blue water coves of the Mediterranean coastline. There was something slightly sinister about the Smugglers Arms, however. The place reminded him of an old pub in Cornwall, with the same mysterious atmosphere, pervaded by the ghosts of ancient mariners, good and bad, risen from their graveyards to hatch plots in the drinking dens of their prime.

Lindsey had decreed that the evening's entertainment should be paid for by the army. The bosun, as paymaster, was therefore the focal point for the girls who periodically turned up at the counter with empty glasses before disappearing back into the throng. Sometimes they stayed behind to tease him.

'Fancy one of those, bosun?' said Pippa pointing to a group of the powdered and scented ladies.

'You could take one to your barge,' said Megan.

'For a short time,' said Pippa.

'Or a long time,' said Megan.

'How about the one in the pink skirt, bosun?' said April.

'We won't tell anyone,' said Pippa.

'Except Mrs Meredith,' said April.

'Oh yes, we'd have to her, naturally,' said Pippa.

And the girls mimicked the sly wink that the personnel manager had given the bosun during dinner at the Market Hotel the previous week.

Basking in their attention, the bosun grinned merrily. Who would have predicted he would end up one summer evening in a pub on the Thames, drinking beer at the expense of the army, being ribbed by three attractive young ladies? Well, maybe it was stretching a point to call Miss Megan attractive. Plump, cheerful and a trifle bossy, that was more like it. But the other two were lovely young things. Miss Pippa, dark-eyed and rascally. Miss April, sweet-natured and divinely pretty. It crossed his mind that the sub-lieutenant would find it difficult in pursuance of his duties as commanding officer to remain aloof from his crew and, as a bachelor, to keep such delightful females at arm's length.

The sub-lieutenant appeared to be enjoying the party nonetheless. By the movements of his hands, it looked like he was demonstrating to the first mate of the Jamaican freighter the tiller sequence for berthing a canal barge in a lock.

Woolwich Arsenal

April insisted on accompanying Lindsey to the medical unit at Woolwich Arsenal in case he changed his mind and limped off to the canteen, the sort of thing men were capable of doing. He protested that his knee was much better but April had placed her hands on her hips so Lindsey yielded in case she made a scene, which women were capable of doing.

In the medical unit a nurse sat Lindsey in a wheelchair and pushed him to the X-ray room leaving April in the lobby with his walking stick.

'Where was your leg treated?' asked the army doctor examining the X-ray prints fifteen minutes later.

'Ipswich,' said Lindsey.

'Nothing but the best for the Royal Navy,' said the doctor.

Hands thrust in the pockets of his white coat the doctor stared at the pattern of lines representing the steel pins in Lindsey's knee.

'I can't see anything out of place. Nothing broken. What happened?' said the doctor.

'I jumped from my bunk and landed heavily on my leg,' said Lindsey.

The doctor scribbled a prescription.

'To reduce the inflammation,' he said.

Lindsey hobbled back to the wheelchair.

'In the army, we advise people with leg injuries to roll out of bed, not jump. It's a slower process but the results are less painful,' said the doctor as the nurse wheeled Lindsey to the door.

'What happened?' said April leaping from her seat in the lobby as the wheelchair approached.

Lindsey showed her the packet of aspirins he'd been given at the dispensary.

'Aspirins!' cried April.

MV 'Sea Snake'

The weather could have been worse, muttered Captain Binbow swinging the wheel of the converted trawler and setting course for the mouth of the estuary. The sea was smooth, clouds concealed the midnight moon and the tide was running in the right direction. At the rendezvous point he would cut the engines and drift.

'You'll be wanting your cocoa?' said O'Reilly the deckhand through the open wheelhouse window.

'Since when did I not want it?' said Binbow.

'Such a fine night it is, I thought you might like something different, cap'n.'

'Like what?'

'Lemonade'

'O'Reilly.'

'Yes, cap'n?'

'When did I last drink lemonade?'

'Now you mention it, not recently, right enough.'

'You're as much use as a three-legged horse, O'Reilly.'

'It'll be cocoa then, to be sure.'

'And hurry up, or you'll be walking the plank.'

The danger was not so much the destroyers from the naval base at Chatham but motor torpedo boats from Dover slicing through the waves at forty knots looking for trouble. Within ten minutes they would be alongside, searchlights and guns trained on the trawler while boarding parties searched the deck. Well, thought Binbow glancing at the revolver on the chart table, they'd find more than they bargained for.

St James's, London

The two elegantly dressed men dining at their club in St James's Street, betraying evidence of their expensive education by commencing luncheon with brown windsor soup, and hinting at their involvement in the upper echelons of British intelligence by virtue of their discussions, were in celebratory mood. Not everybody had approved of the endeavour. Too expensive, manpower intensive, questionable justification. The first objection had been countered by persuading the War Office to meet the costs of the project on the grounds of improved security at Lee Navigation Canal. The manpower problem had been solved by mobilising the CID in a clandestine manoeuvre of great satisfaction to the instigators. As for justification, well, the case had now been proven, in spades.

The only concern was that the Germans had attacked the convoy earlier than expected. And unfortunately, if recent reports from France were true, the Luftwaffe was commissioning a new delivery system of extraordinary accuracy. They had missed the target last weekend, but would they miss next time or, more pertinently, was there sufficient time and opportunity for the police to make arrests before the next raid? It might be prudent to build another set of CFZ munitions barges, just in case. The safety of personnel on the existing convoy was, of course, of paramount importance. Everything possible was being done to minimise the risk to the crew. Not that much more in the way of safety precautions was, frankly, practicable.

'We all make sacrifices,' they agreed summoning the steward for a decanter of Cockburn's port.

The Ambassador Club, Mayfair

Fingleton Kelly the floor manager at the Ambassador Club bathed his hand in the gentlemen's cloakroom. The water soothed his bruised knuckles and removed the traces of blood. One of the younger members had misbehaved after a win at the baccarat table. Drunk with champagne he had thrust his hand under a hostess's skirt and the person she had been talking to resented the gesture and took a swing at the offender. All three ended up on the floor. Kelly had incurred the bruises while restoring order.

Kelly dried his hands on a towel, checked his bow tie in the cloakroom mirror and returned to the chandeliered-opulence of the gaming rooms. The young man had departed with a group of aristocratic friends to a nearby nightclub and the hostess had left with her gallant protector, presumably to an address of greater privacy. Play in the rooms had continued throughout the incident without interruption.

Descending the carpeted staircase from the bar Kelly observed that Major Macleod had at long last made his return to the Ambassador Club. He was sitting at the central roulette table in the chair closest to the croupier behind a pile of £10 gaming chips. Ten chips, counted Kelly. He watched the major slide two of them on number eighteen and stare intently at the wheel which spun in the glow of the chandeliers.

'*Numéro vingt sept*,' called the croupier.

Kelly watched the major repeat the bet four times, each time on the same number, each time unsuccessfully, each time with increased signs of restlessness. When the last of his chips had gone, the major stared at the board for a while then reached into his mess dress jacket and produced a cheque book. Kelly watched him lean across and speak to the croupier. The croupier lifted his eyes in Kelly's direction.

'Good evening, sir,' said Kelly walking to the table. 'Fifty pounds? Of course, sir.'

Kelly stepped back and nodded at the croupier.

The major placed all five chips onto the black-coloured section of the board then sat back in his chair and stared fiercely at the wheel as the croupier set it in motion. The roulette ball bounced in tantalising little jumps, into a red pocket, into a black pocket and finally, with a graceful little leap, into a red pocket. Kelly saw the major's shoulders slump.

'Don't cash the cheque yet - give me a week,' said the major on his way out.

'With pleasure,' said Kelly.

'I'll get the funds,' said the major.

'Of course you will,' said Kelly opening the door to Park Lane.

Weedon Narrowboats

In accordance with instructions, Lindsey, or a deputised member of the crew, telephoned the ARP control centre every evening to report the position of the barges after mooring. The control room subsequently passed the details to the local emergency services. Not until next morning were the details issued for general circulation, to ARP wardens along the route of the canal, lockkeepers, toll stations and other concerned parties including Weedon Narrowboats.

Mrs Meredith monitored the progress of the flotilla carefully. She needed to know the estimated date of return of the barges to Weedon in order to book rooms at the hotel, check that stores and provisions had been ordered and ensure Mr Browning, who was always so busy, had been in touch with the barracks regarding the date and time for re-loading. She also checked for signs of delay in the progress of the barges that might indicate damage or injury. Shocked at the news of the bombing raid she consoled herself with the thought that the crew must be all right as long as the convoy was reported to be on the move.

Mr Browning was in regular contact with the War Office but she couldn't keep asking him for news because of his tendency to lean back in his chair and examine the ceiling while making references to the natural affinity between personnel managers and naval chief petty officers.

She was in no mood for nonsense this morning however.

'What's this about building spare barges?' she demanded marching into his office.

'Now, now, Maggie. Don't jump to conclusions,' said Mr Browning.

'There's only one to jump to,' she said.

'The War Office is simply investigating the option of holding vessels in reserve, in case, for example, one of our existing barges breaks down,' said Mr Browning.

'Or gets blown up, you mean,' said Mrs Meredith.

Grand Union Canal

Detective Sergeant Quinn tailed the flotilla back up the canal to Stoke Bruerne then changed out of his overalls and headed north on the A5. In the saddle bag of his bicycle was a security pass allowing him entry to the CFZ compound at Weedon Barracks. On arrival he was collected at the guardroom by the unit subaltern, Second Lieutenant Ashworth.

'Our CO, Major Macleod, is in London, but I'll show you around,' said the subaltern as they set off..

'I appreciate that, sir,' said Quinn who had timed his visit to coincide with the major's absence.

'What are you looking for exactly?' said the subaltern.

'Routine familiarisation - on behalf of the civil defence service, sir,' said Quinn.

'Let's start with the store, then,' said the subaltern.

They walked along the paved road beside the ordnance canal between parallel rows of large brick buildings which the subaltern said were storehouses containing small arms, ordnance equipment, bicycles, motor bicycles, armoured vehicle spare parts, clothing and several hundred thousand pairs of army boots. On the other side of the canal a railway line ran past the storehouses into a covered platform with loading ramps. The entire area was surrounded by high walls studded with machine gun posts. Barrage balloons hovered high overhead, twisting in the summer air.

They continued past the magazine blocks with racks of shells and ammunition visible through open doors to a collection of smaller buildings enclosed by a barbed wire fence. The sentry at the entrance to the compound examined Quinn's pass, opened the gate marked 'Danger - Authorised Entry Only' and saluted.

'This is where we keep the finished product,' said the subaltern leading Quinn into the first building. 'Bomb-proof walls, three feet thick, vaulted ceiling, reinforced concrete.'

The material arrived in the store from the adjacent production bays in three foot lengths which were packed into wooden boxes and placed in racks along the wall, explained the subaltern. When required for loading the boxes were transported by trolley to the ordnance canal. The store was ventilated by the cast iron grilles in the walls and ceiling. Temperature was monitored by thermostats which activated an alarm at eighty degrees fahrenheit. Smoking was forbidden inside the building. The only incident so far had involved a dropped box. Fortunately the contents had not detonated otherwise there would have been a large hole in the ground where they were standing. The soldier involved in the incident was still in hospital being treated for shock.

From the store they visited the series of production bays each with bomb-proof walls and roof. Powder 'A' was combined with liquid 'B' in the preparation bay using solvent 'C' to facilitate the mixing process. The mixture was passed to the press bay for extrusion into half inch diameter rods. The rods were transferred to the drying bay and laid in slatted trays through which warm air was passed to drive off the solvent. When the solvent had evaporated the rods were transported to the store by trolley. Quinn asked if he could take one of the fragments of rod lying in a basket in the drying bay as a souvenir. Shaking his head the subaltern told Quinn that a piece of CFZ rod the size of a fingernail could destroy a house. Quinn said he had only been joking.

On the subject of security, said the subaltern as they returned along the paved road beside the ordnance canal, the civil defence service could be assured that the strict movement control measures witnessed by Quinn during the course of his visit were diligently enforced at all times and that there was no possibility of access by unauthorised personnel into the compound for the purpose of sabotage or theft.

'The CO's office is through there,' said the subaltern pointing down a gloomy corridor as they passed through the main lodge.

'Easy to get on with, is he, sir?' asked Quinn.

'Not always,' grinned the subaltern.

'Eccentric, I gather, sir.'

'Yes, he lets his hair down sometimes. Mind you, we all do, don't we, from time to time?'

'Dead drunk on Saturday night,' laughed Quinn.

'I don't think he was completely drunk,' said the subaltern cautiously.

'I meant me,' said Quinn.

'Oh, I see. I thought perhaps you were referring to the dance the other weekend. It's a stressful job looking after a new project, you understand, particularly when explosives are involved.'

'Now you mention it, I do remember hearing something about that dance. One of the girls from the munition barges was involved, isn't that right? It's amazing what people talk about in the pubs,' prompted Quinn.

'I think he just loaned her some money. Now, anything else you'd like to see?' said the subaltern changing the subject, already regretting that he had allowed himself to comment on his commanding officer's private life.

'You've covered everything, thank you, sir.'

'What about the external defences, do you want to see the anti-aircraft batteries?'

'No need. That will do nicely. Thank you for your time, sir.'

Quinn shook hands with the subaltern and surrendered his pass in the guardroom. Before mounting his bicycle he inserted the fragment of CFZ rod he had pocketed from the drying bay into the bundle of overalls in his saddle bag. It might reduce blast damage to his posterior, he thought, if the bicycle hit a bump.

Weedon Narrowboats

Mrs Meredith greeted the girls with open arms. She thought about embracing the bosun too but changed her mind and shook his hand coyly. She didn't know how to greet the sub-lieutenant either so she shook his hand too and said how wonderful it was that everyone looked so well. In truth she was amazed at the high-spirits of the girls who were laughing and chatting gleefully.

'We're so looking forward to a bath, Maggie,' they cried.

'Your rooms are ready. We'll have dinner in the hotel tonight, and Mr Browning will be there to pay the bill as usual,' said Mrs Meredith.

She had lectured herself firmly beforehand about not discussing the bombing raid in case the subject distressed the girls. She need not have worried. They seemed to regard the incident as an amusing adventure.

They're so young, of course, thought Mrs Meredith who personally would have died of fright if a bomb had dropped fifty yards from her bed. At dinner the girls talked openly about the raid and teased the bosun for sleeping through the explosions. Apparently when he had woken up and found Megan and Pippa in his cabin he accused them of trying to steal his precious barrel of rum! April, the darling girl, had made the sub-lieutenant visit the clinic in Woolwich Arsenal on account of him landing heavily on his wounded leg. Laughing, April recounted how the army medical officer had given Lindsey a few aspirins and a lecture on how to get out of his bunk.

In fact the girls were far more interested in talking about Saturday's dance at Weedon Barracks than the raid. They declared that Mrs Meredith must accompany the officers and crew to the party. The bosun, said the girls, was tired of feminine chatter and needed someone intelligent of the opposite sex to converse with. Beaming the bosun said the girls were talking nonsense but nevertheless he would be delighted if Mrs Meredith would join them at the dance whereupon Mrs Meredith became coy and said she would need to check her diary.

Mr Browning declined the invitation on the grounds that his mother-in-law would be in Weedon over the weekend and she caused enough trouble without him disappearing on Saturday evening to dance with his personnel manager and three charming young ladies from the flotilla.

'What about you, sub-lieutenant?' said Mrs Meredith.

'I'll be there,' smiled Lindsey.

'You'd better be,' said April softly under her breath.

Aylesbury Product Analytics

The man in the laboratory coat stared suspiciously at the open package.

'What is it?' he said.

'A fragment of CFZ rod,' said Detective Sergeant Quinn.

'What's CFZ?'

'A powerful cordite-based explosive.'

'For me, or my kids?'

'They dropped a full box, and nothing happened. If CFZ is as stable as they say, I need to know why the soldier who dropped the box is in hospital suffering from shock.'

'Who's they?'

'The Ordnance Depot at Weedon Barracks.'

'Good grief, Sam, this is a forensic laboratory not a military research station.'

'I need the answer by Monday.'

'Why Monday, as a matter of interest?'

'That's when the next convoy sails.'

The man peered further into the package.

'Powerful, you say?'

'Very.'

'Why did you choose us, Sam?'

'Well . . .'

'Let me guess. We were the last laboratory on your list, and you've blown up the others?'

'You're top of my list,' grinned Quinn. 'But if you detonate your premises over the weekend, I'll try Oxford next.'

Weedon Barracks

The ground floor of Storehouse 2 in Weedon Barracks had been converted at the start of the war into a recreation hall for dances and concerts. Coloured balloons and streamers were draped across the hall to alleviate the drabness of the grey painted walls. Ducking under a string of balloons Lindsey propped his walking stick behind a chair and looked around. On the elevated stage at the far end of the vast space an eight-piece band was playing songs from the latest Cole Porter musical. On the opposite side of the hall white-coated stewards were dispensing beer and spirits from a makeshift bar consisting of trestle tables covered in army issue tablecloths. Between the bar and the stage the dance floor was packed with girls in pretty dresses and soldiers in khaki uniforms, stamping and twirling, bobbing up and down, boots and shoes drumming on the wooden planks.

It was different from the dances to which he was accustomed, where the girls wore long gowns and the men preened themselves in white ties and tails, where the guests danced in baronial ballrooms and flower-decked marquees erected on the lawns of grand estates, and where the music was provided by orchestras of violins, oboes and clarinets.

Different but no less enjoyable. In fact some of the girls were worthy of pursuit, he thought, mourning the constraints of his appointment. Unencumbered by the responsibilities of command he could have flirted with some of these pretty village maidens and dallied with them afterwards in the moonlight. Now they were untouchable. As untouchable as the girls in his crew.

'Here you are, sir,' said the bosun emerging from the crowd with a tray of beer glasses.

'Well done, bosun. Are we safe, do you think, in our naval uniforms? We might have to fight our way out. You know what soldiers are like.'

'Safe enough, sir,' said the bosun merrily.

'We'll fight back to back, if necessary. Keep in touch with Mrs Meredith. She might need to clear a path for us with her handbag.'

'I'll instruct her accordingly, sir.'

Lindsey scanned the crowd. Megan and Pippa were at the bar. Mrs Meredith had gone to the ladies cloakroom to powder her nose. Where was April? There, emerging from a group of soldiers, advancing towards him with the palms of her hands upwards in radiant supplication.

'Come on, skipper. You promised,' she said.

'I only promised to try,' said Lindsey.

'Come on,' she repeated extending her hand.

'I might fall over.'

'Of course you won't. Here, hold onto me, like this.'

The last time he'd danced was six months ago at a hunt ball in Dorset. His partner that evening had been beautiful but not half so lovely as the girl on whose shoulder he now leaned, whose silky hair swung prettily, whose eyes glowed lustrously at him through the haze of cigarette smoke, whose skin was so soft and smooth and whose lips resembled a Cupid's bow as she responded to his questions, describing her life as a child afloat on English canals, how her father had read Goethe to her at bedtime and played Brahms on gramophone records. There was a scent of flowers in her hair. He found himself leaning forward slightly as they danced, his nostrils twitching. That would be the extent of his pleasure tonight, he thought grimly, sniffing the fragrance of a girl.

'There, you see, you've done it - a complete circuit,' said April when the music stopped.

'Thanks entirely to you,' said Lindsey.

'I want the last waltz too, please,' said April tucking her arm into his on the way back to the chair.

'Last waltzes are for boyfriends.'

April lifted herself up on her toes and spoke into his ear. 'I don't have one.'

'They're definitely not for crippled sub-lieutenants,' he said.

'You're not crippled.'

'Let me find someone more suitable for you. Look, there's one, a handsome subaltern, at the bar.'

'Listen to me, skipper. I'm a member of your crew - you're supposed to protect me, not offer me to other men.'

April looked at him beseechingly.

'Very well,' smiled Lindsey.

'Promise?'

Lindsey promised and sank sideways into the chair with his right leg stretched out along the wall where it could not be kicked by soldiers lumbering to the bar or swerving off the dance floor. In this comfortable position, drinking from his beer glass, he was approached by Major Macleod.

'Don't get up, my boy,' said the major swaying slightly.

'Good evening, sir.'

'Enjoying the fun? Damned nice girl you were dancing with just now.'

'One of my crew, sir.'

'Got you, my boy. Damned difficult, isn't it, when you're in charge of them?'

'It certainly is, sir.'

'Need to go to London, that's the answer. Plenty of them there, fillies,' said the major tapping his nose.

'Yes, sir.'

'Well, I mustn't keep you. You're looking well.'

'Thank you, sir.'

'Time for another,' said the major stumbling slightly. 'Oh, meant to tell you. She found the purse.'

'Purse, sir?'

'That other filly of yours.' The major fumbled in his pockets. 'Stroke of luck,' he said waving a ten shilling note above his head.

In another part of the hall the bosun swept Mrs Meredith onto the dance floor. As a boy seaman on wooden ships with tall sails crossing the Atlantic he had learned the hornpipe, in the ports of South America he had mastered the tango and in Cuba dusky maidens had taught him the calypso. Foxtrots and quicksteps presented no difficulty to him. Gracefully he propelled Mrs Meredith around the hall. They were a warm-hearted couple and conversed easily with one another. Mrs Meredith described her bungalow and invited the bosun for tea next time the barges returned to Weedon. Her lawn ran down to the canal, he would enjoy sitting in a deckchair sampling her scones and watching the swans, said Mrs Meredith.

The bosun also dutifully invited the girls to dance. Megan planted a kiss on his forehead and said she didn't want to lose her position at the bar, Pippa hugged him and said she was too drunk, April said thank you very much and took his arm. She badly needed his advice.

'I like the skipper so much, bosun, but he's not the least bit interested in me,' she told him as they circled the room.

'What makes you think so, miss?'

'He's so brusque.'

'Begging your pardon, miss, but the flotilla's a heavy responsibility for him.'

'I don't speak as well as Megan and Pippa, perhaps that's the problem. They're so sophisticated.'

'You have a charming voice, miss.'

'But not like theirs.'

'With a slight foreign accent, miss. Which Mrs Meredith and I both find delightful.'

'Do you think it sounds foreign?'

'Yes, miss.'

'But not very smart.'

'Smart to my ears, miss.'

'What am I going to do about him, bosun?'

'The sub-lieutenant is in a difficult position, miss. Commanding officers have to avoid personal relationships with the crew.'

'He could at least smile occasionally.'

'But he does, miss. What's more,' said the bosun coughing discreetly, 'I have often seen him look favourably in your direction.'

'Really, bosun?'

'He likes you for sure, miss, but can't do anything about it - at least not yet, if you get my drift.'

'It all sounds pretty hopeless.'

'As long as you're one of his crew, miss.'

'Oh dear,' sighed April. 'I've got one more chance tonight. If that doesn't work, I'll just have to wait. But he can't stop me trying to look after him.'

As midnight approached Lindsey became increasingly uneasy. The last waltz was a pre-mating ritual at these kind of events. The lights were dimmed, the male circled his partner's waist and the female snuggled close sighing under the spell of soft romantic music from the band. Unfortunately there was no provision in the ritual for the male, forced by circumstances beyond his control, to keep the female at arm's length.

Smiling expectantly April collected him from his chair. On the dance floor, with his weight on her left shoulder, she tried to move closer but Lindsey stiffened his arm and held her apart. Far from the hoped-for murmurs of affectionate small talk as they danced, Lindsey treated her to an offhand account of a skiing holiday in Switzerland the previous winter which disturbed the other dancers and attracted hostile stares and 'shhhhs'. Hurt and embarrassed April lowered her eyes. When the waltz ended the couple parted in silence.

She walked back miserably to the hotel with Megan and Pippa who tried to cheer her by describing the expensive cocktails they had charmed from senior army officers at the bar particularly from the adorable old major with the eyepatch who was so intoxicated he could scarcely stand. Mrs Meredith and the bosun followed the girls, engrossed in a discussion about strawberry sponge cakes. Lindsey made up the rear, glaring angrily up at the moon.

Weedon Narrowboats

The bosun took the girls shopping on Monday morning. Lindsey was alone when the security guard at the boatyard escorted an elderly man with weather-beaten face to the quay.

'Says he's April's father, sir,' said the guard.

Lindsey looked up in surprise from the requisition forms he'd been signing in the cockpit of his barge.

'Thank you,' Lindsey said to the guard. 'How very nice to meet you, sir,' he said to the visitor.

'I came as soon as I heard,' said Mr Tree.

Lindsey cleared a space in the cockpit and invited April's father onboard. He could see the likeness to April immediately. His leathery face and rough clothes marked him as a working man but his eyes were deep and intelligent and he moved with the steady grace of a person not born to manual labour. His voice was cultured, with an accent far removed from the dialect of local boatmen, continental, definitely not English.

'Heard what, sir?'

'About my daughter April. That she's working on munitions barges, here. Is that true?'

'Yes,' nodded Lindsey.

'On one of these?' Mr Tree scanned the line of barges with red and yellow lines under their gunwales.

'You didn't know, sir?'

April's father shook his head. 'She didn't tell us. My wife and I are worried. We heard what happened, about the bombs.'

'Missed by miles,' smiled Lindsey. 'Let me get you some tea.'

They sat together in the cockpit drinking from enamel mugs while Lindsey explained the role of the CFZ convoy vessels to Mr Tree who stared with anxious eyes at the polite young naval officer who was transparently attempting to alleviate his concerns by conveying a picture of munitions barges drifting peacefully down the canal between stops at picturesque taverns and convivial dinners in the cabins and glasses of rum on grassy banks under willow trees at sunset as if describing afternoons on the river in Oxford on punts loaded with hampers and bottles of champagne.

'From our discussions, I gather she's saving up to attend secretarial college after the war. She gets well paid for this kind of work, ' said Lindsey.

'She's so young,' said Mr Tree.

'But an indispensable and thoroughly charming member of the crew nonetheless, sir. You can be proud of her,' said Lindsey.

April's father gazed at the white ensign on the stern of the barge. 'We assumed she was somewhere safe.'

'Nobody is completely safe in wartime, are they, sir?' said Lindsey. 'However I'm sure your daughter is better off on the canals than working in London, for example.'

'I hope you're right.'

Lindsey enquired after April's mother and sister and Mr Tree talked of his decision to abandon piano tuning and become a canal boatman and how despite early difficulties he had been able to keep his family together and provide his children with the fundamentals of a classical education. Lindsey suggested he might like to see his daughter's barge and perhaps wait for her in the cabin she had so decorated so artistically. Mr Tree thanked Lindsey for his hospitality and they walked together along the quay to the barge with the hand-painted *Daisy* name-board where the two men shook hands.

'Look after her, please,' said April's father.

Grand Union Canal

'We told you!' cried Megan and Pippa.

They were addressing April after the departure of her father who had been impressed at being called 'sir' by the young naval officer in charge of the convoy and he kept shaking his head and saying good manners were in short supply these days and that if April insisted on getting herself blown up by the Germans at least she would depart this earth in the company of a gentleman.

'Told me what?' said April.

'That the skipper likes you. He said that to your father.'

'Maybe he did, but it doesn't make any difference,' said April. 'Even if he does like me, he won't do anything about it - he can't, according to the bosun.'

'Then you'll have to do something.'

April shrugged her shoulders helplessly. 'Like what?'

'Girlish tactics.'

Megan and Pippa explained that the simplest place to secure a male's affection was in his bed which ordinarily posed logistical problems but not here because Lindsey's cabin was only a few yards away and he always kept the door unlocked when onboard, all she had to do was to arrive in the middle of the night in an alluring nightgown shivering with fright at a make-believe dream about air raids and ask to be comforted until the memory of the dream had passed.

'I couldn't do that!' said April.

'Of course you could, darling.'

'What if he said no!'

'Oh April,' sighed Megan and Pippa. 'You have so much to learn.'

West End Central Police Station, London

The duty constable at the front desk of West End Central Police Station was talking to his friend from the squad car division about the diabolical lack of ventilation in the station seeing that the windows had been sealed with adhesive tape to prevent the glass blowing in during air raids, and his friend said what they needed was a nice drop of beer from that blue and white brewery lorry that always seemed to be delivering to public houses when the squad cars were out looking for the source of the Mayfair wireless transmissions.

'Say that again,' said the constable.

His friend repeated his observation and said that perhaps they should get in touch with the brewery and arrange for a regular delivery of beer to the police station.

'Sergeant,' called out the constable.

The duty sergeant lifted his head from the newspaper he had been studying in order to familiarise himself for official purposes with the reasons why the girl on the centre page was unclothed.

'Yes?'

'We could be onto something, sergeant.'

''You haven't been thinking again, Johnson?'

Five minutes later a general alert was issued to regional police stations regarding the investigation and search of all blue and white brewery lorries in the London area.

Bletchley Park

The head of the signals intelligence and traffic analysis section at Bletchley Park walked through Hut 15 to inform his communications analyst of the prospective breakthrough in the search for the Mayfair wireless transmission source.

'Brewery lorry, you say?'

'Yes, Rupert.'

'That's interesting.'

'Why, Rupert?'

The communications analyst pointed to the map on his desk.

'According to the map references in the intercept I have received from next door, one of the radio transmission sources is here.'

'Where is that, exactly?' said the section head squinting at the map.

'A hilltop settlement fifty miles from the Uganda border in the Belgian Congo.'

'Africa?'

'So it couldn't be the central source of the transmissions,' said the communications analyst, 'because by the time the brewery lorry had left the settlement and crossed the Sahara desert on its way to London the beer would have gone flat.'

'So you can rule that source out, Rupert?'

'Almost certainly.'

'Are you on the right track with the map references generally, do you think?'

'It's difficult to say,' said the communications analyst, 'at this stage.'

Special Air Operations, Berlin

Fist raised at eye level the Abwehr colonel responsible for German air intelligence acknowledged the salute of the guard at the door and marched into the lavender-smelling conference room on the third floor of the Abwehr special air operations building in Berlin.

'Pleased with yourselves?'

The members the air intelligence committee taking their seats at the conference table did indeed look smugly satisfied. Nodding and smiling they reached for their pencils and entered the date of the meeting on their notepads.

The Luftwaffe captain standing beside the large-scale map of England commenced the briefing with a recapitulation of the constraints of the delivery system. For accuracy within the defined limits the aircraft had to approach the target in level flight at a maximum altitude of 250 feet and optimum altitude of 200 feet which ruled out targets defended by barrage balloons. For the safety of the pilots the targets had to be a reasonable distance from RAF airfields with night fighter capability. And the cloud base had to be sufficiently high and visibility sufficiently good for low level flight.

Subject to those constraints the system had demonstrated its effectiveness during last week's CFZ convoy raid. Pictures taken by agents on the ground showed the remarkable accuracy of the deliveries, each crater being equidistant to the next and each within five degrees of the attack line. The Luftwaffe captain pointed at the photographs pinned to the map and swept the tip of his cane across the surface of the largest photograph to indicate the distance between the craters and the canal bank.

'Fifty yards exactly,' he said.

'Pleased with yourselves, then?' said the Abwehr colonel.

The Luftwaffe captain nodded. 'Appropriate adjustments have been made. They'll get it right next time.'

Aylesbury Central Police Station

'Inert?'

'According to the forensics laboratory.'

'Completely harmless?'

'Totally.'

Detective Chief Inspector Standish of Buckinghamshire CID was accustomed to spectacular shifts of direction during the course of police investigations but this one left him almost speechless.

'No wonder the box didn't explode!'

'The soldier was obviously misinformed, sir.'

'Especially now, in the light of this information.'

'Quite, sir.'

'Well done, Sam.'

'Thank you, sir.'

The chief inspector offered a cigarette to Quinn, who shook his head.

'So, it's more than a fishing expedition for enemy agents, Sam, they've set us up too.'

'It looks like it, sir.'

The deliberations of the two detectives were interrupted by a pigeon which alighted on the window ledge outside the room and preened itself noisily, admiring its reflection in the glass. The chief inspector threw a matchbox at the window and the bird fluttered off into the cloudless sky.

'In which case, what's their objective? Expense, low cost operation?' said the chief inspector retrieving the matchbox and lighting a cigarette.

'Damage control, minimum loss of infrastructure from bomb strikes?' suggested Quinn.

'Probably a mixture of both,' said the chief inspector. 'A typical Whitehall scheme, divert attention from the Lee Navigation Canal, reduce the prospect of major damage to the Grand Union Canal and simultaneously earn applause from the Treasury for masterminding low cost counter-espionage measures. Quite clever really, unless you happen to be on one of the barges.'

Quinn pulled one of his ears.

'Something's wrong though, sir. I can't quite put my finger on it, but there's something strange about those barges.'

'You think the Germans have planted an agent in the convoy, Sam?'

'I wouldn't rule anything out at the moment, sir.'

'There's not much point in planting people, Sam, then bombing them.'

Quinn shuffled his feet.

'You're right, sir,' he said sheepishly.

'So, what do we do now?' said the chief inspector rubbing his chin.

'Warn the crew, sir?'

'You mean, tell them they're risking their lives transporting boxes of inert dried paste?'

'They might feel more comfortable during air raids, sir.'

The chief inspector stubbed out his cigarette.

'No, Sam. One of them might talk and accidentally give the game away. Keep it to yourself for the moment.'

Luftwaffe Base, Carbon-Dreyville

Mademoiselle Marie Pretot had left school at seventeen to help her mother cope with six children, several dozen hens, pigs and a flock of ducks at the family smallholding in the village of Carbon-Dreyville. When the Germans requisitioned the chateau she applied for the position of kitchen maid there. Not everyone in the village approved of activities which sustained the German military machine and muttered in doorways about fraternization and the penalties to be inflicted on collaborators after the war. Others in the village, including the Pretot family, were aware of infiltration by the Maquis into the chateau.

Marie's innocent-looking demeanour persuaded the Germans to approve her application and after a probationary period as scullery maid during which her performance was jointly monitored by the Luftwaffe stewards in the chateau and members of the local French resistance movement she was promoted to kitchen maid by the Germans, and to junior espionage operative by the Maquis.

She was not particularly beautiful but possessed the redeeming feature of youth. Nor was she particularly intelligent but worldly enough to recognise that, as a pubescent female, her knickers could be deployed to the benefit of France.

Despatched to the herb garden that summer evening, the air heavy with the scent of rosemary and thyme, finches singing in the branches of the chestnut tree which overhung the walled garden, the sun still warm as it dropped into the distant green forest, she lifted her dress and squatted legs apart at the parsley bed, slowly snipping the stalks. Her position coincided with a gap in the wall. Beyond the gap stood the guard house. Inside the guard house the sentries trained their binoculars in the direction of the parsley bed.

To the irritation of the sentries Maurice, one of the gardeners, chose that very moment to wheel his battered old bicycle past the guard house thereby blocking the sentries' view of the kitchen maid's underwear. 'Get on with it, you imbecile!' they shouted waving the gardener through the checkpoint. Maurice plodded to the gate, not changing his pace less it aroused suspicion, then mounted the battered old machine and wobbled off towards the village. The message concealed inside the bicycle seat stated that a special Luftwaffe mission was planned that night, time of takeoff approximately 0130 hours, destination unknown, code reference CFZ.

Grand Union Canal

Lindsey didn't much care for the squint-eyed landlord of the Horseshoe Inn but yielded to the girls' request and agreed to stop there for the first night, providing the barges moored further along the bank. If the bombers returned he didn't want to make the pilots' job easier by maintaining the same berthing pattern. For the same reason he decreed that the barges should moor two hundred yards upstream of the twin locks at Pitstone on the second night instead of trying to reach Marsworth before the 1900 hour curfew where they had berthed last time.

The decision was more or less forced on him anyway because of the hour lost retrieving *Buttercup's* hawser at Slapton. The bosun had been forced to dive into the murky waters of the canal to retrieve the rope and Pippa had fallen in trying to grab the end from him and April had grounded *Daisy* while doubled up with laughter watching the two of them spluttering in the water with strands of weed in their hair. Not, reflected Lindsey observing the shambles from the cockpit of his barge, an occasion of which Admiral Nelson would have been proud.

In view of the wet clothes and general exhaustion everybody stayed onboard after dinner playing cards and listening to the bosun's yarns until, yawning heavily, they dispersed to their respective bunks and were asleep by midnight. April dreamt of wedding dresses, the bosun dreamt of the deckchairs on Mrs Meredith's lawn, Megan and Pippa dreamt of money and Lindsey dreamt of an angel beckoning him into the sky where she waited with outstretched arms on a dance floor sparkling with starlight which he was just about to reach when a fist crashed against the cabin door.

'Get out!'

The fist continued hammering while Lindsey leapt out of his bunk, on his good leg, and hopped to the door.

'Move your barges!'

Opening the door Lindsey encountered a bristling moustache

attached to the face of a large figure in military uniform with three stars and a crown on each shoulder. The brim of the figure's cap shaded his face from the moonlight but Lindsey made out a pair of large eyebrows bristling in unison with the moustache and further down a huge pair of fists which clenched and unclenched impatiently as Lindsey clambered into his clothes.

'For the record, who are you, and what are you doing on this vessel, sir?' said Lindsey buttoning his jacket.

'Brigadier Smythe, Buckinghamshire Civil Defence and, by virtue of the flagpole on the stern of your barge, I assume you are Sub-Lieutenant Lindsey?'

'Yes, sir.'

'Well, Lindsey, you've got fifteen minutes to move. The Luftwaffe are after your cargo again.'

Glancing up at the sky Lindsey climbed from the cabin into the cockpit. Not a cloud in sight. If the Luftwaffe knew the convoy's position, they were sitting ducks. There was no chance of escape to open country south of the locks because the gates were closed. The barges would have to turn in the narrow stretch of water here and head upstream where unfortunately, Lindsey explained to the brigadier, the options were limited because of the residential area beyond the toll point at Greenbrook.

'How far to the toll point?' said the brigadier squinting upstream at the copse of trees where the silver ribbon of water narrowed.

'Two hundred yards beyond the copse, sir,' said Lindsey.

'The toll point is unoccupied presumably? You'd better moor opposite it. Too bad if it gets blown up.'

'I'm sure the toll collector won't mind, sir,' said Lindsey.

The brigadier looked suspiciously at the young naval officer. There had been a hint of sarcasm in that reply but with German bombers on the way it was an inappropriate moment to pursue the issue.

'As soon as you've moored, run like hell,' said the brigadier.

'Actually we've been advised to remain on the barges, but I appreciate your concern, sir.'

The brigadier looked suspiciously again at Lindsey. 'Please yourselves. But hurry up. I'll get the emergency services organised.'

Woken by the noise of the banging on the cockpit door the girls were already on deck. Lindsey shouted at them to cast off and moor upstream opposite the toll booth while he hopped over the gunwales, woke the bosun, returned to his barge and started the engine. The noise of the diesels on both motor boats coughing and belching into life drowned the sound of the brigadier's powerful motorbike disappearing into the night.

Greenbrook Toll Point

On Tuesday evenings Bert Simkins played dominoes with his friends at the Coach & Horses and slept away from home. The old octagonal toll booth was closer to the pub than his house. It was pleasantly cool in summer with the windows open, warm in winter with the stove alight and as comfortable as his bedroom at home thanks to the mattress which during the day stood rolled up in a corner. To be truthful it was quieter too, without the coughs and snuffles of his wife, and pleasant being lulled to sleep by the sound of water lapping the quay and owls hooting in the copse of trees further down the canal.

But bless my soul there was something afoot tonight and no mistake, he muttered sitting up in his makeshift bed disturbed by the noise of fire engines racing along the road clanging their bells. He stood up and checked the windows. There was no sign of smoke or flames in the direction of the village but good grief, he muttered rubbing his eyes, what was going on in the canal?

Barges were on the move. Turning here, at the toll point! Munitions barges, no mistaking them with those red and yellow danger markings visible in the moonlight. They were heading for the bank on the other side of the canal but why for goodness sake, he muttered, would they be mooring there in the middle of the night?

A thunderous roar from the devil himself made the toll collector step back. Long black shapes with swastikas on their fuselages flashed past the window. He ducked at the sound of explosions and looked up again to see Bert Barnham's turnip field on the other side of the canal erupting into the night sky. And then, if that was not enough to scare the wits out of a person, more thunderous roars and more aircraft hurtling past, this time in the opposite direction, curling up over the copse to reveal RAF markings on their wings.

Shaking his head, he reached for his pipe and stood at the window amidst a cloud of aromatic tobacco smoke wondering why the Germans had wanted to destroy Bert's nice crop of turnips. It was more likely, he concluded, they were trying to hit the munitions barges. In which case it was just as well they'd missed because if the barges had exploded the toll booth would have disintegrated in the blast and Mrs Simkins would have ended up a grieving widow or, if not exactly grieving, hopping mad at the loss of his wages.

The fire engines arrived, brakes squealing. They were lining up along the quay either side of the toll booth aiming their water cannons at the barges. The fire engines were followed by a truck load of ARP wardens who jumped out waving and shouting at the firemen not to discharge their cannons until orders were received from the senior officer at the incident site who seemed to be the large figure on the other side of the canal dismounting from a motorbike.

Grand Union Canal

Brigadier Smythe stepped across the grass from his motorbike to the barges lolling gently in the water.

'Good show, well done. Anybody hurt?' he said returning Lindsey's salute.

'No casualties, sir,' said Lindsey. He introduced the brigadier to the girls who had already initiated the CFZ convoy process for celebrating unsuccessful Luftwaffe raids, namely the liberal consumption of alcohol.

'Would you care to join us, sir?' said Lindsey.

'Don't mind if I do. What is it?' The brigadier sniffed at the glass given to him by the bosun.

'Jamaican rum, sir Seventy five percent proof,' said the bosun.

'Good god,' said the brigadier.

'How about your batman, sir? said Lindsey indicating the wiry-looking lance corporal standing beside the motorbike with a thirsty expression on his face.

'Barker? He doesn't drink,' said the brigadier.

The lance corporal gave Lindsey a pleading look.

'It's a chilly night, sir,' said Lindsey.

'Oh, very well, but not too much. I don't want him toppling off the bike again' said the brigadier.

The head of Buckinghamshire's civil defence service propped himself against *Daisy's* gunwale next to Megan and surveyed the moonlit scene critically. Soldiers from the local home guard unit were trampling across the field looking for unexploded bombs, illuminating the soil and scattered remains of shredded turnips with their torches. ARP wardens with tape measures were recording the size and position of the bomb craters in the middle of the field approximately a hundred yards in from the canal. On the road beyond the field a row of ambulances waited patiently.

'Rotten aim. No wonder they're losing the war,' said the brigadier.

'Perhaps they're trying to starve us into submission, sir,' suggested Lindsey.

'By destroying our turnips, eh? Can't think why the farmer grows them, nobody eats turnips nowadays, except the Scots,' said the brigadier.

'And cattle, sir,' said Lindsey.

'I suppose so. I say, this is a damn fine drink.' The brigadier held out his glass to the bosun, then turned to Megan. 'How about you, my dear, you must be getting used to air raids?

'I can't wait for the next one,' said Megan sweetly.

'That's the stuff. Damned courageous, all of you,' said the brigadier patting her arm.

The old goat, thought Megan! Making passes at his age, in the middle of a battlefield too.

'Excuse me, sir,' said a home guard captain running towards them saluting. 'The area is clear - no casualties - damage confined to the field - the farmer's been contacted - permission to stand down the medical and fire services?'

'Very good, captain,' said the brigadier.

'Another nightcap, sir?' said Lindsey as the home guard captain ran off making semaphore signs with his arms.

'Just a small one,' said the brigadier. 'Anti-aircraft guns. That's what you need, mounted on your barges, then you wouldn't have to rely on the RAF. They're always late anyway. What do you think, my dear?' he said to Megan.

'Someone would have to teach us how to fire them,' pouted Megan.

'Glad to be of service personally, any time, my dear,' said the brigadier twirling his moustache.

He swallowed the last drop of rum.

'Excellent,' he said handing the empty glass to the bosun. 'Fine drink.'

The officers and crew of the CFZ flotilla watched the brigadier's motorbike accelerate into the early dawn mist bumping over the uneven ground of the turnip field with the lance corporal behind him clinging precariously to the pillion seat.

Aylesbury Central Police Station

Baffled by the sequence of events Quinn looked uncharacteristically despondent as he bicycled back to Aylesbury through the same early morning mist to report details of the latest bombing raid to Chief Inspector Standish.

'Why did the barges move their moorings?' said the chief inspector.

'Brigadier Smythe told them to,' said Quinn.

'How did he know the Luftwaffe were coming?'

'From an intelligence report, sir.'

'Cutting it a bit fine,' said the chief inspector.

'I agree, sir, but the point is that the Luftwaffe still found the convoy, in the middle of the night, amidst all the other barges on the canal.'

'And missed, again?'

'Only just. A hundred yards to the right and the bombs would have blown them up, inert cargo or not.'

The telephone rang. The chief inspector listened to the voice at the other end of the line. 'Thank you,' he said replacing the receiver.

'No unauthorised radio transmissions were reported in the region of the canal immediately before or during the raid,' said the chief inspector.

Quinn stared gloomily at the floor.

'Could anyone else have known about the move? How about our suspicious army major?' said the chief inspector.

'Possibly, sir. He's on the distribution list.'

'Should we question him?'

Quinn shook his head.

'Why not?'

'Major Macleod is working for MI5, sir, in my opinion. His

uncharacteristic behaviour is typical of a spy catcher, sir.'

'You're confident of that, Sam?'

Quinn nodded.

'In which case,' said the chief inspector, 'we must conclude that the bombers are being guided to the target by person or persons unknown, from somewhere on the ground. You're going to need support, Sam. Let me have a list of people you would like on your team.'

Quinn stood up and made for the door.

'Incidentally,' said the chief inspector, 'Bletchley are working on radio intercepts for the CFZ project. They want dates and locations of convoy movements. Help them out, will you?'

Barclays Bank, Aylesbury

A routine check of new accounts at the main branch of Barclays Bank in Aylesbury revealed two large payments within the space of a fortnight to Miss April Tree. Her account had been opened by Weedon Narrowboats. Corresponding accounts had been opened for Miss Megan Leigh-Harvey and Miss Pippa Howland. The deputy manager of the branch conducting the check noted that the purpose of the accounts was to meet War Office regulations regarding disbursement of funds to employees undertaking certain categories of hazardous work. All three accounts had been credited with salary payments from Weedon Narrowboats at end June. The additional substantial sums remitted to Miss Tree's account from a London branch of Westminster Bank had been made in late June and early July.

Delphinium Cottage

In the local tea shop Alice Macleod unburdened her woes to her friend Priscilla Prescott-Overton whose husband's infantry battalion was fighting the Germans somewhere in North Africa.

'The telephone calls, I simply dread them - that awful boorish voice.'

'Who is he?'

'I've no idea. He can't be army.'

'Have you asked Alasdair?'

'Not directly. You know what he's like. I'm so afraid he's mixed up in something, well, unsuitable. All those trips to London.'

'How very worrying for you.'

'I think he's given up hope of promotion, and I'm rather giving up hope of buying the lovely little cottage we're renting. I do so want to settle down, after all those years in India.'

'Chin up, Alice, we're bred to suffer.'

A shadow fell across the table as the proprietress of 'Ye Olde Tea Shoppe' arrived to refill their teapot with hot water and enquire if everything was to the ladies' satisfaction.

'The cream cakes were heavenly, Mrs Suggins,' said Priscilla Prescott-Overton.

'I'm glad you like them, I'm sure. We reserve the real cream items,' said the proprietress lowering her voice, 'for our genteel customers.'

St James's Street, London

The pair of senior civil servants from the counter-espionage division of military intelligence who lunched frequently together agreed that whereas oxtail soup was in most respects appetizing and full-bodied it lacked the subtle quintessence of the brown windsor soup for which the club was rightly renowned. Comfortably seated at their usual window table overlooking St James's Street the day after what they whimsically referred to as *L'Affaire Navets* (loose translation 'turnip field raid') they discussed a wide range of subjects including the disappointing lack of progress on the Mayfair radio transmissions and the equally disappointing absence of results from the CID's unwitting contribution to the CFZ project.

'No trace of the blue and white lorry yet?'

'None.'

'It's probably green and white. The constabulary are fixated on blue.'

'They don't seem to be fixated on anything at all in Aylesbury. Up the creek without a paddle, by the sound of it.'

'Up the canal, more like.'

'That's very good. I wonder if we shouldn't take over? Our man's doing very well.'

'I didn't think we had anyone . . .'

'Oh, yes, he's close to reeling in a very big fish indeed. Now, what would you like, Stilton or Cheddar? It's such a relief not having to rely on the French for cheese.'

Weedon Narrowboats

Mrs Meredith's hand leapt to her mouth when she learned about the second raid. Those poor girls! What a terrifying experience! It was bad enough being at the end of indiscriminate bombing in the big cities but these were deliberate attacks on the CFZ barges. No casualties, said the report. What about the after-effects? How were the girls handling the pressure? She forced herself not to think about the bosun. At least he and sub-lieutenant were trained in warfare.

'It's not fair. We didn't tell them that hazardous transportation meant being dive-bombed every week!' she said storming into Mr Browning's office.

'We didn't know, Maggie,' soothed Mr Browning.

'When the barges return, I'm going to interview each of the girls and let them quit, if they want to, with full payment,' said Mrs Meredith defiantly.

'I agree,' said Mr Browning.

'You do?' said Mrs Meredith brightening. 'Oh, I'm so glad. They're are scarcely out of school, you know. They're young enough to be our daughters.'

'Mrs Browning mustn't hear of this,' said Mr Browning.

'Hear what?' said Mrs Meredith puzzled.

Mr Browning leaned back in his chair and examined the ceiling.

'That you and I have three children.'

Mrs Meredith stared at her boss, then a smile burst out on her face.

'You and your little jokes!' she chuckled.

Listening to the click of high heels in the corridor as Mrs Meredith returned to her office Mr Browning reflected yet again that his personnel manager was an attractive woman for her age and that Chief Petty Officer Jones could do a lot worse than settle down with her. If he survived.

Greenbrook Toll Point

The youth temporarily assigned to Greenbrook toll point to assist old Bert Simkins gawped at the turnip mounted in a glass-fronted case on the shelf containing the toll booth registers. He was not tall enough to read the inscription on the brass frame but the meaning would have eluded the youth anyway seeing he generally had trouble with written words.

'It says *In Memoriam*, lad,' said Mr Simkins. 'That's what goes on tombstones. And that's how close I was to the hereafter when Jerry tried to bomb the munitions barges.'

Mr Simkins pointed across the canal at the bank where the convoy had moored.

'I wish I'd been there, and seen it all,' said the youth.

'It was like this, lad,' said Mr Simkins indicating with his arms how the German aircraft had come in at low level from Pitstone travelling faster than the speed of light and how the RAF fighters had swooped down out of the sky even faster and how the noise of the aircraft had been so loud that the windows rattled and made his ears ring so much he could scarcely hear what Mrs Simkins shouted at him when he returned home.

'I'll never forget the sight of those turnips floating through the air, lad,' said Mr Simkins shaking his head. 'Like a fountain, it was.'

'Crikey,' marvelled the youth.

'And the crews of the munitions barges, lad. Didn't turn a hair. Standing on the grass after the event as cool as you like, laughing and drinking. Army uniforms, Navy uniforms, girls in pretty clothes. You'd think they were attending a garden party in Buckingham Palace.'

Grosvenor House Hotel, Mayfair

Mario the head barman in the Grosvenor House Hotel added a second olive to the martini cocktail and placed the glass on the tray alongside the whisky and soda for Mr Kelly's guest, the military gentleman with the eyepatch. Mr Kelly always had two olives in his cocktails because they reminded him of certain aspects of the female anatomy. Personally speaking, Mario did not find the association tasteful. Mr Kelly was not a person of great refinement. However he tipped generously and last year had found employment for Mario's youngest cousin as a steward in the Ambassador Club.

'Thank you, Mario,' said Kelly ostentatiously placing a one pound note on the tray.

'My pleasure, always,' said Mario bowing and reversing from the pair of armchairs in the lobby.

'The staff know me here. It's a second home really,' said Kelly to Major Macleod. 'I come here most days for a break from the club, when the tables are quiet, to relax for half an hour and think back to my youth in Dublin. Those were hard times. I can truthfully say, in all honesty, that they were the hardest times of my life. Up the Khyber.'

Kelly raised his glass. The major reciprocated half-heartedly and took a gulp of whisky.

'Mind you, it was a good training ground. You learned how to look after yourself. Broken bottles, knives if you could get hold of them. Attack, that was the best form of defense. Straight for the eyes or, if you had a knife, slash them across the face. I was quite good at that. Did I tell you about the cabbage leaves? There was this greengrocer where . .'

'Can we get back to the point, Kelly?' said the major.

'I was just going to say, there was this greengrocer, and he had a large garbage bin at the back of the shop, full of rotting cabbage leaves and we used to fight for the privilege of scrambling inside. Can you imagine that? Poverty is not a desirable institution,' said Kelly shaking his head.

'It was very stupid of me,' said the major. 'I should never have returned to the club. Obviously I'll sort out the problem with my bank - and settle the interest on the loan agreement - but I need time.'

Kelly speared one of the olives

'Time?' he said holding the olive up to the light.

'I've got friends. I'll borrow from them. But it will take a few weeks,' said the major.

'Friends?' said Kelly dropping the olive into his mouth and sucking it noisily.

'Unfortunately most of them are abroad right now - you know, the war,' said the major. 'But I'm sure I can find someone.'

'Given time?' said Kelly.

'Precisely.'

'The problem is, you see,' said Kelly, 'that, under the circumstances, the club finds itself unable to grant you an extension, this being the second offence, so to speak. I'm afraid you've rather lost credibility. Isn't there something you could sell, valuables, jewellery?'

The major shook his head fiercely.

'I can't ask my wife to sell her jewellery.'

'Better than selling your house.'

'We're in the army - we don't own, we rent.'

'Pity,' said Kelly spearing the second olive.

'How about that charitable foundation, couldn't they help with another loan, to tide me over?' said the major.

'What does this remind you of?' said Kelly holding up the olive.

The major glared at the little grey shape with pink pimento tip.

'It looks like something out of a martini glass,' he said irritably.

'Nipple,' said Kelly dropping the olive into his mouth. 'The problem is, you see, the foundation has lost confidence in you too. Which is a pity, a great pity, seeing that the club has instructed me to commence proceedings through our solicitors if your cheque is not cleared by the weekend.'

The major sank back in his chair.

'Well, that's it then,' he said.

He reached for his whisky glass and emptied the contents in one gulp.

'I've been a bloody fool,' he said standing up. 'Thanks for the drink.'

'You've got until the weekend,' said Kelly.

The major ignored Kelly's outstretched hand and set off towards the cloakroom to collect his cap and gloves. He walked slowly over the sumptuously thick carpet, head bowed. He was half way across when Kelly called him back.

'I've got an idea,' said Kelly.

Woolwich Arsenal

While the cargo was being unloaded at Woolwich Arsenal by soldiers stripped to the waist in the fierce summer sun April attempted to persuade Lindsey to revisit the medical unit. His knee was not improving, she could see that from the way he limped and the tightening of his eyes when he hoisted himself over the gunwales.

But he shook his head. 'Thanks, April. It's getting better, really,' he said.

The relationship between the two had ostensibly settled. April had accepted the bosun's advice and avoided outward displays of affection confining herself to expressions of feminine anxiety over the condition of his knee and the pain he was obviously enduring. On Lindsey's part the close proximity in the evenings when everyone gathered in the cabin for supper, and in the taverns where they drank side by side, had forced him to replace his pretence of aloofness with an attitude of semi-formal affability appropriate to his position as commanding officer. He was very careful not to sit next to April at table, however, or stand too close to her in the pub lest he should yield to temptation.

Sometimes the urge to reach out and take April's hand became so intolerable that he resolved to transfer her with the bosun to the standby barges being prepared by Weedon Narrowboats. The two of them could get the boats ready in the event of problems with the main convoy. The idea was strategically valid. If the flotilla suffered a major breakdown or the Luftwaffe's aim improved enough to cause damage the standby barges would be able to maintain a flow of CFZ cargo until additional vessel were constructed. But when the opportunity arose to discuss the transfer proposal with Mr Browning, he faltered. He would miss April too much.

It was not just the sheer loveliness of her presence. She was amusing company too. After supper the other night, for example, the girls had been discussing dates of important historical events and asked the bosun to contribute to their list.

'I know only two dates, the Battle of Trafalgar, and the date my pension is due,' he said.

April had tilted her head and said innocently 'Which comes first, bosun?'

'You young ladies will be the death of me,' laughed the bosun pretending to throw a cushion in April's direction.

Fortunately Lindsey was separated from her during the day being at the helm of the motor boat at the rear of the flotilla, and April being on *Daisy* at the front. Between them lay a stretch of open water. When the barges nestled together in the locks, Lindsey needed all his will power to stop him from hobbling over the deck towards *Daisy's* cockpit on the pretence of checking with April that the pair of forward boats were in good shape.

MV 'Sea Snake'

The converted trawler *Sea Snake* lolled in the light swell twenty miles north east of Margate. Inside the wheelhouse Binbow scanned the horizon. The cloud cover was intermittent. The moon kept breaking free and illuminating the ocean. They would be in trouble if a ship from the wrong navy appeared.

'It's a grand night, to be sure,' said O'Reilly the deckhand through the open wheelhouse window.

'No it isn't, you idiot,' snapped Binbow.

'You'll be worrying about the moon, right enough?' said the deckhand.

'I'll be wondering why I ever hired you. Have you released the hatches?'

'That I have, indeed.'

'What about the fenders?'

'You'll be wanting them as well?'

'Give me patience. Check they're all properly secured,' shouted Binbow.

He swept the eastern horizon with his binoculars. Was that a speck? He adjusted the focus and trained the binoculars on the small dark shape with a white crescent indicating a vessel travelling at high speed. He swung round and checked the coastline to the west. All clear, for the moment. He looked at his watch. They were late. At forty knots it would take them ten minutes to close the gap. He could feel the muscles contracting in his chest. He forced himself to think of the prize, the villa he would build in an orange grove in a country where the winters were warm and the girls obliging. He would need three of them, one to pick the oranges, one to cook, one to share his bed. No, he thought reaching for the revolver on the chart table, three were not enough. With the money he was making he could afford six, and change them every week.

'That's what we're waiting for, I'll be thinking,' said O'Reilly the deckhand through the open wheelhouse window pointing at the approaching vessel.

'Drop the fenders, starboard side,' snapped Binbow.

The roar of the twin-engine exhausts died to a growl as the large sleek craft drew alongside *Sea Snake*. Sailors stood fore and aft waiting to throw mooring lines across to the trawler. Other sailors crouched behind the deck-mounted Oerlikon 20 mm cannon. Binbow stepped out of the wheelhouse to receive the forward line.

'*Guten abend, Herr Kapitän*,' shouted a voice from the bridge of the E-boat.

West End Central Police Station, London

'I've got some disappointing news for you, Johnson,' said the duty sergeant at West End Central Police Station.

'You're going to be posted here indefinitely, sergeant?' said the duty constable.

'None of your lip, my lad.'

'I am speaking, of course, on behalf of the constables at other police stations who would be deprived of your competence and experience, sergeant.'

'The blue and white brewery lorry has been discovered . . .'

'That's not disappointing, sergeant!'

'. . . in Birmingham. The vehicle was on temporary assignment to London apparently. The brewery says it was in Birmingham during all but two of the Mayfair radio transmissions, and there was no radio equipment in the lorry when searched.'

'That's a pity, sergeant.'

'Never mind. It's a useful lesson in competence and experience, Johnson.'

Bletchley Park

The head of the signals intelligence and traffic analysis section at Bletchley Park leaned over the communications analyst's desk and peered at the first of three typewritten sheets.

'What am I looking at, Rupert?' he said

'The relationship between the dates of the Mayfair radio transmissions and corresponding CFZ convoy movements, as supplied by Buckinghamshire CID. Note the increased levels of radio activity each time the convoy approaches London. The levels are identical, in both cases.'

'So what conclusions can we draw, Rupert?'

'I don't know yet.'

'At least we know the subject of the transmissions, surely?'

'I suppose so. That's not much help, though, until they decipher the intercepts.'

'What's on the second sheet, Rupert?'

'Map references.'

'And the third?'

'I thought it would be useful to prepare a list of callsigns on the transmissions, in date order.'

'Why, Rupert?

'It passes the time between opening hours.'

'Yes, Rupert, but does the list tell us anything?'

'Apart from the fact that every callsign includes the initials "AT", not much.'

Aylesbury Central Police Station

'You were right, Sam,' said Detective Chief Inspector Standish.

'Sir?' said Quinn.

'There has been a descent from heaven over Whitehall. You are invited to attend Major Macleod's office in Weedon Barracks to discuss matters of mutual interest,' said the chief inspector.

Weedon Barracks

Driving an unmarked police car along the A5 road past hedgerows heavy with summer flowers Quinn permitted himself a sigh of relief at the prospect of help arriving from an unexpected quarter. The absence of progress in his investigations so far, his failure to make any sense of the evidence, weighed heavily on his conscience. The lives of the people on the CFZ barges depended on the prompt capture of one or more of the enemy agents now known to be lurking in the grass, for which he was primarily responsible. He had begun to suffer nightmares of girls' bodies exploding over the Grand Union Canal.

At Weedon he reported to the guardroom and was escorted into the bleak stone building to a door marked O/C CFZ.

'Come in and shut the door.'

To Quinn's surprise the person behind the desk instructing him to sit down was slim and smartly dressed, and the gaze from his uncovered eye was sharp and direct. From the reports of the person's behaviour Quinn had imagined someone portly and red-faced.

'Identification?' said Major Macleod.

Quinn showed the major his badge and papers.

'None of this goes beyond these walls, Detective Sergeant Quinn, is that understood?'

'Yes, sir.'

'The CFZ project in the Grand Union Canal is a feint. The real action is taking place in the Lee Navigation Canal.'

Waltham Abbey gunpowder mill had developed a powerful new propellant, explained Major Macleod, which was being shipped by night along the Lee Navigation Canal to Woolwich Arsenal. To divert enemy attention from the area he, Major Macleod, had been given the task of setting up a spurious operation in the Grand Union Canal. Specially-modified barges had been hired from a local boatyard and the navy had assigned personnel to the project as part of the subterfuge. None of the officers or crew on the barges were aware of the deception, and none of the officers or soldiers in Weedon Barracks knew that CFZ was a specially engineered but harmless derivative of chemical waste from a paint factory. So far, at least, nobody had seen through the guise. Externally the project had proved its worth in dramatic fashion by virtue of the bombing raids on the barges. Fortunately the Luftwaffe had missed the target on both occasions and thanks to a clandestine source in France it was hoped that the RAF would be able to intercept future raids.

Meanwhile he, Major Macleod on behalf of military intelligence, had been attempting to snare a suspected enemy agent in London. In the guise of a disaffected officer, passed-over for promotion and drinking too much, he had become a member of the gambling club in London where the man worked. The suspected agent had taken the bait of a bounced cheque but the operation had nearly come to grief during a meeting with the suspect when he, Major Macleod, had spotted a Special Branch officer lurking at the hotel bar and realised he was in danger of being arrested by his own side. Informed of the danger, his masters in Whitehall had warned off the Special Branch and, incidentally, had acquainted him of CID's operation along the Grand Union Canal.

'Which is one reason you're here,' he said to Quinn.

The suspected agent had responded to the bounced cheque by offering him, Major Macleod, a loan at exorbitant rates of interest. In his evolving role as a reckless gambler with serious financial problems he, Major Macleod, had returned to the club, lost heavily again and bounced another cheque. Closing in on his prey the suspected agent made his move. No link had been previously been established between the suspect and the canal operations but at a meeting two days ago in the Grosvenor House Hotel the proposal made by the man, surname Kelly, not only confirmed he was an enemy agent but that the Germans possessed detailed information on the CFZ project.

'Which is the second reason you're here,' said Major Macleod.

Confident that Kelly was not acting alone and could lead them deeper into the nest of infiltration he, Major Macleod, had played along with Kelly's proposal. Although the Germans had amassed a significant amount of data they still believed the CFZ operation was genuine and that the flotilla was carrying a strategically important new type of explosive, as evidenced by the air raids. There was no indication they knew anything about the real operation in the Lee Navigation canal. To keep it that way he, Major Macleod, had persuaded Whitehall that all parties involved - MI5, Special Branch and CID - should cooperate more closely and keep each other informed of their respective activities. Until the time came to arrest Kelly he, Major Macleod, would continue to play the role of a disaffected officer and, in case the Germans had planted someone in Weedon Barracks, continue to make a spectacle of himself on Saturday evenings at the weekly dance.

'Now,' said Major Macleod, 'let me tell you about Kelly's proposal.'

'I was hoping you would, sir,' said Quinn.

'In exchange for cancelling my debts, Kelly has requested that I supply him with details of CFZ convoy departure dates and, when instructed by him, that I re-arrange loading schedules and delay shipments to meet his requirements.'

Quinn stared in astonishment at the major.

'Would you mind repeating that, sir?' said Quinn.

'Through me, they want to control the departure dates for the flotilla.'

Quinn looked baffled.

'It doesn't make sense, sir. They don't need to worry about the barges, with you in their pocket. Why not take the obvious step of persuading you to let them into the barracks, then blowing up the CFZ compound and terminating the entire project?'

'I was rather hoping you could help me answer that question,' said Major Macleod.

Weedon Narrowboats

Mrs Meredith interviewed the girls as soon as the empty barges returned and tied up alongside the boatyard. She spoke to Sub-Lieutenant Lindsey first, such a charming person, and told him that Weedon Narrowboats intended to release, without penalty, any member of the civilian crew concerned about the bombing raids on the grounds that the girls had not been warned of that particular hazard and it was unfair to hold them to an imperfect contract, for which Weedon Narrowboats accepted full responsibility. Sub-Lieutenant Lindsey said he heartily agreed and although he would be very sorry to lose any member of the crew he considered it right and proper that the girls should be given the opportunity of resigning from the convoy on grounds of misrepresentation if they wanted to, assuming of course that Weedon Narrowboats would be able to replace them?

Mrs Meredith assured Sub-Lieutenant Lindsey that there had been numerous applications for crew positions on the new barges being prepared by Weedon Narrowboats at the request of the War Office. The vacant positions should therefore be filled promptly, assuming that the applicants, who were all female, accepted the risk of bombing raids.

Sub-Lieutenant Lindsey agreed with Mrs Meredith it was a pity that applications for dangerous work always seemed to come from females, but then Mrs Meredith observed that most of the males were in the armed forces nowadays, so perhaps it wasn't so surprising after all. Mrs Meredith also observed that Sub-Lieutenant Lindsey's leg didn't seem to be getting better and suggested she arrange a hospital appointment for him. Sub-Lieutenant Lindsey said he was already under pressure from Miss Tree in that respect and had promised to report to the medical unit at Woolwich Arsenal if his knee hadn't improved by the end of the next convoy.

Mrs Meredith interviewed Megan first. Megan was the most difficult of the girls to manage, in Mrs Meredith's opinion. She was cheerful and friendly enough, yet somehow distant. Perhaps because of the girl's eyes which were really quite steely. Anyway Megan firmly declined the offer of honourable release from her contract. The job was the greatest fun ever, she declared. Pippa said exactly the same thing at her interview. Where else in the middle of a war, she asked, could you get paid to drink rum cocktails while cruising in a comfortable boat on one of England's most beautiful waterways?!

April hesitated, however. She became very quiet and thoughtful when Mrs Meredith made the offer. You mustn't worry, my dear, said Mrs Meredith, what people might think. It was no disgrace to decline conditions of employment which had been inadequately represented. Weedon Narrowboats would provide excellent references if she chose to go. April still hesitated. She was concerned about her family, thought Mrs Meredith. Perhaps her father's recent visit to Weedon had fostered feelings of guilt? No, said April, shaking her head at the suggestion. April was quiet again for a while then suddenly perked up and, thanking Mrs Meredith profusely for the considerate offer, confirmed that she wanted to continue working in the convoy.

Finally Mrs Meredith talked to Chief Petty Officer Jones, not about leaving the convoy, heavens alive, that was not up to her, anyway a gallant sailor like the bosun would scoff at such a suggestion, no, she talked to him about a new recipe for strawberry jam which included infusions of elderberry and invited him to tea on Saturday, an invitation he duly accepted and arrived clutching a bunch of flowers picked from the banks of the canal and sat in a deckchair on her lawn while she fed him watercress sandwiches and sponge cake and they talked without break all afternoon, content in each other's company.

Aylesbury Central Police Station

At the central police station in Aylesbury the pigeon was back on the window ledge preening and cooing at itself in the glass.

'That damn bird's in love with its own reflection,' said the detective chief inspector hurling a box of paperclips at the window. The box burst open, spraying metal over the room. Quinn joined the chief inspector on the floor.

'There's no possibility of a mistake, sir?'

Quinn was referring to a report received from France over the weekend to the effect that the German pilots returning from what British military intelligence clearly identified as the latest attack on the CFZ convoy had celebrated extensively through the night toasting the "success and accuracy" of the bombing raid.

'The report came from a normally reliable source, I am informed,' said the chief inspector.

'In which case there are only two logical conclusions, either the aircraft couldn't see the target clearly - which is ridiculous, the conditions were perfect that night, no clouds and a bright moon - or they missed the barges deliberately.'

'Strange, isn't it, Sam?'

Frowning with concentration, eyes down searching for paperclips, Quinn did not reply.

'Almost as strange as Major Macleod's report that the Germans are trying to control departure dates for the flotilla,' said the chief inspector.

Quinn suddenly straightened up.

His eyes narrowed.

'I've got it!' he said slamming his fist into the open palm of his other hand.

Grand Union Canal

Propped comfortably against the stern board cushion of his barge the bosun watched the changing patterns of light on the water as the convoy headed south. The sun flickered through the branches of the willow trees casting shadows on the ripples from the boats. Nothing could beat the deep blue sea, of course, where dolphins sometimes played in a ship's wake but the patterns on the surface of a canal on a warm summer morning were an agreeable alternative and frankly, reflected the bosun, he was getting to the age when the tranquility of life on a narrowboat compared favourably with the bustle of a warship.

There was also the matter of future arrangements. His daughter had emigrated to New Zealand before the war taking his grandchildren with her, his small terraced property in Plymouth had been destroyed during the blitz and his possessions amounted to an alarm clock, christening mug, prayer book and sundry items of kit and clothing all of which fitted in a single duffel bag. His intention on retirement had been to rent lodgings somewhere in Devon overlooking the sea with taverns along the harbour wall where he could play draughts and swap yarns with shipmates but fate had now presented him with an alternative. Instead of a landlady clucking at him and chiding him in rented quarters, a comely property-owning widow had beckoned him into her life. Instead of cold nights in a drafty boarding house, the prospect had arisen of spending winter evenings in an armchair beside a glowing fire with slippers on his feet. What possible reason, he reflected ducking under the low-hanging branches of a willow tree, could there be for not responding to the overtures of a warm-hearted woman with whom he found himself completely at ease?

A noise disturbed the bosun's thoughts. He glanced sideways at the skipper who was steering the rear pair of barges with his arm crooked over the motor boat's tiller.

'Did you hear that, sir?'

'Hear what, bosun?'

The bosun stood up and shielded his eyes against the sun.

'Police boat ahead, sir.'

Greenbrook Toll Point

The youth temporarily assigned to Greenbrook toll point to assist the lumbago-afflicted toll collector burst into the booth.

'Soldiers, Mr Simkins!'

'Where, lad?' said the toll collector.

The youth waved his arms.

'All around us, Mr Simkins. Soldiers, with guns.'

The door from the road swung open and an army captain with a revolver entered the booth. Motioning the toll collector and youth to get down the captain strode to the window.

'What's going on here?' demanded Mr Simkins.

'Military operation. Keep below the level of the window, please,' said the captain.

The toll collector lowered himself to the floor muttering that what with bombing raids, flying turnips and army officers barging in with revolvers the world was going to the dogs and no mistake. The youth, with the bold curiosity of teenage years, knelt down but kept his eyes level with the window. Upstream of the toll point he could see the CFZ munitions barges approaching. Waiting for them in the middle of the canal was a police boat. In the stern of the police boat someone was shouting instructions at the flotilla though a loud hailer.

Grand Union Canal

There must have been an accident at one of the Pitstone locks, thought Lindsey. The police were halting traffic until the damage had been repaired. One of the coal barges had probably rammed a lock gate. In which case the repairs would take all day and the convoy would probably have to moor at Greenbrook for the night. But why were the police directing the convoy barges to the toll point quay on the public side of the canal, not to the bank on the opposite side which was out of harm's way? And what were those soldiers doing on the quay? It must have been a serious accident.

Lindsey watched April swing the front pair of barges, lashed together in the usual abreast formation, towards the quay. Lindsey reached for the throttle and reduced speed. At the same distance from the toll point he pushed the tiller over and followed April's course to the shore. As the bows swung, the bosun stepped across the deck to prepare the mooring ropes.

The soldiers don't look very friendly, thought Lindsey. There were dozens of them, lined up along the quay with rifles in their hands. Something must be really seriously wrong, thought Lindsey, reversing the engine and bringing the second pair of barges alongside the concrete wall ten yards astern of *Daisy* and *Buttercup*.

The bosun jumped ashore, secured the mooring ropes, extended his hand and pulled Lindsey up from the inboard barge. The girls were already the quay, looking around at the soldiers, spreading their arms in "what's going on?" gestures. Lindsey collected his walking stick and limped towards the two figures disembarking from the police boat, one in uniform, the other in plain clothes.

Lindsey recognised the figure in plain clothes.

'Detective Sergeant Quinn. Tell me what's happening, please.'

'Good morning, sir. I'm sorry about this but I must ask you to step back with your crew, to the end of the quay, while we conduct a search of your vessels.'

'Search? On whose authority?' demanded Lindsey.

'Government orders, sir,' said Quinn indicating the line of soldiers and the army captain who had stepped out from the toll booth holding his revolver. 'We have reason to believe that one or more of your vessels may be engaged in illegal activities.'

'Illegal activities!' said Lindsey. 'We're transporting explosives!'

The two men stared at each other.

Lindsey looked round at the army captain standing impassively in front of the toll booth, then swung back to meet Quinn's unflinching gaze.

'Very well,' said Lindsey. 'Who's conducting the search, and are they aware of the hazardous nature of the cargo?'

'Captain Letchworth's men will carry out the search. They are appropriately aware and qualified, sir.'

Lindsey motioned the bosun and girls to follow him and limped to the end of the quay where he turned, propped himself on his walking stick and watched in bemused anger as a group of soldiers in khaki overalls advanced cautiously towards the barges, covered by the rifles of the soldiers lining the quay, and led by the army captain brandishing his revolver.

'What in heaven's name are they looking for, bosun?' said Lindsey.

'The rum barrel, probably, sir,' said the bosun cheerfully.

The searchers started on motor boat W3, Lindsey's barge. They unfastened the straps, hoisted the inboard tarpaulins revealing the racks of munitions boxes, clambered down into the ventilation channels and clambered out again. Shaking their heads they climbed into the cockpit, disappeared into the cabin and reappeared, again shaking their heads.

From motor boat W3 they moved across to butty boat W4, the bosun's barge, and repeated the process, clambering in and out of the cargo hold and cabin, shaking their heads once more as they came out. On butty boat W2 (*Buttercup*) the straps on the central tarpaulin had fused onto the brackets and had to be cut free with a knife. Lindsey noticed that Quinn had the decency to nod in his direction acknowledging the damage being caused to flotilla property. Megan and Pippa were more concerned about the amount of time the searchers spent in their cabin.

'I hope they're not going through our underwear,' said Pippa.

When the searchers moved to motor boat W1 (*Daisy*) and hoisted the tarpaulins the army captain stepped backwards so suddenly that Lindsey thought he was going to topple into the canal. Clutching at a stanchion the captain steadied himself, raised his revolver and shouted 'Come out!'

To the astonishment of almost everyone on the quay, a man emerged from the depths of the barge holding his hands above his head, blinking at the sunlight. He was followed by a further five men also blinking at the sudden transition from night to day. All except the first were wearing German air force or naval uniforms.

It was Quinn who found the metal plate. While the captured men were being lined up on the quay he joined the search party in *Daisy's* cabin and found a red and yellow fluorescent rectangle hidden in a groove behind the cupboard. Quinn had guessed he would find something like that, something bright enough to mark the position of the convoy for the Luftwaffe on their diversionary raids.

Quinn walked grimly to the end of the quay carrying the plate under his arm.

'Please identify for me the person or persons residing in motor barge GUC/W1, sir,' he said to Lindsey.

'That's me,' said April raising her hand.

Protesting at the implications of Quinn's question Lindsey took a step forward and tripped over a mooring rope. The last thing he saw before his head struck the bollard was the look of bewilderment on April's face as she was marched off by soldiers to the police car waiting behind Greenbrook toll booth.

PART 2 PROSECUTION

The process of rounding up the enemy agents associated with the Grand Union Canal escape route for German prisoners of war commenced with the interrogation of the man in plain clothes captured during the combined police-military operation at Greenbrook toll point.

Interrogation of Hans Schneider

According to the documents found in his possession the man's name was Ansgar Erling, age 48, nationality Swedish, profession timber merchant. The documents included business cards describing him as sales director of the Anglo-Swedish Timber Products Company of Kensington in London. The man was medium height, suave, with blond hair. He wore a white polo-neck shirt and grey slacks.

The interrogation was conducted by a Special Branch superintendent and a military intelligence officer at an undisclosed location in north London. Both interrogators spoke German. The prisoner was not handcuffed or constrained in any way although the window of the room was barred and the door locked. The prisoner and interrogators faced each other across a pinewood table with an ashtray in the middle. Drinking water was available in paper cups.

The superintendent, speaking English, asked the questions. The military intelligence officer looked on languidly, legs crossed.

'You are Ansgar Erling, and you're from Sweden?' said the superintendent.

'Yes,' said the prisoner.

'You work for the Anglo-Swedish Timber Products Company in Kensington?'

'Yes.'

'From an office?'

'Yes.'

The superintendent consulted his notebook.

'We seem to have difficulty tracing it.'

'Quite understandable,' said the prisoner. 'My apartment is a combination of office and living quarters.'

'That's the difficulty, you see. We couldn't find a signboard or nameplate outside the premises.'

The prisoner smiled.

'You've been doing your homework,' he said.

'Which, combined with the fact that your identification papers are forgeries,' said the superintendent, 'indicates you're probably not a timber merchant. Shall we start again? Are you Ansgar Erling?'

'No.'

'What is your real name?'

The prisoner stared in the direction of the barred window for a while, stroking his chin while evidently evaluating his odds of survival if he refused to answer.

'Hans Schneider,' he said.

'What is your nationality?'

'German.'

'How long have you been in England?'

'Approximately six months.'

'How did you got here?'

'Sorry, I can't tell you that.'

The superintendent paused.

'You do understand, Herr Schneider, that the British government discourages illegal entry to this country, particularly from nations with which we are at war?' he said.

'Certainly. We feel the same about it in Germany.'

'Presumably you are not here on vacation?'

'Correct.'

'And you were not on vacation when discovered in the cargo hold of one of our munitions barges?'

'Correct.'

'Can you explain what you were doing in the barge?'

'Acting as escort.'

'Please explain.'

'My role was to look after the first stage of the journey, from the assembly point to London, loading our people onto the barge and travelling with them to Woolwich.'

'Please elaborate.'

The prisoner stared at the window again, then shrugged his shoulders.

'Our original intention was to use commercial vessels on the Grand Union Canal. Then we learned about the CFZ project and realised you were unlikely to search your own munitions carriers. Even more unlikely if we arranged spurious bombing raids, which we did, although that nearly went wrong.'

'In what way?'

'We requested a hundred metre safety margin. The pilots dropped the bombs too close on the first raid and nearly blew the tarpaulins off.'

'We wondered about that,' said the superintendent.

The prisoner shrugged his shoulders again.

'You would have worked it out eventually,' he said.

'When you say "we", who were you working with?' said the superintendent offering the prisoner a cigarette.

'Sobranie? How very nice, thank you. When discussing names, I must of course be careful,' said the prisoner blowing smoke at the ceiling, 'to remain within the limits of confidentiality.'

He's not frightened, thought the superintendent. The suave manners indicated an upper class background, appropriate for the noble tradition of rescuing captive countrymen from foreign lands, a tradition stretching back to antiquity and practiced famously during the French Revolution by the Scarlet Pimpernel, Sir Percy Blakeney. Sir Percy, however, had been more successful overall than Schneider and not fallen foul of the French equivalent of Buckinghamshire CID.

'Let me help you,' said the superintendent reading from his notebook. 'We calculate you must have embarked during night stops of the convoy at the Horseshoe Inn near Grafton Regis owned by Mr Sid Prone, that you subsequently disembarked at the Smugglers Arms in Woolwich owned by Mr Jake Hawkins and the escaping POWs were then transported to sea by the converted trawler MV *Sea Snake* owned by Captain Charles Binbow for rendezvous with one of your vessels, presumably a submarine or E-boat. How are we doing?'

'Most impressive,' said the prisoner.

'The persons mentioned above are all now in custody. They protest they were acting under threat of violence. Were you the instigator of the threats?'

'Certainly not.'

'You were in overall charge of the operation?'

'Yes.'

'You indicated you were not working alone?'

'I delegated recruitment and management of local personnel to someone else.'

'What was his name?'

'I don't know.'

'You delegated local activities to someone you didn't know?'

'I said, I didn't know his name.'

'Presumably you were in regular contact. When you were together, what did you call him?'

'Stupid.'

'Why? Didn't you get on?'

'He was not the sort of person I normally like to associate with. I felt quite sorry for his employees who incidentally, if it helps, referred to him as "The Gambler".'

'Is this the man?' said the superintendent passing a photograph across the table.

The prisoner glanced at the picture of Fingelton Kelly.

'Yes,' he nodded.

'He controlled the local hirings, but responded to your instructions, would that be correct?' said the superintendent.

'I set the objectives, he executed them, then I paid him,' said the prisoner.

'Was anybody else involved in the decision making process?'

'Not on my side.'

'What about his side?' said the superintendent indicating the photograph.

'I don't know.'

'Was he in charge of the local operation?

The prisoner reached for the ashtray and stubbed out his cigarette.

'It's possible.'

'Why did you call him stupid?'

'Because he insisted on trying to recruit a British army officer, who was obviously being used as bait.'

'Why didn't you stop him?'

'I thought I had.'

'Who operated the radio?'

'I did.'

'Did you have any direct dealings with the crews of the munitions barges?'

'No?'

'Did you ever meet with, or speak to, Miss April Tree?'

'No.'

'That will do for the moment,' said the superintendent closing his notebook and looking enquiringly at the military intelligence officer.

'I realise you're probably going to shoot me,' said the prisoner. 'Which is a pity. There's so much more to do, so much more to enjoy. All those lovely Greek islands, for example. So it occurs to me you might be interested in some information I've picked up while working for the Abwehr. Really quite important information. Do you suppose someone on your side might want to consider exploring the possibility of an arrangement agreeable to both sides? At an appropriate time and place, of course.'

The military intelligence officer languidly uncoiled his legs.

'My department is always interested in possibilities,' he drawled.

Interrogation of Jed Boult

Surveillance in the vicinity of the Smugglers Arms in Woolwich led to the arrest of the driver of a grey Bedford van with 'Emergency Blitz Repair Unit' painted on the doors and side panels.

He was Jed Boult, 19, British, born in Liverpool, religion Roman Catholic. He had left school early and moved to London where he worked as a porter in Billingsgate fish market. The fish merchants who knew him declared he was honest and reliable though he liked to bet on horses and was always short of money. At the outbreak of war he had disappeared. The assumption at Billingsgate was that he'd gone underground to avoid conscription. There was no police record in his name. To all intents and purposes Boult was one of the many young men Britain living off their wits rather than fighting for their country.

The interrogation was conducted in Pentonville Prison by the Special Branch superintendent who had interviewed Hans Schneider.

Boult was nervous and evidently shaken by his arrest. He kept shifting in his chair and biting his lip. The interrogation took place in one of the caged interview rooms, with a warder visible throughout in the passage outside.

'You're not going to shoot me, are you? You can't shoot someone who's been blackmailed, isn't that right?' said Boult.

'Calm down, Jed,' said the superintendent. 'You'll get a fair trial. Just answer my questions truthfully, and I'll do my best for you,' he said.

'It wasn't my fault. He would have killed me if I didn't.'

'Tell me what happened when you left Billingsgate, Jed. Where did you go?' said the superintendent.

'A job.'

He had owed money to a man who frequented the public houses around the fish market. The man lent to the porters at a reasonable rate of interest, at least it seemed reasonable until you added it up properly, and when you couldn't repay the loan he introduced you to another man who pretended to be nice and friendly but when you couldn't pay him back he threatened to hurt you, badly, unless you agreed to carry out little jobs which, in his case, involved driving a van through London at night delivering sealed packages to different addresses. That way you got to pay off the loan gradually but you also got very tired because the porters started work at half past four in the morning.

When the war started he still owed money to the man who said he could pay off the debt by leaving the fish market and driving the van full time, only this time it would be official because he would have a trades union card for London docks, which suited him fine because he didn't want to be called up. The only trouble was he never seemed to be able to pay off the debt and when he complained about the situation he ended up half scared to death in a warehouse talking with a man you wouldn't want to meet on a dark night alone.

The new man, evil looking, with a scar on his cheek, told him that the sealed packages he'd been delivering contained contraband goods and people who dealt in contraband goods during the war got the death penalty. The man said that fortunately he was of a generous nature and wouldn't report Jed to the authorities, and that Jed was now working for him, and that Jed would get a reasonable wage but, if Jed tried to be smart, what was left of him after the man had finished carving him with his knife would be dropped off at the nearest police station. If Jed behaved himself, said the man, he would get paid well for continuing to make special deliveries around London plus some additional work of an unspecified nature. He would be given forged papers and a new van, painted grey with emergency service signs to help him through road blocks. The van would contain valves, pipes, and electrical equipment with enough space in the middle for the additional work.

'I didn't have a choice, did I?' said Boult.

'Is this the man?' said the superintendent producing the photograph of Fingleton Kelly.

Boult stared at the photograph and grimaced.

'Yes.'

'Don't worry. He's safely behind bars. You won't see him, except in court, when you may have to identify him. Tell me about the special deliveries.'

'They were the same as before, at night.'

'What was in the packages?'

'I don't know.'

'Where did you deliver them?'

'All around, pubs mostly.'

'Did the packages contained bottles?'

'Might have done, I didn't open them.'

'Where did you collect the packages?'

'The warehouse.'

Occasionally he was required to report to the warehouse in the morning, about eleven, where a man, a different man, would load radio equipment into the space in the middle of the van. Jed's job was to drive to Hyde Park Corner, keep in the traffic, go round the roundabout, drive to Piccadilly Circus, go round the roundabout and repeat the circuit until the man told him to return. If stopped by the police, Jed was to stick his head out of the window and shout "Sorry mate, unexploded bomb emergency in Pimlico" and put his foot down. Back at the warehouse Jed was to lower and lock the roller door, let the man out of the van and run like hell from the rear exit of the building. That never happened, fortunately, and the man always gave him a tip afterwards. Nice person, he was.

'He sat in the middle of the van with the radio equipment, while you drove around London?'

'Yes.'

'Could you hear him talking?'
Boult nodded. 'In a foreign language.'
'Is this the man?'
Boult looked at the photograph of Hans Schneider.
'That's him.'

Trial of Binbow and O'Reilly

Captain Charles Binbow and deckhand Seamus O'Reilly were the first to be tried in the case of the Grand Union Canal escape route. The hearing took place in closed session at the Old Bailey in London, with reporters and the general public excluded from the court.

The prosecuting counsel, one of England's most eminent barristers, started by pointing at the two men in the dock - one burly and grim, the other bald and grinning - and emphasising to the jury the seriousness of the charges. Captain Binbow was the owner and master of an old coastal trawler MV *Sea Snake*. The vessel had been converted for general haulage and tug boat duties within the Port of London and adjacent waters including the Medway river. The vessel had been surveyed by the Admiralty at the outbreak of war and rejected as suitable for escort or minesweeping duties. In May, Captain Binbow had notified the Port of London coastguard that he intended transporting consignments of electrical motors from the Thames to the naval dockyard at Chatham. The trips were to take place at night to minimise the risk of being strafed by enemy aircraft, a hazard increasingly faced by coastal vessels.

The coastguard station duly noted the passage of MV *Sea Snake* eastward to sea on three occasions during June and July. The court will hear, said the prosecuting counsel, that instead of delivering electric motors to Chatham the trawler proceeded to sea and rendezvoused with an enemy vessel, believed to have been an E-boat or submarine, for the purpose of handing over German prisoners of war who had escaped from British detention camps.

The first witness called by the prosecution was the Special Branch superintendent leading the police investigation. The superintendent told the court that during interrogation the German agent running the escape route had provided details of Captain Binbow's role in the operation, together with dates of the three occasions that MV *Sea Snake* had handed over escaping POWs to a German warship, dates arranged by the agent himself via radio to Berlin. For security reasons the agent could not be named or appear in court.

Captain Binbow's defence counsel, a forceful young barrister exempt from war service by virtue of his profession, challenged the evidence.

'Did your so-called agent claim to have met my client?' said the barrister.

'He met Captain Binbow on several occasions,' said the superintendent.

'Yet he is not prepared to identify my client in court?'

'Unfortunately he cannot appear here, for reasons I have explained.'

'How very convenient. The jury will not then have the opportunity of determining if your so-called agent was lying.'

'We have every reason to believe he was telling the truth.'

'Have you any other evidence connecting my client with the escape route operation?'

'Yes - the intercepts of the radio communications with Berlin,' said the superintendent.

'Are they being produced in court?'

'The documents are classified, and have not yet been fully deciphered,' said the superintendent.

'So you can produce nothing tangible to link your so-called agent with my client,' said the defence counsel sitting down scornfully.

Re-examined by the prosecution, the superintendent confirmed that the evidence from the agent had been validated by the radio intercepts, and was believed to be correct beyond all reasonable doubt.

The second witness for the prosecution was an officer from the Port of London coastguard station who submitted certified copies of the station logbook. The dates of the logbook entries for the nights in June and July when MV *Sea Snake* had been seen departing from the port coincided with the dates the captured agent declared had been arranged for the handover of POWs from the trawler to a German warship.

Captain Binbow's defence counsel again challenged the evidence.

'Did you personally see MV *Sea Snake* alongside the alleged warship?' he said.

'No.'

'How then do you conclude that MV *Sea Snake* was engaged in unlawful activities?'

'We don't. The coastguard service is here simply to present the station logbook and respond to associated questions.'

'You had no way of knowing what cargo was onboard the trawler on the nights in question?'

'None.'

'Captain Binbow asserts he was transporting electric motors to Chatham. Is there any reason to disbelieve the assertion?'

'No.'

'Thank you,' said the defence counsel sitting down.

The prosecuting counsel concluded his case against Captain Binbow and the deckhand Seamus O'Reilly by emphasising to the jury that the dates of trawler's night sailings as recorded in the coastguard logbook coincided exactly with the dates that the German agent had given for the handover of the POWs to a German warship.

Captain Binbow's defence counsel called only one witness, a man of furtive demeanour from Chatham who told the court he specialised in second hand electric motors and had received three consignments from MV *Sea Snake* during the nights in question. The credibility of the witness was diminished when he admitted to the prosecuting counsel that the papers covering the transactions had inadvertently been misplaced, most likely eaten by his dog which was given to bouts of random consumption.

Nonetheless Captain Binbow's counsel appeared satisfied. He declared to the judge that the case for the defence of his client was concluded, and sat down giving the jury a knowing look.

Seamus O'Reilly's defence counsel, an equally young and energetic barrister, called his client to the witness box.

Presented by the clerk of court with the bible and card containing the judicial oath, O'Reilly turned to the warder who had accompanied him from the dock and whispered that he couldn't read. The taking of the oath was thereby administered by the accused chanting loudly the words whispered to him by the warder.

Returning the bible to the clerk of court, O'Reilly stood upright in the witness box and surveyed the court with cheerful interest, apparently pleased to be centre of attention. He seemed especially interested in the judge, and turned in his direction with such frequency that the judge was forced to comment.

'Is something bothering you, Mr O'Reilly?'

The accused beamed at him.

'It's a fine looking robe you're wearing, your grace.'

The judge lifted his distinguished eyebrows.

'I am not a bishop, Mr O'Reilly, I am a judge.'

'And a grand job you'll be making of it, right enough,' said the accused.

O'Reilly's defence counsel asked the accused to tell the court about his duties onboard MV *Sea Snake*. The request confused the deckhand who described his job on a building site in Dulwich, which had been very vexatious on account of the condition of the food at dinnertime, especially the soup which contained bones and even, on one occasion, a beak which could have been chicken but most likely was crow. Glared at by the judge the energetic young defence counsel struggled to focus his client's attention on his job on the trawler. The jury would particularly like to know, prodded the counsel, about the events on the three occasions in June and July when MV *Sea Snake* had gone to sea at night.

If Captain Binbow had nurtured hopes that O'Reilly would remember what he was supposed to say, the hopes were dashed as soon as the accused stopped scratching his head and launched into a description of the guns on the large boat which had come alongside the trawler. Captain Binbow's head dropped as the accused described the transfer of men in uniform from the trawler to the large boat and how there'd been a lot of shouting in a foreign language.

'What uniforms were the men wearing?' said O'Reilly's defence counsel.

The accused shook his head. 'I couldn't rightly say.'

'What about the large boat, did you recognise the markings, or the uniforms of the sailors?'

'Captain Binbow told me the boat was from Spain, which is near India,' said the accused helpfully.

'What else did Captain Binbow tell you?'

'That the boat was taking British soldiers to fight the Germans.'

'Captain Binbow told you that the men on MV *Sea Snake* being handed over to the large boat were British soldiers, and the boat was

Spanish?'

'Very precise about it, he was,' said O'Reilly, suddenly clutching the back of his trousers.

'Is something the matter?' said the defence counsel to his client. The warder standing behind the accused leaned forward and spoke into his ear. The accused turned and spoke back, clutching at his trousers with increased urgency.

The warder leaned out of the witness box and spoke to the court usher.

'The accused wishes to go the lavatory, my lord,' announced the court usher to the judge.

The judge clucked his tongue irritably.

'Very well,' he scowled. 'The court will remain in session, so be quick about it.'

The accused was smiling broadly when he returned to the courtroom. Followed by the warder he walked from the door with an amiable swagger, nodding cheerfully at the assembly of lawyers, attorneys and court officials lining the benches. When the usher opened the witness box door for him, he stopped, shook his hand and told him confidentially but loud enough for everyone in the court to hear 'You'd travel a long way to beat a good shit.'

'Silence in court,' shouted the judge banging his gavel.

The judge waited for the coughs and suppressed guffaws on the benches to subside.

'There are ladies present, Mr O'Reilly,' he said. 'I don't want to hear remarks of that nature again in my court. Is that quite clear?'

'Begging your pardon, I'm sure, your grace,' mumbled the accused.

He was subdued for the rest of his evidence. Not until the prosecuting counsel took over and accused him of pretending not to understand what had taken place on the trawler did he come back to life.

'That is a terrible sinful thing for you to say, you being in the priesthood,' said O'Reilly wagging his finger.

'I am not a priest,' said the prosecuting counsel through clenched teeth, 'and this is not a church.'

'Then what was the bible for, tell me that?' demanded O'Reilly. 'And me thinking it not polite to ask about my wages.'

'What wages?' sighed the prosecuting counsel.

'The wages he hasn't paid me,' said O'Reilly pointing at Captain Binbow who was holding his head in his hands.

'I have no further questions, my lord,' said the prosecuting counsel sitting down wearily.

In his address to the jury the judge made the point that the evidence of the Special Branch superintendent should not be discounted on the basis that the superintendent's source, the captured German agent, had not been produced in court. You may wish to assume, said the judge, that the Special Branch had good reasons for withholding the agent's presence. The point was especially important, said the judge, because of the contrasting evidence of the defendants.

The members of the jury took less than an hour to return their verdicts.

'Do you find Captain Charles Binbow guilty or not guilty of the charges against him?' said the clerk of court to the jury foreman.

'Guilty.'

'Do you find Seamus O'Reilly guilty or not guilty of the charges against him?'

'Not guilty.'

Grinning broadly the former deckhand of MV *Sea Snake* turned and offered his hand to Captain Binbow who had to be restrained by warders from grabbing his former employee by the throat.

'You are free to go, Mr O'Reilly,' said the judge. 'In future, you will perhaps be more careful with whom you associate.'

'That I'll be doing, right enough,' said the deckhand scrambling for the door.

'Captain Binbow,' said the judge to the burly figure who remained in the dock. 'You have been found guilty of consorting with the enemy in a reprehensible contravention of the Official Secrets Act.'

The judge placed a black cap on his head.

'The sentence of this court is that you shall be taken from here to a place of execution where you shall be hanged by the neck until you are dead. May God have mercy upon your soul.'

Trial of the Innkeepers

The innkeepers were next to be summoned to the Old Bailey,

charged with harbouring the enemy in contravention of the Official Secrets Act. The accused, Sidney Prone of the Horseshoe Inn near Grafton Regis and Jake Hawkins of the Smugglers Arms in Woolwich, shared the same defence counsel. Prone's unattractive squint and Hawkins' black scowl made an unfavourable impression on the jury.

Both men pleaded not guilty. The prosecuting counsel told the jury he would produce evidence that the accused, far from being innocent, were part of a network of persons involved in traitorous subterfuge. He said he would demonstrate beyond reasonable doubt that the accused had knowingly accommodated German prisoners of war and cooperated in arranging onward transport for them, by canal barge to London from the Horseshoe Inn and by trawler to sea and safety from the Smugglers Arms.

The first witness for the prosecution was a small lady with a loud voice and disapproving countenance.

'Are you Mrs Helen MacTavish of Slate Road, Grafton Regis?' said the prosecuting counsel.

'Aye.'

'Have you until recently been employed as a general help in the Horseshoe Inn near Grafton Regis?'

'Aye.'

'What were your duties, Mrs MacTavish?'

'Keeping the place tidy and cooking meals for folk.'

'What kind of meals?'

'Egg and chips, in the main.'

'Did you cook frequently?'

'No.'

'Why not?'

'Because not many people came to the place, on account of him being so disagreaable,' said the witness nodding in the direction of the accused Sidney Prone in the dock.

'Would you please tell the court what happened on three occasions, during June and July of this year, that caused you surprise?' said the prosecuting counsel.

'Aye, multiple orders for egg and chips.'

'Why did that surprise you?'

'Because not that many people were in the pub.'

'Did you question the orders with the accused, Mr Boult?'

'Aye.'

'And what did he say?'

'That they were for the army.'

'Were any army personnel in the pub at the time?'

'None that I could see.'

'You kept a record of the dates in question, didn't you, Mrs MacTavish. Would you tell the court why?'

'Because I got paid extra for the eggs. I mean, I'm no daft.'

'Would you please inform the court of the dates?'

The witness rummaged in her handbag and produced a small diary. Licking her fingers, she flipped through the pages.

'18 June, 2 July and 16 July,' she read out.

'The court will learn,' said the prosecuting counsel to the jury, 'that the dates in the witness's diary coincide precisely with the dates that canal barge GUC/WO/W1 moored opposite the Horseshoe Inn.'

The defence counsel declined to cross-examine the witness. Faced with the evidence he knew was about to be produced, and the private confessions of his clients, he was concerned only to save the innkeepers from the gallows by proving they had acted under duress.

The second witness for the prosecution was a pert and buxom teenage girl.

'Are you Miss Lily Foster of Dock Lane in Woolwich?' said the prosecuting counsel.

'Yes.'

'What is your occupation?'

'I do lots of things.'

'You're no longer in school?'

'Nope.'

'Then shall we say you are a casual worker?'

'If you like,' smirked the witness.

'Will you tell the court where you were on the night of 5 July?'

'In the Smugglers Arms. Black Jake didn't mind me being under age,' said the witness defiantly. 'He'd wink and pat my bum, and give me gin and orange. I had to pay for it, mind.'

'By Black Jake, you mean the accused, Jake Hawkins?' said the prosecuting counsel.

'Yes.'

'Please tell the court what happened after you left the Smugglers Arms?'

'After the drinking?'

'Yes.'

'When I was nosing with my boyfriend in the alleyway outside?'

'Yes.'

'Nosing?' said the judge.

'Embracing, my lord,' said the prosecuting counsel. 'Carry on, please, Miss Foster.'

'Well, there was this noise from the back of the pub. A sort of grating noise, like a heavy door being opened. Anyway, it went quiet for a while, and after about five minutes, when my boyfriend and I were ramming it, the gate at the back . . .'

'Ramming it?' said the judge.

'A deeper embrace, my lord,' explained the prosecuting counsel.

'You can say that again,' said the witness. 'It was dead embarrassing because, as I was saying, the gate at the back of the pub suddenly opened and Black Jake appeared. He looked round, obviously didn't see us in the alleyway, made a waving motion with his hand and, well, we couldn't believe our eyes, because half a dozen men in German uniforms crept out onto the quay, and disappeared out of sight.'

'They were definitely wearing German uniforms?'

The witness nodded. 'Just like in the flicks.'

'What did you do then?'

'Waited for Black Jake to return through the gate, then I lifted my things and scarpered.'

'You didn't think of going to the police?'

'My boyfriend said it would be too dangerous. It was unhealthy to get on the wrong side of Black Jake, he said.'

'The court will learn,' said the prosecuting counsel to the jury, 'that on the same night of 5 July arrangements had been made by the German agent running the Grand Union Canal escape route for a group of escaping POWs to be transported offshore from Woolwich and delivered to a German warship. Thank you, Miss Foster.'

'Do you wish to cross-examine the witness?' said the judge to the defence counsel.

The defence counsel shook his head.

The third witness for the prosecution was the Special Branch superintendent in charge of the police investigation into the case. Responding to questions he informed the court that from a series of interviews with the captured German agent it had been verified that the two innkeepers were part of the network which assisted POWs to escape back to Germany. The Horseshoe Inn was the assembly point. The inn's role and location had been broadcast to internment camps throughout England via coded messages in German radio programmes.

'Did your agent refer to the accused by name?' said the prosecuting counsel.

'Yes.'

'Did your agent ever meet the accused?'

'Yes.'

'So he would be able to identify them?'

'Yes, though for reasons of security I'm afraid he cannot appear here in court.'

'Thank you, inspector,' said the prosecuting counsel. 'That concludes the case for the prosecution.'

The defence counsel didn't challenge the superintendent's evidence or attempt to devalue the German agent's testimony. He concentrated solely on the aspect of duress.

'Is the man Fingleton Kelly known to you?' said the defence counsel.

'Yes, he has been a subject of our investigations,' said the superintendent.

'What was his relationship with my clients, the accused?'

'Fingleton Kelly was the ringleader of the local support group for the German agent.'

'He employed my clients, in other words?'

'Yes.'

'Fingleton Kelly had a reputation for violence, isn't that right?'

'We believe so.'

'Isn't it the case, inspector, that during interrogation your German agent expressed sympathy for Fingleton Kelly's employees?'

'Yes.'

'You see, my clients assert they owed money to Fingleton Kelly and were blackmailed into sheltering the escaping prisoners of war during transit, and threatened with violence if they didn't. In Mr Hawkins' case, when he protested, he found his dog hanging from the ceiling in the Smugglers Arms with its throat cut. Does that surprise you, superintendent?'

'No.'

'Is it not also true that other employees of Fingleton Kelly were threatened with violence?'

'We have some evidence to that effect,' said the superintendent.

'Is it not reasonable to conclude, therefore, that my clients' actions were governed by fear of violence?'

'It is possible.'

'Thank you, inspector,' said the defence counsel. 'No further questions, my lord.'

The prosecuting counsel returned to his feet.

'As a result of your investigations, can you prove that the accused were blackmailed, superintendent?' he said.

'We have conclusive evidence of blackmail and violence on the part of Fingleton Kelly, and conclusive evidence of association between him and the accused,' said the superintendent

'That's not what I asked.'

'The evidence that the accused were coerced is substantial, but not proven.'

'Thank you, inspector.'

Despite the efforts of the prosecution the jury sided with the defence and returned verdicts of guilty under duress. The judge spared the innkeepers the death penalty, sentencing each of them to twenty years in prison.

Trial of Jed Boult

The van driver Jed Boult faced three charges at the Old Bailey, aiding and abetting the enemy in contravention of the Official Secrets Act, distributing black market goods and evading conscription. He pleaded not guilty on all counts.

The prosecuting counsel described to the jury how the accused had been caught in possession of a grey Bedford van used by an enemy agent to evade detection whilst in radio communication with Berlin, how he had been identified as the driver of the vehicle while the German agent was making and receiving the radio transmissions, how the accused had used the vehicle for distribution of contraband goods and how by means of forged papers he had avoided conscription.

For corroboration the prosecuting counsel called the Special Branch superintendent in charge of the Grand Union Canal escape route investigation. The superintendent confirmed that the accused had admitted using forged documents and driving the van in the circumstances described. The prosecuting counsel thanked the superintendent, told the judge that the case for the prosecution was concluded and sat down.

The defence counsel used the same strategy as the defence attorney in the previous trial.

'Is the man Fingleton Kelly known to you?' he asked the superintendent.

'Yes, he has been a subject of our investigations,' said the superintendent.

'What was his relationship with my client?'

'Fingleton Kelly was the ringleader of the local support group for the German agent.'

'He employed my client, in other words?'

'Yes.'

'Fingleton Kelly had a reputation for violence?'

'We believe so.'

'Is it true, superintendent, that during interrogation the German agent expressed sympathy for Fingleton Kelly's employees?'

'Yes.'

'My client asserts he was threatened with violence by Fingleton Kelly. Does that surprise you, superintendent?'

'No.'

'Is it not also true that other employees of Fingleton Kelly were threatened with violence?'

'We have some evidence to that effect,' said the superintendent.

'Is it not reasonable to conclude, therefore, that my client's actions were governed by fear of violence?'

'It is possible.'

'Thank you, superintendent,' said the defence counsel.

The prosecuting counsel returned to his feet.

'We've been here before, superintendent, so you know what I'm going to say?'

'I think so,' smiled the superintendent.

'Can you prove that the accused was blackmailed, superintendent? Please just answer yes or no,' said the prosecuting counsel.

'No.'

The defence counsel called two character witnesses. The first was a well-known Billingsgate fish merchant.

'How long did the accused, Jed Boult, work for you?' said the defence counsel.

'Approximately two years.'

'Were you satisfied with the quality of his work?'

'He was an excellent porter, one of the best.'

'Was he reliable?'

'Yes.'

'Honest?'

'Yes.'

'Did he ever give you cause for concern?'

'He liked to bet on the horses, but it never affected his work.'

'Would you employ him again?'

'Certainly.'

The second character witness was Mrs Ethel Plumtree, a large lady in a floral dress and hat of the type regularly observed in the pews of churches on Sunday mornings.

'When did Jed become a lodger in your house, Mrs Plumtree?'

'Let me see now, it was just after the sirens started, the sirens right at the beginning that is. They did give us a fright, didn't they? Mrs Perkins, my neighbour at the time, said we'd better be going down to the cellars and I said . . .'

'Was it during September 1939, Mrs Plumtree?'

'I suppose you're right. My goodness, how time flies.'

'So he's been a lodger with you for nearly two years?'

'Until they took him away last week, poor lamb,' said Mrs Plumtree looking solicitously across the court at the accused. 'Proper disgrace, if you ask me, he never did anyone any harm.'

'Did he inform you of his occupation?'

'He said he was a van driver for the docks.'

'Did you have any reason to doubt that?'

'Why should I? He showed me his union card, and gave me his ration book. Proper generous he was. Always insisted I took his share of eggs and milk. Mind you, I always made sure he had bacon in his sandwiches when he worked nights.'

'Did he talk about his work?'

'Not much. He slept a lot.'

'Do you know why he's here in court today?'

'Draft evasion, they told me. But that couldn't be right, could it? He was in a reserved occupation, working for the docks.'

'The prosecution claims he was working for the Germans.'

Mrs Plumtree snorted.

'That's be the day! A nice lad like Jed.'

'Would it surprise you to learn that Jed admits associating with undesirable people, who blackmailed him into illegal activities, and threated him with violence if he didn't cooperate?'

'You could knock me down with a feather. Mind you, he did sometimes look very pale and worried, poor lamb. I put it down to the strain of the war, I mean it affects all of us, doesn't it?'

'You think highly of Jed, Mrs Plumtree?'

'Like he was my own son,' said Mrs Plumtree with an affectionate look at the dock.

Finally the defence counsel called the accused himself to the witness stand.

'Why did you not join up at the start of the war, Jed?' asked the defence counsel.

'I was offered a job to pay off a debt.'

'At the time, did you believe the job was genuine?'

'Yes.'

'Did you believe that the job entitled you to reserved occupation status?'

'Yes.'

'When you realised that the job was not genuine, why didn't you go to the police?'

'I was frightened.'

'Why were you frightened?'

'Because the person I worked for said he would cut me to pieces with a knife.'

The jury listened sympathetically to the pleasant looking young man whose anxious expression and quiet demeanour coupled with the opinions expressed by his landlady and Billingsgate employer hinted that the accused's troubles had arisen more from naivety than deliberate intent. The prosecuting counsel thought differently.

'You delivered packages, by night?' said the prosecuting counsel rising for cross-examination.

'Yes.'

'Why not by day?'

'Because there was less chance of getting caught, I suppose.'

'Exactly. You knew from the start what was going on.'

'I didn't know what was in the packages.'

'But you knew the packages didn't contain, for example, tins of baby food?'

'I guessed they probably contained alcohol, but that didn't seem too bad, not with bombs falling and people needing a drink.'

'Driving an enemy agent around London didn't seem too bad either, is that right?'

'I've already explained, I didn't know who he was, and I was scared for my life by then.'

'I suggest you've told the court a pack of lies, Jed. You took the job, knowing it involved criminal activities, to avoid conscription. You quite enjoyed the freedom and the money, didn't you? You enjoyed being tipped by a man with a foreign accent who made radio transmissions while you drove him around London, transmissions that may result in the death of your countrymen at the hands of the German pilots who escaped from this country, thanks to your cooperation. That doesn't seem too bad either, does it, Jed?'

'Yes,' said the accused, white-faced, gripping the sides of the witness box.

'Yes? Yes, you evaded the draft? Yes, you knowingly distributed contraband goods? Yes, you knowingly assisted a German agent?'

'No,' whispered the accused.

'No? Make up your mind, Jed.'

'I mean . . .'

'Speak up, Jed, so the jury can hear you.'

'I mean, I did all those things, but I was forced to.'

'Unfortunately for you, Jed, there's no one here to prove it.'

Summing up, the prosecuting counsel told the jury that the accused's plea of not guilty had been contradicted by his admissions in the witness box. There was no proof that the accused had been subject to duress and the jury would therefore be in no doubt of the need to return verdicts of guilty without qualification.

The defence counsel stressed the youthfulness of his client and the insidiousness of the small gambling debt which had resulted in a downward spiral into misfortune at the hands of a vicious extortionist.

The judge reminded the jury that unless the prosecution had established beyond all reasonable doubt that the offences had been committed then the accused must be acquitted.

When the time came for the jury to pronounce its verdict the young man rose slowly from his chair in the dock. His shoulders sagged as the foreman declared him guilty on all three counts and when the judge pronounced a sentence of five years imprisonment his lips wobbled. 'I'm sorry, I'm sorry,' he burbled across the court at his landlady Mrs Crump.

'However,' said the judge to Jed Boult, 'there is credible indication of duress so I shall suspend the sentence for two years if you proceed forthwith under escort to enlist in His Majesty's armed forces.'

Trial of Fingleton Kelly

Fingleton Kelly refused to talk. He stared straight through the Special Branch officers during interrogation, through the chaplain at Pentonville Prison during visits, through the lawyer appointed to represent him and through the clerk of court in the Old Bailey when the charges were read out and he was asked how he intended to plead.

'Enter a plea of not guilty on his behalf,' the judge instructed the clerk of court.

The prosecuting counsel told the jury that the accused had conspired with the enemy to recruit and administer by blackmail and violence sundry persons to help him support an escape route for German prisoners of war via the Grand Union Canal. Evidence that the accused had conducted a support operation by means of extortion was manifest in the court records of the previous trials associated with the case.

For evidence of the accused's recruitment activities the prosecuting counsel called to the witness box an army officer referred to, for security reasons, as Major X.

The witness walked briskly into the courtroom adjusting his eyepatch. He identified the accused as Fingleton Kelly, floor manager of the Ambassador Club in Mayfair, and explained that the accused had been under surveillance by the security services since the start of the war for suspected links with the underworld.

'What was your role in the case, major?' asked the prosecuting counsel.

'To act as bait, in the guise of a disaffected army officer with financial problems, to see where it got us.'

'The court appreciates that certain aspects of the army's involvement are confidential, major, but will you please tell the jury where it did get you?'

'The significant result was that, after several weeks of meetings and pretence on my part, the accused requested information which linked him directly with enemy activities.'

'Proving in effect, to the satisfaction of the security services, that the accused was spying for the Germans?'

'Yes,' said the major looking across the court at Fingleton Kelly who ignored him and continued to stare into the middle distance.

'Thank you, major,' said the prosecuting counsel. He turned towards the judge. 'I have no further questions, my lord. That is the case for the prosecution.'

'Do you wish to cross-examine the witness?' said the judge to the defence counsel.

'My lord, my client has refused to provide testimony relating to the charges against him,' said the barrister retained by the accused's lawyer.

The judge addressed the prisoner in the dock. 'Mr Kelly, is there anything you wish to say to the court?'

The accused stared straight through the judge without speaking.

In his summing up the judge told the jury that the accused's refusal to defend himself should not be taken as evidence of guilt. It was up to the prosecution to prove beyond all reasonable doubt that the offences had been committed and that unless the prosecution had succeeded in doing so the jury must acquit the accused.

The verdict from the jury was unanimous.

'Fingleton Kelly, you have been found guilty of capital offences under the Official Secrets Act,' said the judge placing a black cap on his head. 'You are a traitor and extreme danger to the State and Crown. The judgement of this court is that you be taken from here to a place of execution and hanged by your neck until you are dead. May God have mercy upon your soul.'

'May God have mercy on yours,' shouted the accused from the dock, 'you fat arrogant bastard son of Cromwell's army!'

Trial of April Tree

The evidence against April Tree was so overwhelming that the judge's preparations for the case included advancing the date of his golfing holiday, due to commence after the trial.

Photographers waiting outside the Old Bailey jostled for position as the prison van arrived. April stepped out awkwardly from the rear of the vehicle handcuffed to a warder. She was dressed in a blue suit several sizes too large supplied by the prison authorities in preference to the casual clothes she had worn at the time of her arrest. The jacket drooped over her shoulders, and the hem of the skirt reached almost to her ankles. She wore no jewellery around her neck, no lipstick on her lips, no powder on her face. Despite the absence of fashion or adornment, however, there was an audible intake of breath from the men in the courtroom as she entered the dock.

The prosecuting counsel, the same eminent barrister who had represented the Attorney General throughout the series of Grand Union Canal escape route indictments, explained to the jury why April's quietly-spoken plea of not guilty was spurious, and called his first witness.

'Are you Miss Sally Fields, wages clerk, of Weedon Narrowboats?'

'Yes,' said the wages clerk, a young woman in a grey dress.

'Did you open a bank account for the accused, April Tree, on commencement of her employment in June?'

'Yes, with Barclays Bank in Aylesbury.'

'Is it usual to pay wages that way?'

'No, but the girls in the munitions barges received special danger allowances, which the War Office wanted to audit. So we paid them monthly by remittance to their accounts.'

'Would you please tell the court how much Weedon Narrowboats paid the accused, April Tree?'

'£1.10s per week wages, plus 12/6d per week danger money.'

'£8.10s per month. A good salary?'

'Oh yes, I should say so!' said the young woman. 'They deserved it though, on those barges.'

The prosecuting counsel's second witness was a bespectacled middle-aged man wearing a striped suit.

'Are you Mr Dennis Lamont, deputy manager, Barclays Bank, Aylesbury?'

'Yes.'

'Is this document,' said the prosecuting counsel showing Exhibit A to the witness, 'a copy of the bank statement for the accused, Miss April Tree?'

'Yes.'

'Would you please read out, to the jury, the entries on the statement?'

'19 June £250, 30 June £8.10s, 4 July £250.'

'Three entries?'

'Yes.'

'Do the amounts surprise you?'

'They certainly do.'

'In what way?'

'Sums of £250 are unusually large for an employee of the company in question.'

'Unusually large in any circumstances, would you say?'

'Well, yes.'

The men in the jury kept glancing sideways at April. What was such a young and lovely woman doing in the dock? Someone must have made a mistake. The silky-smooth and irritatingly pompous prosecuting counsel who looked down his nose at everyone was apparently trying to link the dates of the £250 payments with the dates of the dummy bombing raids on the munitions barges. Did he seriously suppose that a girl with the face of an angel had been responsible for unleashing the fury of the German air force!?

'Are you Rupert Maynard, a communications analyst at Bletchley Park?'

'I am,' said the third witness, a studious-looking person with a fountain pen in the top pocket of his tweed jacket.

'Are these documents respectively a schedule of callsigns and schedule of map references from intercepted German radio messages associated with the Grand Union Canal escape route operation?' said the prosecuting counsel to the witness.

'Yes.'

'Exhibit B, my lord,' said the prosecuting counsel to the judge.

'Very well,' said the judge.

'From the first document would you please read to the jury the callsign terminating each series of letters,' said the prosecuting counsel to the witness.

'AT'

'As in April Tree, for example?'

'Objection!' said the defence counsel.

'Can you support that interpretation?' said the judge to the prosecuting counsel.

The prosecuting counsel shook his head. 'Unfortunately we have been informed that the intercepts which form the basis of the schedules in Exhibit B have not yet been fully deciphered, my lord.'

'In which case the objection is sustained, and you,' said the judge turning to the jurors, 'are instructed to disregard the prosecuting counsel's last question to the witness.'

Dressed in smart town clothes Megan looked quite different from the country girl who had sluiced the decks of canal boats in dungarees and an old shirt. She wore a tailored suit, hat and platform shoes and strode confidently into the court pausing momentarily to cast a sympathetic glance towards April in the dock.

'You are Miss Megan Leigh-Harvey, lately employed by Weedon Narrowboats?' said the prosecuting counsel.

'I am.'

'Until recently you worked alongside the accused, April Tree, on a munitions barge on the Grand Union Canal?'

'On adjoining barges,' said the witness. 'April was on *Daisy*, I was on *Buttercup* with Pippa Howland.'

'Those were the names of your barges?'

'Yes.'

'Were you friendly with the accused?'

'Yes, we all got on well together. Pippa and I absolutely adored April. We simply can't believe what's happened.'

'Your barges were moored side by side at night, is that correct?'

'Yes.'

'Would you please tell the jury what happened the night before the convoy was stopped by the police?'

'It wasn't so much that particular night, it happened several times.'

'What happened?'

'Noises from April's barge.'

'Go on, please.'

'It's hard to explain. It was as if people were moving about in there, in the middle of the night.'

'Did you ask the accused about the noises?'

'No.'

'Why not?'

The witness hesitated. 'Because . . .'

'Because what, Miss Leigh-Harvey?'

'You see, April was extremely attractive. We thought that, perhaps, she was, well . . '

'Well what?'

'That she was perhaps - that she had - I know it sounds awful,' said the witness lowering her eyes, 'but we thought that April was perhaps entertaining someone in her cabin.'

There was a loud gasp from the dock.

'But you were wrong, weren't you, Miss Leigh-Harvey? The noises you heard were from enemy prisoners of war, inside the accused's barge, being transported to safety through the canal, isn't that right?'

'Unfortunately, that turned out to be the case,' said the witness.

The men in the jury looked glum as Miss Leigh-Harvey's exquisitely dressed and equally well-spoken friend Miss Pippa Howland confirmed the bit about noises in the night and how the two friends had thought that the accused had been indulging in a bit of hanky-panky. It was going to take some explaining by the lovely girl in the dock why her barge had been full of Germans.

Detective Sergeant Quinn was the final witness for the prosecution.

'After you had arrested the men found in the cargo hold of the accused's boat, sergeant, did you conduct a search of Miss Tree's cabin?' said the prosecuting counsel'

'Yes.'

'What did you find?'

'A plate fitted with reflectors.'

'Is this the plate?' said the prosecuting counsel handing Exhibit C to the witness.

"Yes.'

'Please tell the jury the purpose of the device, in your opinion.'

The sergeant held up the plate, pointed at the studs on the bottom and explained how the plate, attached to the superstructure of the barge, could be seen from the air but not from the ground.

'On a moonlit night,' he said, 'the glass reflectors would be visible to aircraft from miles away, thereby identifying the position of the munitions convoy for the Luftwaffe.'

'As a result of your discovery, sergeant, what action did you take?'

'I arrested the accused.'

'That is the case for the prosecution, my lord,' said the prosecuting counsel as the detective sergeant descended from the witness box.

The defence counsel had tried very hard in the weeks before the trial to believe his client's story, indeed it would be true to say he had struggled harder than at any time in his career to find evidence of a client's innocence. His heart had melted at every meeting with April Tree in Holloway Prison, she was so sweet and helpless, or appeared to be, but the facts were damning.

His strategy was to avoid cross-questioning the prosecution witnesses in case he ended up emphasising the force of their testimony and making April's position worse. Instead he proposed calling her to the witness box in the hope that she could somehow persuade the jury, if not himself, of her innocence. Before doing that, before throwing her to the wolves so to speak, he attempted to demonstrate that the accused was not, by character or temperament, a person capable of the treacherous crimes with which she was charged.

'Are you Mrs Margaret Meredith, personnel manager of Weedon Narrowboats?' he asked the matronly lady in a summer frock and feathered hat now standing in the witness box.

'I am.'

'Are you acquainted with the accused, Miss April Tree?'

'Yes.'

'In what respect?'

'She is one of our employees.'

'How long have you known her?'

'Approximately two and a half months.'

'How long have you been a personnel manager, Mrs Meredith?'

'Nearly twenty years.'

'You have considerable experience, then, of assessing personalities?'

'I would say so.'

'How would you assess the personality of the accused?'

'April is one of the nicest, kindest girls you could possibly meet.'

'Not someone likely to engage in criminal or traitorous activities, would you say?'

'Absolutely not,' bristled Mrs Meredith. 'The charges against her are ridiculous.'

'Why do you consider them ridiculous?'

'For a start, why would she nearly quit the job half way through?'

'Please explain what you mean.'

'After the second bombing raid, we offered to release the girls from their contracts without penalty on the grounds that the danger was greater than we had originally predicted. April was the only one who hesitated before refusing.'

'Did she give a reason for hesitating?'

'No, but she would hardly leave if she was supposed to be working for the Germans, would she?' demanded Mrs Meredith.

The prosecuting counsel had little difficulty dismantling the personnel manager's evidence.

'Would you agree with me, Mrs Meredith,' he said rising from the benches of the court for cross-examination, 'that there could be a number of reasons for the accused's hesitation in the circumstances you describe?'

'Yes, of course.'

'Sickness?'

'Yes.'

'Worry?'

'Yes.'

'Bluff?'

'Certainly not bluff,' protested Mrs Meredith.

'Why not?'

'I know her too well for that.'

'You've been acquainted with the accused for two and a half months, you say?'

Mrs Meredith nodded. 'Yes.'

'Would you marry someone in that period?'

'I beg your pardon!'

'If you were single, and were courted by a stranger, would you learn enough about him in two and a half months to accept a proposal of marriage?'

Mrs Meredith looked flustered.

'It would depend, but I don't see what that's got to do with April,' she said.

'On the contrary. By your hesitation you have demonstrated to the jury the sheer improbability of accomplishing a comprehensive assessment of a person's character in such a short period,' said the prosecuting counsel sitting down.

The defence counsel sighed and returned to his feet.

'In your position as personnel manager, Mrs Meredith, you will inevitably have gained considerable experience, over the years, in assessing the character of employees and applicants for positions in your company?'

'Yes,' said Mrs Meredith defiantly, 'and April is a darling, darling girl who wouldn't hurt a fly.'

The sub-lieutenant in charge of the Grand Union Canal munitions convoy was unfortunately immobilised in hospital so the defence counsel called CPO Jones to support Mrs Meredith's testimony.

'You are Chief Petty Officer Herbert Jones, Royal Navy, currently based in Weedon?'

'I am, sir.'

'You worked alongside the accused, Miss April Tree?'

'I did, sir.'

'Was she a competent member of the crew of the munitions barges?

'A fine young lady, sir. Always smiling and willing to help. A pleasure to work with, sir.'

'Are you surprised to find her in the dock here, accused of assisting the enemy?'

'I am, sir.'

'Why, chief petty officer?'

'A number of reasons, sir. For instance she was far too nice a person. She didn't act strangely either, if you know what I mean, always singing and happy. There was another reason too, sir.'

'Yes?'

CPO Jones hesitated, then turned towards the dock.

'I'm sorry, miss, if this embarrasses you,' he said to April across the court. 'The fact is,' he said turning back to the defence counsel, 'Miss April was in love with someone. She told me about it, and asked my advice. Very stricken she was, and you don't go about betraying your country if you're in that sort of condition, in my opinion, if you know what I mean, sir.'

'I'm sure everybody in the court understands what you mean,' said the defence counsel looking pointedly at the jury.

'I can't give the person's name, I'm afraid, if you don't mind, sir.'

'That's not necessary. Thank you, chief petty officer. Your testimony has been most valuable,' said the defence counsel.

'So the accused was in love?' said the prosecuting counsel on his feet again.

'Yes, sir.'

'Have you heard of Mata Hari, chief petty officer? I'm sure you have. Allow me to refresh your memory. A thoroughly nice person, everybody said, very beautiful, always singing and happy and so forth. The trouble was, she was spying for the Germans against the Allies. And do you recall her method of operation? Let me remind you - love affairs and seduction. Thank you, chief petty officer. Your testimony has been most valuable,' said the prosecuting counsel sitting down.

That probably does it, reflected the defence counsel gloomily.

The men in the jury, outwardly compassionate at the commencement of the trial, had steadily progressed from varying states of incredulity at the charges against April to one of morbid fascination. There was no longer any doubt about her guilt. All that remained was to see how she handled herself in the witness box and how she might seek to excuse her treacherous conduct. They watched her walk, graceful as a fawn, accompanied by two female warders, across the old wooden floor of the courtroom. The bewildered expression on her face they attributed to masquerade.

'Are you Miss April Tree, an employee of Weedon Narrowboats?' said the defence counsel.

'Yes,' said April quietly but with sufficient firmness for everyone to hear. She held her head up. She was determined not to cry.

'You've heard the evidence against you. Is there anything you want to say?'

'It's not true, any of it.'

'The payments of £250. Where did they come from?'

'I don't know.'

'The prosecuting counsel maintains the payments coincided with the dates of the dummy-bombing raids on the convoy, and were thus rewards for your involvement. What do you say to that?'

'He's wrong.'

'Did you use the reflective plate, Exhibit C, to guide enemy aircraft to the target?'

'No.'

'Were you aware of the presence of the plate in your cabin, or of German prisoners of war in the cargo hold?'

'No.'

'Did you hear, at any time, noises of movement in the cargo hold?'

No.'

'Did you, at any time during the night, entertain a person in your cabin alone?'

'No!'

'Did you ever receive coded radio transmissions from Germany with, or without, the callsign "AT"?'

'No.'

'Can you explain to the court how the subversive activities with which you are charged were performed, if not by you?'

'No.'

'If not by you, they must have been carried out by someone else?'

'Isn't that,' said April looking at him with imploring eyes, 'terribly obvious?'

The prosecuting counsel rose imperiously from the benches, collected his robes around his shoulders and stared at April down his nose without speaking, an oppressive technique favoured by barristers, particularly eminent ones of notoriously arrogant and pompous disposition. Sniffing contemptuously his eyes travelled down from the witness box to the notes in his hands, and slowly upwards again. Then suddenly:

'*Guten tag Fräulein*,' he barked.

'*Guten tag Herr*,' said April instinctively.

The shocked silence in the court lasted a few minutes. Even the judge was taken aback, staring with the rest of the court at the witness box until eventually, with an imperceptible shrug, he collected himself and addressed the prosecuting counsel who had resumed his seat.

'Do you intend continuing your cross-examination, Sir Robert?' said the judge.

'I see no point in wasting the court's time with further demonstrations of the accused's guilt, my lord,' said the prosecuting counsel with a dismissive flap of his hand.

The defence counsel returned valiantly to his hopeless task.

'Where did you learn to speak German, Miss Tree?' he said.

'From my father.'

'And where did he . . ?'

'My father is Austrian. I learned some words from him, and from books, but I was born in England. I am British not German. I love Milton as much as Goethe, and Elgar as much as Brahms,' she said looking helplessly around the court for someone to step forward and stand beside her in the witness box and proclaim in a bold and powerful voice 'Enough! This young woman is guilty only of love! If you don't stop this trial, you will be committing in this court today, in the name of justice, a horrendous crime!'

But none stepped forward. And when, not much later, the judge placed a black cap on his head and pronounced that April was to be taken from the dock and hanged by her neck until dead her legs finally gave way.

PART 3 REDEMPTION

Stoke Mandeville Hospital

Lindsey had awakened to find himself in a room looking out over wide lawns. His right leg was suspended in a sling and his head was bandaged. Nurses on either side of the bed were adjusting his pillows.

'There you are,' said the nurse on the left with cute dimpled cheeks.

'How are you feeling, sub-lieutenant?' said the second nurse, older and briskly efficient. 'Keep still now, while we prop you up.'

The nurses placed their arms behind his back, eased him forward and slipped another pillow behind his shoulders.

'Where am I?' said Lindsey.

'Stoke Mandeville Hospital, home of the best surgeons and doctors in the world,' said the older nurse.

'And the best staff. I'm Nurse Trims and that's Nurse Doolittle,' said the nurse with the dimpled cheeks. 'We look after the private rooms. The main wards are full so matron put you in here, with us. Quite taken with you, she was, when you arrived with that lump on your head. How are you feeling, are you comfortable?'

'Where's April?' said Lindsey.

'Who's that? Is she your sweetheart?' said Nurse Trims filling the glass on the bedside table.

'She's got hazel eyes,' said Lindsey. 'I've got to see her.'

'We will check for you,' said Nurse Doolittle patting Lindsey's hand. 'Try to get some rest. Mr Jameson, the surgeon, will be here shortly.'

Next time Lindsey awoke there was a man in a white coat beside his bed.

'We reopened your knee. There was some infection, and the pins had gone awry. It must have been hurting. I'm Jameson, by the way. You're going to have a headache for a while too. Luckily, you didn't break your skull.'

'When can I get up?' said Lindsey.

The surgeon shook his head.

'Not for a while, I'm afraid,' he said.

'I've got to find April,' said Lindsey urgently.

'You've just returned from the operating theatre,' said the surgeon. 'Your knee has been immobilised. You'll be lying here like this for several weeks. If you try to put pressure on your knee too soon you might lose the entire leg. So be patient. On the bright side, if you let your knee mend properly and do what the nurses say, you should be walking again, without a stick, within a couple of months.'

'Months,' groaned Lindsey.

'The nurses will take details of your next of kin, and the addresses of people you want to see, and we'll do our best to trace your friend April.'

'I must find her,' said Lindsey closing his eyes and falling back asleep.

The handsome young naval officer set hearts fluttering amongst the day and night staff, especially the heart of Nurse Trims who spent as much time as possible in his room, smoothing the sheets, checking the tension of the sling, helping him sit up as he recovered from the impact of the drugs, adjusting the window blinds, refilling the water jar and arranging into a flower vase the bouquet of roses delivered to the hospital with a card from his mother saying "Keep warm, darling. Coming soon".

It was Nurse Trims who, on the third day, brought Quinn to his room.

'Thank god, I've been tearing my hair out,' said Lindsey indicating the bandage around his head. 'Trims, bring a chair for Detective Sergeant Quinn and please open the blinds, let the sun in. Sit down, Quinn. Thanks so much for coming. Where's April, and what's happening to her?'

Nurse Trims transferred a chair to the side of the bed, opened the blinds and pretended to be checking the medicine trolley while the large plain-clothes policeman spoke to Lindsey. Unfortunately the ward sister called for her soon afterwards and all Nurse Trims managed to learn before leaving the room was that April was someone who'd been working for the sub-lieutenant and was now in prison, for some reason.

'She couldn't have done it,' said Lindsey shaking his head.

'What makes you so certain, sir?' said Quinn.

'Her attitude. She didn't behave like a spy.'

'Unfortunately there's a great deal of evidence to the contrary, sir.'

'She was far too affectionate.'

'To you, sir?'

Lindsey shifted awkwardly amidst the pillows.

'Well, yes. But . . .'

'Affection is not much of a defence, sir.'

'Someone must have placed that plate in her cabin.'

'If it was just the matter of the plate, sir, then one would have to explain what the German POWs were doing in her barge, and why she got paid for guiding the bombers in for their spurious runs.'

'Paid!'

'We have determined that a large sum of money was deposited in her bank account directly after each raid.'

'Oh god,' groaned Lindsey.

'A problem shared is a problem halved,' said Nurse Trims when she returned after Quinn's visit and found Lindsey staring miserably out of the window.

'Sometimes it helps to talk,' she encouraged whereupon Lindsey told her everything, or as much as he could within the constraints of the Official Secrets Act, how it was impossible for April to be guilty of the shocking charges against her, how he was responsible for having allowed the situation to develop unchecked, how he felt so helpless with his knee in a sling, ordered by the surgeon to remain in bed when he should be out challenging the evidence against April and doing everything possible to set her free.

'She's in Holloway Prison. Holloway! It's like nailing a butterfly to a concrete wall,' said Lindsey miserably.

'She's going to be tried in court?'

'Yes.'

'Well then, the judge will set her free,' said Nurse Trims to whom optimism came naturally.

'I most certainly hope so.'

'Until then, I'll pray for her,' said Nurse Trims tidying Lindsey's pillows.

In the weeks before April's trial Lindsey received visits from policemen, lawyers, Special Branch officers, naval officers and, on one memorable occasion, his mother who arrived in a chauffeur-driven limousine with Lindsey's elder brother, an army officer with red tabs on his shoulders, greeted personally by the matron who accompanied them along the corridor to Lindsey's room and glowed with pleasure when Lindsey's mother said that the view from the room was simply divine.

The most interesting visitor in terms of understanding what had happened on the Grand Union Canal was a cosy person called Mrs Meredith who told Nurse Trims in confidence that the air had crackled with romantic tension whenever the sub-lieutenant and April were together and that it must have been so difficult for them in view of the sub-lieutenant's position. They had behaved heroically, both of them, for demonstrating such great restraint. As for April, the charges against her were outrageous. She was the sweetest, most darling girl you could possibly imagine and Mrs Meredith proposed giving the judge a piece of her mind when she attended April's trial as a defence witness at the Old Bailey.

As the day of the trial approached Lindsey's attempts to persuade Mr Jameson to let him out of bed became increasingly desperate and the surgeon's admonishments became equivalently severe. Matron was summoned to deliver a warning.

'What's this I've been hearing, sub-lieutenant? Applying to get out of bed indeed! Do you realise how much time and trouble has been taken by the surgical and nursing staff here to repair your knee, and the damage you would cause by premature movement? I'm very disappointed in you, sub-lieutenant. I don't want to hear any more nonsense from your room, please.'

Nurse Trims, who was in the room at the time of the scolding, had great difficulty maintaining a straight face. 'Stop smirking, Trims,' said Lindsey when the matron stalked out. 'If they won't let me up, you're going to have to help with telephone calls.'

On the day of the trial Lindsey sat taut and motionless in bed, his ears straining for the sound of the telephone in the ward sister's office. Nurse Trims had been despatched to stand outside the office with instructions to answer the phone immediately. She was to run back with whatever messages arrived from Chief Petty Officer Jones who was appearing as a witness in the court. Separately the bosun had been requested by Lindsey to call the hospital whenever there was anything to report and to bring April immediately to Stoke Mandeville when she was freed.

To keep the line clear Nurse Trims was further instructed to dissuade people from using the ward sister's telephone on the grounds that calls of national importance were expected which, as she explained to

Lindsey who was too busy worrying about April to pay attention, would not cut much ice if matron happened to be passing.

Only one message arrived from Chief Petty Officer Jones. It came late in the afternoon when shadows from the trees in the garden were lengthening on the lawns.

'I am so, so sorry,' said Nurse Trims.

Transit to Weedon Bec

Mrs Meredith sobbed and dabbed her eyes all the way back to Weedon, accompanied in the train by the wages clerk Miss Sally Fields. There was no consoling the personnel manager. Miss Fields tried to point out that Mrs Meredith had impressed everybody with the force of her testimony in the witness box but the personnel manager shook her head and wailed that her failure to answer the prosecuting counsel's questions properly had resulted in April being sent to the gallows and that she alone was responsible.

'That horrible man - when he mentioned marriage . . . How could he have known about me and the bosun?' wept Mrs Meredith.

'There, there,' said Miss Fields.

'Not that there's anything between Chief Petty Officer Jones and myself, of course. Not formally, I mean.'

'Of course.'

'I should have said immediately that two and a half months is quite long enough to get to know a person, regardless of circumstance, but the question took me off guard, you see.'

'It would have taken anyone off guard.'

'Perhaps he was just guessing. But even then . . . I shouldn't have hesitated, that was my mistake.'

'You mustn't blame yourself.'

'They're so terribly clever, lawyers. They know how to trip people up.'

'They certainly do.'

'That poor darling child . . .' sobbed Mrs Meredith.

'Hush now, you can have a nice cup of tea when you get home, and you'll feel much better,' said Miss Fields.

Transit to Plymouth

The bosun was equally disconsolate. On the train journey to Plymouth, where he'd been recalled following the return of the munitions barges to Weedon and cancellation of the CFZ project, he stared glumly through the carriage window at the transit of farms and meadows intermittently veiled by puffs of smoke from the locomotive.

Over and over again he replayed the prosecuting counsel's sarcastic comment. "Have you heard of Mata Hari? Allow me to refresh your memory." The bosun's well-meaning revelation of April's love for someone had ended up not only embarrassing the poor girl but allowing the prosecuting counsel to mock his naivety. Fortunately the trial had been held in closed session. The morning newspapers had merely reported the successful prosecution of yet another of, what Fleet Street now called, the "Water Spies". If journalists had been allowed into the court and printed details of the bosun's flawed performance in the witness box he would have been the laughing stock of the CPO's mess in Plymouth Barracks, where he was probably now doomed to spend the rest of his working life.

That was bad enough. As for April . . . Well, words couldn't describe his anger and astonishment at the outcome of the trial. It was inconceivable that someone so sweet and gentle, so charming and considerate, could have been involved in treachery. Why hadn't the judge stopped the trial? The evidence was clearly bogus. Did anyone seriously believe that April would have sneaked out from her cabin in the middle of the night to fix a plate onto *Daisy's* superstructure in order to pinpoint the convoy's position for German bombers?! Just because her father was Austrian didn't mean she was Adolf Hitler's niece. And why hadn't the judge reversed his sentence the moment he saw April faint? A real spy would never have collapsed in the dock like that.

Then, to cap it all, there was the scene with Mrs Meredith outside the Old Bailey afterwards. She had clung to him sobbing, looking at him with tearful eyes as he explained he'd been ordered back to Plymouth and couldn't accompany her to Weedon. They had parted without even shaking hands. Goodbye to romance and evenings in front of a log fire with slippers on his feet. Separated by two hundred miles she would find someone else to spoil with sandwiches and sponge cakes and pamper in the pleasant garden overlooking ducks and willow trees on the banks of the canal.

Weedon Narrowboats

Notice of the cancellation of the CFZ project had been received by the board of Weedon Narrowboats with disappointment and apprehension. The cash flow projections for the company had assumed continuity of payments from the War Office for a minimum of twelve months, and the projections had formed the basis of loans from Barclays Bank in Aylesbury against the costs of modifying six traditional barges for munitions transport.

However the managing director, Mr Browning, had proved his worth by extracting a substantial penalty from the army. The sum in question not only allowed the company to pay off the loans to Barclays Bank but covered the expense of reconverting the six barges, the original four plus the two standby vessels, from munitions duty to commercial carriage. And to the relief of the company chairman and his fellow board members, Mr Browning followed his coup by negotiating a contract for haulage of airframe parts from Rickmansworth to Birmingham via the Grand Union Canal thereby making full and immediate use of the company's expanded resources.

In genial mood Mr Browning summoned Mrs Meredith to his office to discuss the manpower requirements for the contract. The personnel manager had just returned from a couple of days at home, where he'd sent her to recover from her distress at the conviction of the traitorous ex-employee Miss April Tree.

'Glad to see you back, how are you feeling, Maggie?' he enquired sympathetically.

'Better,' lied Mrs Meredith. She was not better at all, and never would be, but there was no point in saying so or moping at home. There was a war to be won, and work to be done.

'Excellent. Now, crews for the airframe contract.'

Together they reviewed the options for recruiting the necessary manpower. Barraclough Brothers in Birmingham had offered crews on a temporary release basis but at exorbitant rates, and Mrs Meredith was suspicious of the qualifications of the men being proposed. The Ministry of Supply was looking into the company's request for labour and had promised to give the application favourable consideration in view of the strategic nature of the cargo. The Ministry of Aircraft Production had not yet responded to Mrs Meredith's letter.

'It's a pity we lost those two girls from the munitions project. What were their names?' said Mr Browning.

'Megan and Pippa,' said Mrs Meredith.

'Where did they go?'

'Back to the Lee Navigation Canal. They wanted to continue working on munitions barges, and earn danger money.'

'Mind you, they probably wouldn't have stayed here anyway, after all that trouble with the other girl . . .'

'Probably not,' said Mrs Meredith reaching for the handkerchief in the sleeve of her cardigan.

'So,' said Mr Browning hurriedly, 'where else can we look for crews?'

Aylesbury Central Police Station

Detective Chief Inspector Standish in charge of Buckinghamshire's CID division stood up and applauded as Detective Sergeant Quinn came into his office.

'Congratulations, Sam. I knew you'd win, well done,' he said.

'Thank you, sir,' said Quinn.

'Sit down. Tell me about it.'

Quinn sank into the chair beside the desk and described the series of trials in London which he'd attended as a technical adviser and witness. The accused were all now either behind bars or awaiting execution except for the simpleton trawler deckhand who had been released with a warning and the driver of the radio transmissions van spared prison on condition he joined the army and who by now was probably being marched around Aldershot parade ground with a rifle on his shoulder. The judge had spared him on strong evidence of duress from his employer, an unpleasant underworld figure called Fingleton Kelly, who in turn had been duped by Major MacLeod into revealing his connections with the canal escape route.

'Well done, Sam, you were right about the major too.'

'Major MacLeod was playing a risky game, sir. Kelly was

dangerous.'

'So I hear. Anyway, that wraps it up. A triumph for the division, and for you personally, Sam. You'll be glad of a break. Spend a few days with your family. Take them on a bicycling holiday!' joked the chief inspector.

'They're not as fond of bicycles as I am, sir,' grinned Quinn.

'You'll have to come back after the weekend I'm afraid, Sam. Inspector Greenough needs help with his investigations.'

'It will make a change from canals, sir,' said Quinn standing up.

He paused at the door.

'The German civilian in the barge, sir. Special Branch didn't produce him in court, and wouldn't say what's happened to him. Is there any way you could find out? I'd be interested to know.'

'I'll do my best, Sam.'

On his desk in the main CID office Quinn found a note. "Sub-Lieutenant Lindsey requests visit, Stoke Mandeville Hospital, very urgent".

The Admiralty, London

Rear Admiral Haldenby, the senior officer in charge of the Admiralty appointments division, was admiring the display of purple and yellow gladioli on the table in his office when the lieutenant responsible for junior officer appointments popped his head round the door.

'Assistant naval attaché, British Embassy, Washington, sir,' said the lieutenant.

'What about it?' said the rear admiral.

'The appointment is still not filled, sir.'

'Well?'

'I was wondering if we should send Lindsey, sir?'

The rear admiral turned slowly from the gladioli-decorated table and viewed the lieutenant through his bushy eyebrows.

'Are you quite serious?'

'I know what you mean, sir, about the CFZ project, but it wasn't his fault.'

'Not his fault? I rather thought we appointed Lindsey to take charge of the barges, not lease them to the Germans.'

'The army told him to keep the tarpaulins closed, and not inspect the cargo holds during the voyage, sir, for safety reasons,' said the lieutenant.

'I know that attachés are notoriously unqualified, but are you seriously suggesting we should send to Washington an officer who has been running excursion trips for German POWs?'

The lieutenant tried again. 'He was obeying army instructions, sir. In all other respects he is highly suited to the post.'

'Do you know him personally?'

'He was in my division at Dartmouth, sir.'

'You liked him?'

'First class man, sir.'

'Still in hospital, is he?'

The lieutenant nodded.

'By the time he gets out, he'll be lucky if he's still in the Royal Navy,' said the rear admiral.

Stoke Mandeville Hospital

Detective Sergeant Quinn was collected from the reception desk at Stoke Mandeville Hospital by Lindsey's cute dimpled-cheek nurse who gave him a welcoming smile and led him along the antiseptic-clean corridor to the private wards.

'I'm glad you've arrived,' she said. 'He's been jumping up and down impatiently waiting for you. I'm worried his bed will collapse.'

'How's his knee?'

'The surgeon says he can start physiotherapy tomorrow. Which means he'll be in a wheelchair, and I can get him out to the garden,' she said opening the door to the sunlit room.

'Quinn!' cried Lindsey. 'I thought you were never coming. Trims, where's that chair? Sit down, sit down. I've got something to tell you - something I remembered last night. I tried getting hold of you but the night staff refused - not their fault, I suppose, not at two o'clock in the morning. I had to wait for Trims. Pull up that chair. Trims, what can we give Detective Sergeant Quinn to drink on this hot afternoon? I've got some whisky here that Trims doesn't know about. No? How about some orange juice?'

Nurse Trims, who knew all about the bottle of whisky in the bedside cabinet, poured a glass of orange juice for the burly detective.

'First, what's happening to April, where is she and how long have we got?' said Lindsey.

'I'll have to check, sir, but I expect she's still in Holloway.'

'How long before the . . . ?'

'A week or two, sir. They normally wait, just in case.'

'In case of what?'

'The Home Secretary has to sign the death warrant. He usually waits a short time to make sure there are no loose ends.'

'Right, here it is then.' said Lindsey. 'I woke last night remembering something April said to me about the squint-eyed proprietor of the Horseshoe Inn. I didn't like the man, he was impertinent and inquisitive. April didn't like him either. Well, apparently he had lent over the bar during her first visit, nodded in her direction and said "She from the munitions barges too?" to Megan and Pippa, which April thought was strange.'

'Why strange, sir?'

'Because the convoy was on its first voyage.'

Quinn looked puzzled.

'Are you sure that's what she said, sir?'

'Her exact words,' nodded Lindsey. 'She was concerned about the security implications. I was too, and kept everybody out of earshot during our visits.'

'It might have been a trick, sir.'

'Think about it, Quinn. Why, if April was a spy, would she have told me that?'

Quinn frowned with concentration.

'I can think of only one reason for the innkeeper's remark,' continued Lindsey. 'Megan and Pippa already knew him.'

'That's not necessarily a crime, sir.'

'Yes, but very suspicious under the circumstances, don't you think?'

Quinn's mind travelled back to the final scene in court when April's legs had buckled. He'd been uncomfortable about that.

'You see what I'm getting at, Quinn? April was set up, I'm convinced of it,' said Lindsey. 'Either by someone following the barges, which would have been difficult in view of the ARP warden security cover, or more likely by someone onboard, which certainly wasn't me or the bosun, which leaves Megan and Pippa.

'They appeared in court as witnesses the other day, sir.'

'Of course they did. They had to. But I bet they didn't hang around afterwards.'

Quinn's mind travelled further back, to the declaration that April had hesitated when offered the opportunity of leaving the flotilla, and the prosecuting counsel's assertion that she had been bluffing. There'd been something unsettling about that too.

'You'd like me to trace the two young ladies, sir?'

'Yes, and my money says you won't find them,' said Lindsey. 'One more thing. The only piece of evidence against April that can't have been faked is the "AT" call sign. So, if I'm right and April's innocent, the call sign must have been misinterpreted. Can you get me copies of the relevant documents?'

Quinn thought wistfully of the short holiday with his family he'd been planning on the way to the hospital.

'I'll do my best, sir.'

'Marvellous!' cried Lindsey.

Weedon Narrowboats

Mrs Meredith was surprised to receive a telephone call from Detective Sergeant Quinn. She remembered him from the Old Bailey, a burly pleasant-faced man sitting behind her in the witness stalls.

'Yes, I do remember you, sergeant,' she said.

'I'm trying to get in touch with Miss Megan Leigh-Harvey. Just a routine enquiry. Is she available to speak on the telephone? '

'I'm afraid she's not here, sergeant.'

'How about her friend Miss Howland?'

'I'm sorry, she's not here either.'

'Are they on holiday?'

'I really don't know, sergeant. They don't work for us any more.'

'They've left your employment?'

'Yes.'

Pause.

'I see. Do you happen to know where they've gone, Mrs Meredith?

Did they leave a forwarding address?'

'Yes, of course. Just a minute . . .'

Mrs Meredith hurried to the filing cabinet by the door and returned with a file.

'Avon Boatyard, Lee Navigation Canal, Waltham Abbey,' she said picking up the receiver and reading from the file. 'They've returned to their old job. They worked on the munitions barges there before joining us at Weedon. I don't have the telephone number, but I'm sure you'll find it in the directory.'

'You've been most helpful,' said the sergeant's voice.

Routine enquiry, thought Mrs Meredith replacing the receiver, what did that mean?

Five minutes later the telephone rang again.

'Maggie?'

Mrs Meredith's hand jumped to her mouth.

'Bosun!'

'It's your old shipmate, Maggie, calling to see how you are.'

'Oh, bosun! I'm so happy to hear you.'

'They're keeping me busy, Maggie, or I would have called sooner.'

'Where are you - what are you doing?'

'I'm in Plymouth, Maggie, like I said. They've given me a job in the dockyard. I check stores on the ships, making sure the contractors don't make off with Navy property, which they do, all the time. You won't believe it, Maggie, but yesterday one of them sneaked into the galley and helped himself to a week's supply of sponge puddings. His face was red all over with strawberry jam, like a clown in a circus. He claimed he'd tripped over a cable and dived head-first into the carton. You've get to watch them the whole time, like a hawk, the thieving blighters, if you pardon my language How are you, Maggie, how are you getting on?'

'Oh, bosun, I miss you. I was in such a state in London. I don't even remember saying goodbye, I was crying so much.'

'You haven't forgotten me then, Maggie? Bother, here come the pips and I've run out of change . . .'

The line went dead.

Replacing the receiver at his end, the bosun's weatherbeaten face broke into a smile. She misses me! At the other end of the line, Mrs Meredith held the receiver in her hand for a few moments and stared mistily through the open window at the swallows swooping over the canal.

Avon Boatyard

The lady at Avon Boatyard confirmed over the telephone that Megan and Pippa were working on the Lee Navigation Canal but couldn't say exactly where they were right now, that being the job of the despatch clerk. The clerk in the despatch booth said he couldn't release that kind of information over the telephone, there was a war on in case Quinn didn't know, and it didn't matter whether the caller was a detective sergeant or a bleeding archbishop, those were his instructions. Sighing, Quinn packed an overnight bag and reached Waltham Abbey in the late evening after a fifty mile cross-country journey involving three different buses.

He booked into a boarding house, signed the register as Mr Sam Quinn and told the landlady he was a surveyor for the Ministry of War Transport. Rightly he should have reported to the local CID office but that meant extending the visit and he wanted to return home as soon as he'd located Megan and Pippa. The landlady recommended the Crown & Anchor pub for a meal. Mind yourself though, she said looking pointedly at the "Strictly No Visitors Allowed in Guests' Bedrooms" notice mounted above the staircase, that's where the barge girls go drinking.

If he was not married, reflected Quinn fighting his way through the throng of girls to the counter in the Crown & Anchor, this would be the place for a night of slap and tickle. Immersing his head in a copy of the local newspaper to feign disinterest in the nubile young bodies around him he consumed a steak and kidney pie and two pints of bitter, intermittently lifting his head to scan the array of girls for the objects of his enquiry. Should I ask the attractive girl standing next to me, whom I am pretending to ignore, if she knows Megan or Pippa? No, he rebuked himself fiercely, that would lead to the purchase of drinks for the informant and possibly, if he was not careful, gross violation of the notice mounted above the staircase in the boarding house.

For the benefit of the despatcher next morning Quinn reverted to the role of detective sergeant.

'Leigh-Harvey and Howland?' said the bespectacled figure in the booth at the entrance to the Powdermill Cut, the short stretch of water connecting the Lee Navigation Canal with Waltham Abbey Barracks.

'Yes.'

'Here we are. Avon-237.'

The despatcher stared at the register in front of him and began muttering. He reached for the telephone. 'Where's 237?' he shouted into the receiver. Quinn couldn't hear the reply. The despatcher slammed the receiver down, reached for an eraser and began rubbing out figures in the register.

'Something the matter?' said Quinn.

'Avon-237 was due for loading yesterday at 1100 hours. Steve must have got it wrong. I'll re-schedule her for 1000 hours today.'

'Whose Steve?' said Quinn.

The despatcher looked up with the resigned expression of someone dealing with persons of subnormal intellect.

'My mate,' said the despatcher.

'So you've changed the loading time to ten o'clock then?' said Quinn.

'That's what I said.'

'How will the crew of Avon-237 know you've changed it?'

The despatcher raised his eyes to the sky. 'They'll come and ask, won't they?' he said nodding irritably at the line of barges moored along the bank of the main canal.

Quinn crossed the bridge onto the picturesque stretch of land between the canal and river. Purple and crimson rhododendron bushes flowered beneath the oak trees and the scent of wild roses hung over the grass in the summer heat. Quinn strolled along the towpath in the shade of the trees checking the name-boards on the barges. Some of the girls were still getting dressed or washing their hair and he grinned at the squeals which accompanied his progress. The Avon boats were coloured blue. A quarter of a mile from the bridge he found barge Avon-237. Above the main name-board was a smaller board with *Donegal* painted in florid green letters.

'Anybody at home?' he called out.

The cabin door was closed. He bent down to look through the porthole but the curtain was drawn. Clambering into the cockpit he knocked on the door.

'Can I help you?' said a voice.

Quinn looked up to see a girl with a towel around her head peering at him from the cockpit of the next boat.

'Just delivering a message,' said Quinn.

'They're late risers. Knock louder,' said the girl returning to her cabin.

Quinn tried the handle. The door was locked. He knocked again. Wondering what to say if Megan and Pippa were still in bed or, even more embarrassing, getting dressed, he forced the lock with his penknife. The door swung open. 'Anybody there?' he called. He stepped down into the cabin and looked around. The stove was cold. The bed was folded up into the bulkhead. The sofa was untouched. There were no clothes, dishes, books, shoes, newspapers, cushions, toothbrushes, hats, flowers, milk bottles or girls. The cabin was completely empty.

Greenbrook Toll Point

The youth temporarily assigned to Greenbrook toll point to assist Bert Simkins burst into the toll booth waving a copy of the local weekly newspaper.

'You're famous, Mr Simkins!' he cried.

'How's that, lad?' said the toll collector.

The youth opened the newspaper and spread the pages onto the walnut bureau. Under the headline HEROIC CHARGE CAPTURES ENEMY SPIES was a full-length photograph of the toll collector in theatrical pose, one hand thrust into his waistcoat, chin erect, eyes ablaze with fortitude. The account of the incident was equally dramatic.

> Cognizant of the dangers inherent in the action which he was about to take, but aware of the responsibilities incumbent upon loyal subjects of His Imperial Majesty the King, Mr Bert Simkins, 62, Toll Collector, Greenbrook Toll Point, sized up the situation in a flash. To his right was a fleet of munitions barges approaching down the canal. To his left were dozens of soldiers armed to the teeth, spread out along the quay outside the toll point. One false step and Mr Bert Simkins knew he would condemn the soldiers and himself to a hideous death in a blazing inferno. Heedless of personal risk, however, Mr Bert

Simkins said to the captain of the soldiers "What are we waiting for?" and led the charge down the quay to the barges which by now were moored alongside the jetty. Mr Bert Simkins leapt onto the foremost vessel and peeled back the tarpaulins to reveal a troop of German agents hiding in the bilges. A shout of "Surrender, you curs!" rent the air. Thanks to his brave initiative the day was saved, not a life was lost, and the cowardly Huns are now safely behind bars where they belong. With characteristic modesty Mr Bert Simkins concluded his interview with your roving reporter by saying "It was nothing really - anyone could have done it".

'They didn't get that completely right, did they Mr Simkins?' said the youth when the toll collector had finished reading out the article.

'No,' admitted the toll collector with a hint of embarrassment.

'I mean, you couldn't really have leapt onto the barge, what with your lumbago and swollen legs?'

'They have to elaborate their stories, to increase circulation,' explained the toll collector.

'You're right, Mr Simkins, because, when you think about it, we were kneeling on the floor in here most of the time, weren't we?'

'Most of the time,' agreed the toll collector.

Stoke Mandeville Hospital

Nurse Trims stopped to catch her breath. She had already pushed Lindsey twice round the twin gardens. Now he wanted her to overtake the lieutenant-colonel in front of them whose wheelchair was being propelled slowly along the path by one of the older nurses.

'Come on, Trims. You'll never get past like that,' cried Lindsey. 'You'll have to go onto the grass.'

Hands on hips Nurse Trims looked down at her patient.

'Sub-Lieutenant Lindsey, this is not a race track, and I'm exhausted.'

'You look very pretty when you're cross, Trims. Hurry up, now. They're getting away.'

Lindsey's spirits had soared when Nurse Trims wheeled him through the double-doors at the end of the private ward corridor into the fresh air. He had inhaled deeply and pleasurably. For the first time in weeks the breeze was in his hair and real sunshine in his eyes. The birds were singing, butterflies were fluttering and bees were dancing on the flowers.

'I say, isn't that Quinn?' he said pointing at the burly figure dismounting from a bicycle in the front of the hospital. 'Over here, Quinn,' he waved.

Quinn approached them across the grass. Lindsey's heart sank when he saw the solemn expression on the detective's face.

'Where can we talk?' said Quinn.

They found a wooden bench in the shade of a chestnut tree. Nurse Trims and Quinn sat side by side. Lindsey faced them, crouching forward anxiously in his wheelchair.

'The good news is that you were right, sir,' said Quinn, 'the girls have disappeared from their place of work. The bad news is that Miss Tree's execution is scheduled for Monday.'

'Oh god,' groaned Lindsey.

'Monday noon,' said Quinn.

'Can't you stop it?' said Lindsey.

Quinn shook his head. 'Not enough proof yet, I'm afraid, sir. With the weight of evidence against Miss Tree, the apparent disappearance of two witnesses would not be considered sufficient justification for a postponement. There might be a perfectly reasonable explanation for their absence from work, a delayed journey on return from holiday, for example, or a visit to a sick relative.'

'Then you must find them,' said Lindsey. 'What day is it today, Trims?'

'Thursday,' said Nurse Trims.

'You've got four days,' said Lindsey.

'Two, discounting the weekend,' said Quinn. 'I've already initiated enquiries, sir. But it's going to take more than a slice of luck to find them by Monday.'

Lindsey groaned.

'You'll do your best, won't you, Quinn? I know you will. God, I wish I could help,' he said. 'But even if they allowed my wheelchair out of the hospital grounds, Trims has run out of steam.'

'That's not fair!' protested Nurse Trims.

'I was only joking,' said Lindsey grimly.

Quinn reached into his pocket. 'I've managed to get copies of the callsign and map reference schedules produced in court.'

'Well done, Quinn!' said Lindsey cheering up. 'At least we can do something while you search for the girls. Come on, Trims, you can help.'

Quinn left the sub-lieutenant and dimple-cheeked nurse in the shade of the chestnut tree examining the documents. He walked purposefully to his bicycle. To avoid raising false hopes he had avoided mentioning the clue that Miss Leigh-Harvey and Miss Howland had left behind. If the young ladies were guilty they should have removed the supplementary name-board from their barge before going on the run.

St James's Street, London

The hot weather had brought about a change of attire in Whitehall. The change started at the Foreign Office where male fashion is so often defined. One of the ministers elected to swap his morning coat for a lightweight fawn-coloured cotton jacket of the type referred to as 'Tropical' by Saville Row tailors. In all other respects his dress remained the same - black shoes, socks, pin-striped trousers, grey waistcoat, white shirt, starched wing collar and grey silk tie - however the effect was so agreeably elegant that similar jackets were quickly adopted throughout the building particularly on Fridays when old school ties, predominantly those of Eton and Harrow, were substituted for the formal grey ones.

From the Foreign Office the fashion spread to other departments in Whitehall. Indeed the two senior civil servants from the counter-espionage division of military intelligence lunching at their club in St James the day Lindsey received from Quinn the papers representing Exhibit B in case of the Crown versus Miss April Tree had also exchanged their morning coats for lightweight cotton jackets. The diners commenced luncheon with brown windsor soup, their usual choice, a concoction regarded as nutritious by those of privileged background and inedible by everyone else. They continued with poached turbot, raspberries and cheese accompanied in due sequence by chilled white Burgundy wine and a decanter of port.

'You've closed the file, I suppose?'

'Not completely.'

'Oh?'

'The chap they've turned - the one that's gone back to Germany - has hinted that his local contact was a comparatively small cog in the wheel, and that someone much bigger is still on the loose.'

'I thought they'd all been caught?'

'Not if the hint is right.'

'Got it. So what's happening?'

'Scratching our heads. Meanwhile Buckinghamshire CID have embarked on a separate chase, looking for a couple of girls from the convoy who have disappeared under suspicious circumstances.'

Belfast Harbour

Constable Fergus Muir of the Belfast Harbour Police waited until the last passenger had disembarked then climbed the gangway onto the Liverpool-Belfast ferry. The stewards were cleaning up around the deckchairs, emptying the ashtrays and litter bins and picking up the detritus discarded by the passengers who had crowded the deck during the crossing in preference to the saloons below, as near to the lifeboats as possible in case of mines or torpedoes.

Clattering down the stairs in his heavy boots the policeman headed for the purser's office. The air was sour in the bowels of the ship - a mixture of stale beer, cigarette smoke and vomit. Wrinkling his nose he ignored the "Private No Entry" sign, opened the door, removed his cap and sprawled into the swivel chair opposite the purser's desk.

'If it isn't Constable Fergus Muir,' said the purser, an affable red-faced man with three stripes on the sleeves of his merchant navy uniform.

'The very same, here to greet you in person, wishing you a pleasant stay in Belfast and promising not to search your vessel for contraband goods in exchange for a modicum of information,' said the constable.

'Modicum?'

'It's a new word I've been rehearsing - for the promotion.'

'You need Latin for promotion in the Harbour Police?'

'I thought it might confuse the examiners.'

'Very likely it will, Fergus.'

'So, have you seen them?' said the policeman pointing at the Missing Persons poster from Buckinghamshire CID on the noticeboard.

'Not on this sailing. But one of the stewards . . . Where is it now? You can never find things when you want them, especially when you're busy and your office is full of uninvited Latin-speaking guests. Here it is. Hang on a minute, Fergus.'

The purser flicked a switch on the tannoy module beside the desk: 'Steward Levitt report to the purser's office immediately.'

He had noticed them on the previous sailing, said Steward Levitt standing in the doorway, because of the comparative size of the two young ladies. One was quite heavily-built with broad shoulders, the other was slim, dark and elegant just like the descriptions on the poster in the stewards' quarters though he hadn't seen the poster at the time otherwise he would have reported the presence of the young ladies to the purser earlier. The poster didn't say anything about the man, though.

'Man?' said the constable.

'He was sitting with them, at the same table.'

The constable pulled a notebook from his pocket. 'Describe him please.'

Steward Levitt frowned with concentration. 'Smart tweed jacket - bald - piercing eyes - talked a lot. That's about it. I wasn't really looking at him, you see. I was more interested in the dark-haired young lady who was,' said the steward clearing his throat, 'a nice bit of crumpet.'

'That's Latin for sexually desirable,' the purser informed the constable.

'Did you hear them say anything of interest?' the constable asked the steward.

'Now you mention it, they always stopped talking when I approached the table. Most people ignore us, you know, carry on chatting when we're around, but not them. Shut up like clams when I got near. Very guarded, they were.'

Aylesbury Central Police Station

Quinn was working at his desk in Aylesbury central police station on Saturday morning when the Detective Chief Inspector Standish passed through the main office.

'What are you doing here at the weekend, Sam - still looking for those girls?'

'Yes, sir.'

The chief inspector walked to his desk.

'The case is supposed to be closed, Sam,' he said gently.

'I know, sir.'

The chief inspector observed the lines on Quinn's face.

'Tell me again, Sam. Why do you think something's wrong?'

'That's the problem, sir. I can't prove it.'

'The girl, April Tree. You know her personally? You're fond of her - is that the problem?'

'I don't know her, sir,' said Quinn shaking his head. 'In fact I didn't give the case a second thought after the trial until the naval officer, Lindsey, remembered something Miss Tree had said to him, which pointed at the possibility she'd been set up. Since then, and since the disappearance of her so-called friends from the Lee Navigation Canal, I have become increasingly convinced that the wrong person is going to be executed on Monday and, right now, there's nothing I can do to prevent it.'

'Unless you find the two girls?'

Quinn nodded.

'Who might be perfectly innocent?' said the chief inspector.

'They might.'

'Did anyone check the girls' backgrounds?'

'Special Branch verified that Miss Leigh-Harvey's father is a Church of England minister working somewhere in Africa, that her mother is dead and Miss Howland's parents are eccentric artists living in London, drinking gin before breakfast and painting peacocks. They also verified that both girls were studying at Cambridge when war broke out, and neither of them has any record of political activity, fascist or otherwise.'

'Not much there, then.'

'No, sir.'

'So, where are they? How's the search going?'

'They were spotted arriving in Ulster yesterday, sir. I have reason to believe they're heading south to Donegal. The local police have been requested to stop them at the border post if they cross there.

Alternatively the girls might try and slip over the hills. Unfortunately the police are busy elsewhere, so I've been looking for Brigadier Smythe's address. The army might be able to help with the search. What do you think, sir?'

The chief inspector looked doubtful. 'The army won't thank you if they find the girls sleeping peacefully in one of their grandmothers' farmhouse.'

'It won't hurt to ask, sir. One of the sightings reported that the girls were travelling with a man, which increases the possibility they might try to skirt around the border post.'

The chief inspector stirred in his chair.

'That's interesting. The other day you asked me about the German agent. He's working for us now, apparently. The interesting thing is they now think that Major Macleod's acquaintance Fingleton Kelly was working for someone higher up, who's still on the loose,' said the chief inspector. 'I wonder if there's a connection?'

Brigadier Smythe's Residence

'My word,' said the brigadier when Quinn had finished talking.

The house was large with parapets on the east wing. A sleek limousine, the brigadier's motorcycle and several open-top touring cars were parked in front. There was a tennis court and croquet lawn running parallel to the remains of a tudor wall. The players wore white flannels and pleated white skirts. Other members of the family and guests congregated in groups on the top lawn, comfortably stretched out in rattan armchairs with colourful striped cushions. Maids circulated with trays of refreshment. The brigadier's batman, the sleeves of his khaki shirt rolled up in concession to the weather, panted in the background from his allotted task of collecting tennis balls from the shrubbery and croquet balls from the rose beds.

The brigadier had detached himself from the cluster of players on the croquet lawn to greet Quinn. Courteously introducing the new arrival to his wife, the brigadier guided Quinn to a vacant pair of chairs where they were served with sherbet by a maid bobbing at the knee.

'So you want me to find out if any of our troops in Ulster are tooling around doing nothing?' said the brigadier.

'Search operations are an army speciality, aren't they, sir?' said Quinn

'Of course they are,' sniffed the brigadier. 'Damned good training for the foot soldier.'

'The local police are overloaded, you see, and time's running out.'

'Monday, you said?'

'Monday noon, sir.'

'These girls,' said the brigadier looking at the missing persons notice handed him by Quinn. 'I've met them before, haven't I?'

'You have, sir. At the site of the second bombing raid.'

'Megan Leigh-Harvey. I remember her, a handsome strapping girl. We drank rum together leaning against the barge. She quite liked me, you know,' said the brigadier adjusting the tips of his moustache. 'You can always tell.'

'It would be an opportunity to clear her name,' encouraged Quinn.

'Quite so. They might be innocent, as you rightly say. Leave it with me, Quinn, I'll see what can be done.'

'Thank you, sir. From tomorrow morning I shall be at the telephone number on the notice.'

Returning along the drive in the shade of giant elms between a paddock enclosed by neat post-and-rail fences on one side and an ornamental lake on the other Quinn reflected on the grandeur of upper class weekends and the beauty of their parkland settings compared with his modest semi-detached house in the suburbs of Aylesbury with a small runner bean, potato and cabbage patch garden in the rear. Never mind, he told himself thrusting his chin out, one step at a time. Meanwhile back to the central police station where a squad car was waiting to take him to Liverpool to catch the night ferry to Belfast.

Stoke Mandeville Hospital

The weather broke again that night. The sky hurled thunderbolts and rain from black clouds awakening the sheep and cattle and rattling the window panes of houses in which children peered fearfully from their beds at the ferocity of the storm. In Stoke Mandeville Hospital the clamour awoke the patients and the nurses hurried through the wards answering the bells, patting pillows and reassuring their charges with murmurs of 'It's just a little thunder storm, nothing to worry about, back to sleep now'.

To Lindsey lying restlessly in his private room the tempest heralded the closing stages of a nightmare in which the cries of help from a distant dungeon grew increasingly faint. The cries mingled with a kaleidoscope of letters and numerals, callsigns and map references, spinning senselessly in his head. There was no pattern to them. They served no purpose but to mock the futility of his attempts to unlock the dungeon door and release the girl who had captured his heart.

'Hello,' he called out to a nurse hurrying past in the corridor.

The nurse stopped, opened the door and hurried to his bed.

'It's just a little thunder storm, nothing to worry about, back to sleep now,' she said patting his pillows.

'I can't sleep,' said Lindsey.

'There, there, I'll get you an aspirin.'

'That won't do any good. I need something stronger.'

The nurse pursed her lips.

'I'll fetch sister,' she said.

The night sister listened sympathetically.

'I can't sleep,' said Lindsey. 'My head's spinning. I need to rest my brain so I can figure out these bloody . . . sorry sister . . . letters and numerals. Time's running out. I've only got one more full day.'

The night sister knew all about the approaching deadline and grieved, with the rest of the hospital staff, for the handsome sub-lieutenant and his doomed sweetheart. She helped him sit upright while he swallowed the little blue pill from the night dispensary.

The pill knocked Lindsey out.

Holloway Prison

The rain continued through Sunday. Damp air permeated the condemned cell in Holloway Prison where April sat eyes down gazing at the stone floor. In the office at the end of the passage the prison chaplain talked with the duty warder.

'Have you started the sedatives yet?' he said.

'She won't take them.'

'Have you put them in her food?'

'She won't eat.'

'In her tea?'

'She won't drink.'

'Poor child,' sighed the chaplain.

'She's stopped reading too. I've never known anyone devour so many books. She said she wanted to learn everything about love before she went. Flaubert, Shelley, Byron, Jane Austen, Bronte, Jean Paul, Heyer, Dickinson, du Maurier, Balzac. The librarian's never been so busy. She stopped reading this morning. Now she just sits, staring at the floor, not moving.'

'She won't pray with me. She told me she didn't want to communicate with such an irresponsible God.'

'You discussed free will, I suppose?' said the warder who was a regular in the condemned cells.

The chaplain nodded.

'She looked at me with those hazel eyes and said that free will had got a lot to answer for.'

The warder, a large woman as befitting her status, with stern but compassionate features, completed the shift report and returned the pen to the inkpot. She tapped her pocket to check that the keys of her house were in place. She would be going home shortly, to cook supper for her family.

'She's only broken down once, to my knowledge,' said the warder. 'I tripped over a pile of books in her cell and she jumped up to steady me. Then before I knew it she was crying in my arms. Do you know what she said? "I so much wanted to dance with him again, just one more time".'

'Him?' said the chaplain.

'The naval officer she's in love with.'

West End Central Police Station, London

The duty constable at the front desk of London West End Central Police in London leaned over the sergeant's shoulder and read the article on the front page of the Monday morning newspaper. The headline, above a photograph of April taken when arriving at the Old Bailey for her trial, announced: GALLOWS TODAY FOR GLAMOROUS WATER SPY

'What a waste,' sighed the constable looking at the photograph.

'I take it you are commenting on the young lady's attributes and not on the dastardly deeds she has committed,' said the sergeant.

'Do you suppose she's really guilty, sergeant?'

'They'd hardly be stringing her up if she wasn't.'

'What if they made a mistake?'

'What you've got to learn, my lad, is that the British judiciary system is the finest in the world and never makes mistakes. If it does, which it doesn't, then it is not for us, as guardians of the law, to comment upon the matter.'

'Yes, but what if they found out they'd made a mistake, afterwards?'

'Then it'd be too late, wouldn't it? Enough of the idle speculation, my lad, and get back to work,' said the sergeant folding the newspaper.

Central Police Station, Belfast

Quinn paced the main hall of Belfast central police station alternately glowering at the telephone on the counter and at the switchboard cubicle beyond the counter where half a dozen telephonists attended to incoming calls from the province. He had slept badly in the hotel, tossing and turning, reaching out regularly to check that the telephone receiver was sitting properly on its cradle and that he had not missed a vital call from the soldiers searching the hills near Donegal.

He checked his watch. 0955 hours. Just two hours to go before they placed the noose around Miss April Tree's neck.

By now, even if the soldiers found the girls, the option of travelling to the point of capture and conducting an investigation had gone. He would have to rely on assurance from Special Branch in London that if the girls were found in circumstances indicating flight from justice, then the Home Office would be requested to postpone the execution pending the results of the interrogation. But if the girls were discovered strolling down a country lane with shopping baskets on their arms, or singing Celtic ballads to boyfriends in a hay cart, well then, it was all over.

He checked his watch again. 1015 hours.

He opened the door and peered into the switchboard cubicle. The telephonists shook their heads.

Stoke Mandeville Hospital

Nurse Trims busied herself in the private rooms trying not to look out at the clump of trees where Lindsey's wheelchair was parked. The storm had passed, the sun was out again but the grass was wet so he was shuffling papers despairingly in his lap instead of laying them on the ground which he normally did in order to get what he called a composite picture of the radio transmission scenario.

She had wheeled him out after breakfast in silence. Avoiding contact with his eyes she had wrapped a blanket around his knees and hurried back inside the hospital. She could not bear the look of misery on his face. To keep her mind occupied she changed the pillow cases in every one of the rooms forcing herself to respond to the banter from her patients with a cheerful smile. Each time she returned to the trolley in the corridor she glanced up at the clock.

It was now 1045 hours.

In just a short time, at midday, the papers would slip from Lindsey's lap, his head would slump forward and she would walk out to perform the most difficult of all nursing tasks, the consolation of the disconsolate. She would hold his hand. If he wept she would dry his eyes and tell him it was no shame for a man to cry. She would listen to the outpourings of his grief and guilt and when they subsided she would wheel him around the grounds, around and around, until he had recovered his composure sufficiently and then it would be her turn. She would find somewhere to hide and, affected by his grief, sob quietly into her handkerchief.

'He's waving at you, nurse,' said the ward sister walking past in the corridor.

Nurse Trims peered through the nearest window. Lindsey had moved the position of his wheelchair. It looked as if he was trying to manoeuvre out of the clump of trees but had got stuck in the long grass. He was waving frantically. His mouth was open and his lips were moving. He's shouting for me, she thought, running down the corridor.

'Trims, Trims, hurry up, for god's sake!' she heard as she flung open the doors to the garden and sprinted across the grass.

'What's the matter?' she cried grasping the handles of the wheelchair.

'Get me to a telephone, quick!'

She heaved the wheelchair out of the long grass onto the lawn.

'Where's the nearest one, Trims?'

'Sister's office.'

'Put your back into it!' he cried urging the nurse forward as she struggled over the wet turf.

They reached the driveway. She could run now, clutching her cap with one hand, the heels of her shoes clattering on the tarmac.

'Hold on!' she cried bouncing the wheelchair up the ramp into the building.

'Faster, Trims!' cried Lindsey steadying the papers in his lap as they sped along the corridor past the private rooms narrowly missing Mrs Edna Perch the cleaning lady who stepped out of the way and flattened herself against the wall with her mop clasped to her bosom.

Nurse Goodrow, an older member of staff, was using the telephone in the ward sister's office. 'Personally I have never cared for that fishmonger, as you very well know, very fond of himself I might say, why just the other day he wrapped a piece of hake into a newspaper, everyone could see it was hake, I'm certain of it, and claimed it was cod. Cod, I exclaimed! Why yes, lady, he said all pert and cocky, straight from the North Sea, as fresh a piece of cod as you are likely to find from here to Grimsby and Hull, and I told him off, I said it was outrageous in these times of trouble when people are . . . '

'Get her off the phone, Trims,' said Lindsey fiercely.

'Goodrow,' said Nurse Trims tugging the older nurse's uniform.

'. . . short of food that fishmongers should be trying to deceive their customers into paying for cod when they're getting hake, there should be a law against it, and he said, all snooty now, take it or leave it, lady, and I told him straight out that I would take my business elsewhere, and that when the war was over, there would be a reckoning because, I said, all those customers you have deceived by substituting inferior fish, which everyone can see . . .'

'If you don't get her off the phone, Trims, I will,' said Lindsey glancing furiously at his watch.

'Goodrow, please,' said Nurse Trims tugging harder at the older nurse's uniform.

'I'd better be going, Mabel. There are some people here with less manners than patience,' said Nurse Goodrow replacing the receiver and stalking out of sister's office, her nose in the air.

Lindsey read out the number.

Nurse Trims dialled it.

The call was answered immediately.

'Belfast central police station,' said a brisk voice.

Lindsey took the receiver from Nurse Trims.

'I need to speak to Detective Sergeant Quinn, urgently. Yes, I'll hold on. Yes, I'm still here. Quinn? It's me, Lindsey. Listen, they're not callsigns and map references. Can you hear me ? I said, they're not callsigns and map references. They're letters and figures representing convoy locations and times, itineraries. I said, itineraries. Call me back if we get cut off, I'm at the hospital. Are you still there? No, not callsigns. A sequence of locations based on initials. The sequence includes "HI" for Horseshoe Inn and ends with "SA" for Smugglers Arms and "T" for trawler. Someone inserted spaces between the wrong groups of letters, which confused the issue. I've only just worked it out. Are you still there, did you hear what I said ? Quinn, listen, we talked about this. The radio transmissions are the only piece of evidence they couldn't have faked. Are we too late?'

Bletchley Park

The head of the signals intelligence and traffic analysis section at Bletchley Park marched sternly through Hut 15 to the desk of his communications analyst.

'Your schedules of the Mayfair intercepts, Rupert,' he said. 'Show them to me, please,' he said.

The communication analyst turned back from the window and drew a file from the top drawer of his desk.

'In here, old duck. What's up?'

The section head opened the file. He pulled out the schedules and associated intercepts.

'What are these spaces for, Rupert?'

'Spaces?'

'There, Rupert, and there,' said the section head pointing at the callsigns schedule.

The communications analyst reached for one of the intercepts and compared it with the entries on the schedule.

'I see what you mean,' he said scratching his head. 'Typing errors, I suppose.'

'Rupert,' said the section head. 'You presented these schedules in court.'

'Yes, I know. I was very unhappy about that. I thought the prosecuting counsel's interpretation was highly speculative. People were liable to draw the wrong conclusion.'

'They certainly were,' said the section head grimly, 'and did.'

'I mean, it takes a trained mind to comprehend these kind of figures properly.'

'They're letters not figures, Rupert. The figures are on the other schedule here and, according to information conveyed to me by telephone just now, they represent dates and times, not map references.'

The communications analyst stared at the schedule.

'I say, that's very shrewd,' he said after a while. 'Someone seems to have scored a winner there. No wonder we didn't manage to work it out. Talk about wandering off in the wrong direction. Never mind, nothing to worry about, give me a few minutes and I'll clean it all up. Well, maybe not immediately,' he said glancing at his watch. 'It's nearly lunchtime. Care to join me for a pint?'

But the signals intelligence and traffic analysis section head was already back in his office.

'I say, what's the matter with him?' said the communications analyst turning to the signals coordinator at the next desk. 'He seems a bit edgy. How about you, Cecil, fancy a drink? There's not much going on at the moment.'

Plymouth Dockyard

Not much of a birthday, thought Chief Petty Officer Jones, watching a group of destroyers leave harbour and sweep across Plymouth Hoe with pennants flying. What a way to celebrate, he thought, checking consignments of nuts and bolts in a dockyard store while the rest of navy chased German battle cruisers and U-boats. His time had passed. He was, in terms of the navy's fighting strength, redundant. At least on the Grand Union Canal he had contributed to the defence of the nation in a tactical role. Here in Plymouth, despite what the supply lieutenant in charge of dockyard stores might say in the way of encouragement 'Senior ratings of your qualifications and experience, Jones, are the mainstay of proper shore support', he was no more than a clerk.

And by macabre coincidence, at noon today, on the occasion of his birthday, the lovely young April Tree, with whom he had been privileged to serve on the CFZ convoys, was to be hanged.

It was enough, he told Chief Engine Room Artificer Brewster and Chief Petty Officer Eccles on their way from the dockyard to the Admiral Collingwood for lunch, to drive a man to drink.

The small hand of the clock above the bar had already passed twelve when they entered the pub and settled at a table in the far corner where they were joined by other shipmates seeing out their days at lowly tasks in the dockyard. To keep the bosun's mind off the scaffold in London they topped up his beer glass and made him recount his days on the China station when the gunboats had patrolled the coast and rivers to protect British cantonments and merchant vessels from pirates, but his self-imposed guilt for failing to rescue April from her fate sat heavily on his shoulders and his reminiscences tailed off.

'The worst thing is,' said the bosun admitting for the first time to his friends his unfortunate lapse in the witness box at the Old Bailey, 'with the right words, I might have saved her.'

'Nonsense!' cried his shipmates comfortingly, 'fiddlesticks, balderdash, poppycock!'

'This is how I shall always remember her,' said the bosun leaning back in his chair. 'We moored one warm evening in the shade of willow trees. I was stretched out on the canal bank like this before supper when she sat down beside me and said "Close your eyes and open your mouth, bosun" and I said "I don't much care for raw frogs, miss" and she laughed with that delightful laugh which I shall never forget, covered my eyes with her hand and dropped some wild strawberries into my mouth.'

'Aww,' murmured his shipmates overwhelmed at the poignant scene.

'If I had a magic wand,' said the bosun rising unsteadily to his feet, 'I would wave it like this and bring her back to life.'

Beer swilling from his glass he dropped back into his chair just as the barmaid switched on the radio.

"Here is the one o'clock news, and this is Alvar Lidell reading it. In a new development concerning the Water Spy Case it has just been announced that the execution of April Tree, originally scheduled for noon today, has been halted pending investigation of new evidence . . ."

The outburst of shouts and cheers from the far corner of the pub drowned the rest of the news and, while his back was being slapped and his mystical powers boisterously applauded, Chief Petty Officer Jones beamed serenely at his shipmates.

Central Police Station, Belfast

In Belfast central police station, Quinn slumped happily into the spare chair in the duty sergeant's office clutching the message from Special Branch in London confirming that the Home Office had been persuaded to halt April Tree's execution pending re-evaluation of the Exhibit B documents. If Lindsey was right about the callsigns then the case against April would almost certainly be reopened and the disappearance of two key witnesses would count in her favour. More significantly, if Megan Leigh-Harvey and Pippa Howland were found to be implicated in the spy ring then the case against April would disintegrate.

'I'll give you two more days, Sam,' Detective Chief Inspector Standish in Aylesbury had told him half an hour ago when he called to request further leave of absence. 'If you haven't caught them by Wednesday, you'll have to hand over to Special Branch.'

Freed from the immediate burden of responsibility for April's life he was stretching his legs out when a head appeared round the door. 'Call for you.' Quinn jumped out of the chair and went to the telephone on the counter.

'Lieutenant Grieves, 6th Battalion Ox and Bucks Regiment. We've caught your suspects, one man, two young women. Where do you want them?'

'You've found them?' cried Quinn.

'Hiding in a barn. Shall we deliver them to you in Belfast? Our chaps were up all night. I'd like to give them a break in town, if it's all the same to you.'

'Well done, sir! Yes, thank you, that would save me a journey.'

'Give us a few hours.'

'Please keep the prisoners apart, sir.'

'We're doing that. They're not very talkative anyway.'

Quinn strode elatedly from the police station to the nearby park to clear his head and plan the next step. The correct procedure would be to receive the prisoners from the soldiers, arrest and caution them, invite statements, initiate investigations into any issues arising from the statements that required local action then hand over the prisoners to Special Branch in London for interrogation and closure of the case. Alternatively, it occurred to him as he strolled along leafy paths amongst mothers with perambulators and children on roller skates, why award the glory to Special Branch and delay April's release? Why not conduct the interrogations here, in Belfast?

The plan could go terribly wrong, Quinn reflected. Defence lawyers would pounce on any mistakes, Special Branch interrogators would sneer sarcastically and he would spend the rest of his career on a bicycle.

There was an additional complication - who was the man with the girls?

Weedon Narrowboats

The one o'clock news announcement had been received with boisterous cheers at Weedon Narrowboats too. Crowded around the bakelite radio that played all day in the covered slipway the men had listened to Alvar Lidell's declaration and thrown their caps in the air. April had been a great favourite amongst the workforce. One of the carpenters hurried into the office building. There was a shriek from Mrs Meredith's office and the personnel manager came stumbling out into the sunshine, tears streaming down her face, to seek confirmation that the news was correct and the execution had been halted.

'I knew it, I knew it!' she cried stumbling back into the building to Mr Browning's office where she collapsed into a chair dabbing her eyes with her lace handkerchief.

'Is something the matter, Maggie?' said Mr Browning gently.

'Matter!' spluttered Mrs Meredith. 'That unctuously disagreeable barrister who made a fool of me in court has just had his comeuppance, and April has been reprieved!'

Mr Browning smiled.

'That's excellent news,' he said.

'The barrister should be strung up, not darling April. I would dance on that man's grave.'

'I take it you're celebrating?' said Mr Browning.

'Of course I am,' sobbed Mrs Meredith.

'Then I presume your celebrations will gradually become less tearful?'

Sobbing and laughing simultaneously Mrs Meredith said, 'She was your employee too, you know.'

'I remember Miss Tree very well. A very nice girl, and I was surprised at the accusations although, regrettably, I was not very sympathetic at the time. One had to assume that the legal profession knew what they're doing,' said Mr Browning.

Central Police Station, Belfast

Three army trucks rolled into the yard behind Belfast central police station and formed a semicircle around the entrance to the detention block where Quinn and a squad of policemen stood waiting. From the rear of the vehicles soldiers dismounted, rifles in their hands. The soldiers formed a guard on the tarmac as the prisoners climbed down, one from each truck.

Quinn barely noted the dishevelled state of the girls. His attention was focused on the man. Medium height, bald, tweed jacket, grey trousers, bow-legged like a jockey, penetrating eyes, face slightly familiar. Where had he seen that face before? Quinn peered at the man then slapped his thigh in astonishment. The Old Bailey!

A fortnight ago in London the man now being forcibly handcuffed at rifle point had convinced a high court judge, barristers and jury that he was a half-witted trawler deckhand!

Briefly it occurred to Quinn as he stood waiting that in different circumstances the man could have made his fortune on the stage. What a waste of talent! Unfortunately the option of a stage career was no longer available to him. The life expectancy of persons caught running spy rings in wartime Britain was markedly short.

Quinn stepped forward.

'Seamus O'Reilly, I arrest you on charges against the Official Secrets Act. Anything you say will be taken down and may be used in evidence against you,' he said to the ringleader of the Grand Union Canal escape route support operation.

'Megan Leigh-Harvey, I arrest you on suspicion of charges against the Official Secrets Act. Anything you say will be taken down and may be used in evidence against you,' he said to the larger girl struggling with the policemen holding her wrists.

'Pippa Howland, I arrest you on suspicion of charges against the Official Secrets Act. Anything you say will be taken down and may be used in evidence against you,' he said to the second girl who had already been handcuffed and was protesting 'I can't smoke a cigarette like this!'

Quinn turned to the army captain.

'I am extremely grateful to you and your men, sir,' he said.

'Nothing to it, really,' said the captain. 'Corporal Edmunds here found them.'

'Thank you, Corporal Edmunds,' said Quinn to the sun-tanned corporal standing to attention beside the captain. 'You have helped overturn a major injustice and bring an important police investigation to a conclusion. You found them in a barn, I gather?'

'Yes, sir. They were pretending to be in what you might say was a,' said the corporal clearing his throat, 'conjugal position but our suspicions were aroused, what with the gentleman's age, and there being two girls, and what with his trousers not being down, if you see what I mean, sir.'

Quinn turned back to the captain.

'I would appreciate you allowing Corporal Edmunds to make a statement inside the station, sir. It won't take long.'

'Of course.'

'You know Brigadier Smythe, sir?'

'He was colonel of my regiment when I was a subaltern. Why?'

'I went to him for help. It was fortunate you were over here, sir.'

'If we weren't, he would have found someone else,' said the captain. 'Very resourceful, my old colonel. As it happened, we were exercising with the Royal Ulster Rifles. They gave us time off to play in the hills on your behalf.'

Stoke Mandeville Hospital

Nurse Trims was hurrying down the corridor carrying a packet of balloons borrowed from the children's ward when the matron stepped out of her office.

'There seems to be a disturbance in Sub-Lieutenant Lindsey's room, nurse. Please arrange for the noise level to be reduced for the benefit of other patients in the hospital, as much as possible,' said matron with a smile.

'Yes, matron,' said Nurse Trims continuing down the corridor to the room in question packed with nurses reaching out with medicine glasses to the bed, from which Lindsey was gaily dispensing measures from the several bottles of whisky that had mysteriously accumulated in his bedside cabinet.

Central Police Station, Belfast

The job of recording the statements from the prisoners was given to Police Cadet Kershaw, a studious young man who had won the sociology prize in school for his essay "Crime and Punishment amongst the Clans of Northern Ireland and Scotland, the Facts". A bright future was predicted for him in the Royal Ulster Constabulary on account of his being able to spell constabulary correctly.

'Mind you listen to what they say, and don't make anything up,' instructed the duty sergeant issuing the cadet with a notebook and pencil.

'Lucky old you, you're going to meet the Water Spies,' cried the other cadets enviously.

'Watch out for the male prisoner, he's IRA for sure,' said one of the constables knowingly.

Overwhelmed by the responsibility of assisting the burly and charismatic detective from England, famous throughout the police force for his breakthrough in the Grand Union Canal spy case, the cadet waited nervously in the main hall waiting to be summoned.

He could hear Quinn's voice in the inspector's office.

What if the pencil broke? The sudden thought made the cadet's knees tremble. He would go down in history as the man who had failed to record the confessions of the most notorious criminals ever captured in Ulster. Frantically he looked around. Darting behind the counter he searched along the shelves. There, a spare pencil, mercifully sharpened. He grabbed it and returned to his position in the hall. Breathing deeply he urged his knees to stop shaking.

The door to the inspector's office opened. Quinn emerged.

'Kershaw, is it? Come on then,' said the detective giving the cadet a friendly smile and beckoning him to follow as he strode off towards the detention block.

Quinn started with O'Reilly.

Two warders with truncheons accompanied the detective and cadet into the cell and locked the door behind them. The prisoner was sitting on the bed manacled to the frame by handcuffs staring into space venomously like a snake. The cadet remained as far away as possible as the detective approached the bed. The cadet recorded the detective's words when he offered the prisoner the opportunity of making a statement. The man didn't answer, just kept staring blankly ahead with those venomous eyes. The detective waited for a couple of minutes, nodded to the warders and returned to the door. The cadet lowered his pencil and followed the detective out into the corridor

They proceeded to Megan Leigh-Harvey's cell further along the corridor out of earshot of O'Reilly's cell.

She looked as dangerous as the man, thought the cadet. She was wearing slacks and a roll-top jumper and her eyes burned with the same malevolent intensity. The prisoners had been caught in a barn apparently. There were traces of straw in her hair and clothing. The cadet wrote into his notebook as the detective asked her if she wanted to make a statement but, like the man, she ignored the question and stared right through him.

'They're not going to talk,' muttered the warders to themselves unlocking the cell door.

'Let's take a break,' said Quinn.

On the way back to the main hall Quinn handed the cadet some coins.

'Step out and buy me a packet of Players, will you?' he said with the same friendly smile.

The cadet returned from the tobacconist to be informed by the constables at the front desk that the detective was in the tea room. He sped along the corridor and found Quinn propped against the wall discussing local rugby fixtures with a group of older policemen. The cadet made his way to the front of the group and handed the packet of cigarettes to the detective who said, 'Well done, Kershaw, let's see if this helps.'

They followed the same routine. The cadet and the two warders remained close to the locked door while Quinn approached the bed. The cadet was especially curious about this prisoner, Pippa Howland. Her good looks and fashionable clothes had attracted considerable attention from the reporters covering the Water Spy trials. "Debutante in the Witness Box" had been one of the headlines. This was the cadet's first encounter with a representative of high society and he was uncertain of what to expect but the young lady sitting dejectedly handcuffed to a prison bed with her hair tangled in knots looked a far cry from the smart world of Harrods and Bond Street in London. Nights on the Ulster hills had obviously taken their toll.

To the cadet's astonishment Quinn said to her, 'We shan't be needing a statement. The other two have talked.'

The debutante's reply was equally astonishing. 'Typical of them. Got a cigarette?'

The cadet watched Quinn open the packet of Players.

'Don't you want my side of the story?' said the debutante reaching with her free hand to take a cigarette from the packet.

'It won't be necessary, thank you, we've got all the information we need,' said Quinn lighting her cigarette with a match.

'It was slightly different for me, you see,' said the debutante blowing smoke at the whitewashed ceiling. 'They told you that, didn't they?'

'They explained your involvement,' lied Quinn.

'I think you'd better hear it from me too, don't you?'

'If you insist,' said Quinn. 'Kindly remember that everything you say will be written down and may be used in evidence against you.'

The detective turned to check that the cadet was ready with his notebook.

'Go ahead,' said Quinn to the prisoner.

'Well,' said the debutante.

She had met Megan at Cambridge and become friends, real friends.

They had studied the same subjects, gone out together and Megan always paid which was very convenient because Pippa was always broke. Megan's name was not Leigh-Harvey and her father was an IRA commander not a missionary vicar in Africa. Pippa learned that at a party when they were working on the Lee Navigation Canal, when Megan said they could both get rich helping German prisoners of war to escape, which sounded like a lark and was actually tremendous fun until everything went wrong.

It was very sad about April, and terrible having to go into the witness box and speak all those lies. Megan's father said they needed to get out of the country after the trial but the ports for Dublin and Ireland were all under surveillance so they took the Belfast ferry, hid for a few days then encountered an army patrol near the border. The final indignity was Megan's father lying on top of her simulating sexual intercourse in a hay loft.

Afterwards, outside the cell, Quinn read through the statement signed by Pippa Howland and clapped the cadet on the back.

'Well done, Kershaw,' he said with a broad grin. 'That should get Miss April Tree out tonight.'

Stoke Mandeville Hospital

Wearing uniform for the first time in weeks, Lindsey descended the steps slowly, one at a time, unaided except for his walking stick which reduced the pressure on his right knee. His progress was watched by the hospital staff assembled on the driveway below.

'I'm sorry for misbehaving so badly,' he said shaking hands with the matron, 'I'm afraid I got carried away.'

'We all understand,' beamed the matron.

'Thank you for mending my knee, Mr Jameson,' he said shaking hands with the surgeon.

'Continue with those exercises and you can throw that stick away soon,' said the surgeon.

'I can't wait,' grinned Lindsey.

He shook hands with the nurses including Nurse Goodrow who had occupied the telephone the morning Lindsey solved the puzzle of the callsigns. She apologised again and said how sorry she was to have delayed the call that turned out to be so important. In future every time she saw a nice piece of cod she would think of the sub-lieutenant, she said.

Finally Nurse Trims.

'I don't know how to thank you, Trims,' he said hugging her.

'Thank me by finding that girl of yours,' she said.

'She's forgotten me by now, I expect. Reserved for senior officers only, that's what they used to say on the canal. Anyway, it will be your turn soon, Trims. You deserve a thoroughly handsome prince.'

With a lump in her throat Nurse Trims waved at the departing Daimler then returned to the private wards where she was uncharacteristically short-tempererd with a Household Cavalry officer who complained of an uncomfortable mattress.

'Northward to Small Heath first, if you please,' said Lindsey to the chauffeur.

'That'll be the top of the Grand Union Canal, Master Edward?' said the chauffeur.

'Just so,' said Lindsey settling himself into the back of the Daimler extending his right leg comfortably along the seat. No more hospital food, he thought thankfully gazing out at the gardens and houses as the car drove through the outskirts of Aylesbury to open country with fields and trees. No more boiled chicken, no more rice pudding. Now then, concentrate. What was he going to say to April? What was the correct way of greeting someone newly released from prison, saved in the nick of time from the gallows? There would be tears, inevitably. Maybe not, perhaps she would see him from a distance and, like Hollywood films, run towards him in slow motion and leap into his arms. In which case, he could dispense with introductory greetings. Hang on, why would she leap into his arms? So far they had barely touched each other, except at that miserable dance in Weedon Barracks. They would probably end up shaking hands, he decided dozing off in the luxurious leather seat.

'Camp Hill Locks, Master Edward.'

Lindsey opened his eyes.

The canal was full of barges loaded with coal, timber, scrap iron and gravel jostling for position at the entrance to the upper lock. Ducks bobbed in the open water and the familiar smell of diesel fumes from ancient marine engines hung in the air as Lindsey climbed out of the limousine and walked slowly towards the first of the boatyards.

The foreman pointed further up the canal.

Lindsey continued along the towpath to the gates of Donaldson's Canal Haulage Ltd where the presence of a tall naval officer leaning on a walking stick resulted in the prompt appearance of no less a person than Mr Donaldson himself, panting and mopping his brow.

'Harold Tree? What a pity, I fear you've missed him. That's his barge over there - he sold it just a few days ago. No, I'm afraid I don't know where he's gone. Very angry, he was, about what happened to his daughter. She was imprisoned, you know, you may have heard . . .'

The Admiralty, London

Rear Admiral Haldenby looked up from the table where he had been admiring the arrangement of pink hydrangeas and white roses and beckoned the lieutenant hovering at the door into his oak-panelled office.

'Yes?'

'Assistant naval attaché, British Embassy, Washington, sir,' said the lieutenant.

'What about him?' said the captain.

'The appointment remains vacant, sir.'

'Well?'

'Lindsey, sir. I know you raised objections earlier, but he has rather redeemed himself.'

'In what way?'

'I thought you knew, sir. He figured out the flaws in the case against the Water Spies and initiated the hunt that led to the capture of the ringleader.'

The rear admiral walked to the window. Hands clasped behind his back he looked out over St James's Park where the leaves on the trees were beginning to change colour.

'It will be autumn soon,' said the rear admiral.

'Yes, sir,' said the lieutenant.

'You know what happens in autumn?'

'Leaves fall off, sir,' said the lieutenant.

'I meant, in this department.'

'No more flowers for your table, sir.'

'Wrong. Increase in requests for warm weather postings.'

'Like Washington, sir.'

'Washington isn't a warm weather posting.'

'No, but there's a vacancy there now, sir.'

The lieutenant waited, wondering if he had overplayed his hand.

'Oh, very well,' said the rear admiral to the window. 'Tell Lindsey to pack his trunk and be pleasant to the Americans.'

PART 4 CONCLUSION

Delphinium Cottage

High on the list of wartime inconveniences was the shortage of Bombay Duck. Fortnum & Mason had run out early in the conflict. The pungent delicacy, which originated not from poultry farms or village ponds as the name suggested but from fermented and dried lizard fish, the smell of which revolted the unwary but represented to those who had served in India an irreplaceable accompaniment to hot curry dishes. As a substitute Alice Macleod bought offcuts of salted fish and dried them in the salmon-smoking device her husband had purchased on their return to England which currently sat idle in the potting shed awaiting the end of hostilities and re-commencement of invitations to fish in the River Spey. The results of her experiment had brought praise from her husband who declared that the substitute, although not entirely of the same flaky consistency as the original, was nevertheless an admirable alternative and Alice as usual had blushed with pleasure at the compliment.

Curry in the Macleod's repatriated household was served at Sunday lunch, with sherry or chilled beer depending on the season. Before leaving India, Alice had studied the recipes for the principal curry dishes and practised them extensively with her native cook. On the menu for lunch today, after an expensive visit to the local butcher yesterday, was her husband's favourite, Chicken Madras.

Through the kitchen window as she stirred the red and yellow spices into hot oil she watched her husband collecting apples from the orchard. He was wearing his panama hat and she felt a shiver of excitement to observe that the hat was tilted over his eyes at a jaunty angle. There had been a noticeable improvement in his demeanour recently. Pressure of work at the barracks and all those exhausting visits to London had taken their toll during the summer months but now, when the leaves were beginning to change colour, he was so much better and, thank heavens, those awful telephone calls had stopped.

'First class,' pronounced her husband savouring the first mouthful of hot chicken curry. 'Oh, my goodness . . '

He stood up from the table and hurried to the door. A few moments later Alice spied him in the garden bent over the stream which burbled through the grass at the foot of the orchard.

'I completely forgot,' he said returning to the dining room holding a bottle of white wine. 'Graves Sec 1938, nicely chilled.'

'What a pleasant surprise, dear!' said Alice.

'We have something to celebrate,' he said inserting the corkscrew.

'My!' exclaimed Alice at the sound of the cork popping from the bottle. 'It's just like Christmas!'

'Several things, actually.'

The worst part of the whole operation, he explained during lunch, had been the need to withhold from Alice the reason for his curious behaviour during the summer - the trail of empty cheque books, the letters from his bank, overnight absences, secretive telephone calls and intermittent heavy drinking. But he was being watched and couldn't risk telling Alice that he was working under cover for military intelligence in case something slipped out or, worse, that she herself became a target. His work had taken him into contact with an extremely unpleasant and dangerous individual who knew the address of the cottage and could have threatened Alice if anything went wrong. Fortunately the operation had been successful and a significant group of spies and traitors - including the disagreeable character whose phone calls had so obviously and regrettably been a source of concern to Alice - had been tracked down and convicted.

'Now that the dust has settled, Alice, I'm pleased to tell you that your husband has been promoted to colonel.'

Alice dropped her fork in astonishment.

'I am being given command of Weedon Barracks in its entirety. Which means we can remain here at Delphinium Cottage. It also means that, as result of recent accumulations of back pay and my new salary grade, we can afford to buy the cottage. Which in turn means . . .'

Major Macleod paused, stood up and hurried to the other end of the table where tears had begun to roll down the face of his beloved wife. Placing his arms fondly around her shoulders he told her again how sorry he was about causing so much distress during the summer.

'It's not that, it's just that . . . . . I'm so happy,' sobbed Alice Macleod.

Bletchley Park

The head of the signals intelligence and traffic analysis section at Bletchley Park summoned the section communications analyst to his office.

'About your work, Rupert,' he said.

'Deep down, I don't think I'm ready for promotion, if that's what you're getting at,' said the communications analyst easing himself into a chair.

'Not quite.'

'Challenges of a different type then?'

'You could put it like that. The point is, Rupert, when we took you on, we were hoping for something rather more in the way of results from your desk.'

'Don't blame yourself. Nobody's perfect.'

'Apart the record-breaking number of hangovers, Rupert, it is actually quite difficult to identify any results at all.'

'The work's not been easy, you know.'

'Although of course you did manage to identify Central Africa as a possible source of the Mayfair radio transmissions.'

'I was slightly out there, I grant you.'

'And nearly got someone hanged.'

'Oh that. Well, we all make mistakes.'

'It's just that we'd prefer the mistakes to be made somewhere else now, Rupert,' said the section head passing a rail voucher across the desk. 'It's for this afternoon.'

The communications analyst examined the voucher.

'Back to Cambridge?' he said.

'Thank you so much for your time with us, Rupert,' said the section head rising.

The communications analyst eased himself out of the chair and shook the section head's hand.

'Right, well, cheerio then.'

'Goodbye, Rupert.'

Brigadier Smythe's Residence

The brigadier's wife remembered Quinn from his previous visit and escorted him to the orchard accompanied by her six year old granddaughter who skipped past the croquet lawn and tennis court and disappeared through the gate to the paddock to talk to her pony.

'We had a houseful of guests at the time of your last visit, I recall. How fortunate we were with the weather this summer. Entertaining is so much easier when you can get people outside. Rainy days are a trial, the men drink too much and the wives squabble at the card table. Here we are. Oh dear, that ladder looks so unsafe. Henry, darling, Inspector Quinn is here to see you. Excuse me, inspector, I'd better rescue that poor pony from Sophie,' said Mrs Smythe departing in the direction of the paddock.

'Come on, there's more along that branch!' Brigadier Smythe was bellowing up at his batman perched precariously in a tree reaching out for apples and dropping them into the brigadier's open hands.

'First class catching practice, Quinn,' said the brigadier. 'Do you play cricket?'

'I'm afraid not, sir,' said Quinn watching the batman claw himself back to a safe position near the ladder.

'Never mind. It's not always a prerequisite for eminence,' said the brigadier doubtfully. 'I say, have you been promoted?'

'Yes, sir,'

'Congratulations, Quinn. Richly deserved.'

'Thank you, sir. I've called to say how much I appreciate your help in arranging military assistance in Ulster. It made all the difference, sir.'

'Not a bit. I was glad to help. You did very well on the case.'

'It aged me a bit, sir,' smiled Quinn.

'What was that Irishman doing, pretending to be a deckhand?' asked the brigadier picking up a basket of apples from the ground and setting off with Quinn back towards the house where Quinn's gleaming new Morris motor car, which came with the rank of detective inspector, was parked.

'The Germans paid the IRA for every prisoner returned to Germany along that route, sir. He wanted to make sure the trawler finished the job properly so that they could claim the money.'

'A high price in the end,' said the brigadier.

'It certainly was, sir. He went to the gallows yesterday, with his daughter.'

'I remember her. Megan, wasn't it? She took quite a shine to me, you know. You can always tell. What happened to the other girl?'

'Pippa Howland, sir. She got twenty years.'

The two men shook hands and Quinn climbed into the car.

'Oh lord, I've left Barker up the tree,' said the brigadier waving Quinn goodbye. 'I suppose I'd better go and get him down.'

Transit to Weedon Bec

A cold wind was blowing from the sea as Chief Petty Officer Jones boarded a train at Plymouth dockyard station. He wore a muffler and navy blue raincoat over his uniform, and carried a duffle bag with his shaving kit and a change of clothes. Tucked into his jacket was a railway warrant for Weedon Bec and a leave pass.

He found a window seat in a third class carriage which gradually filled with able seamen and stokers who would have preferred not to have shared their journey with a CPO but it was better than squatting in the drafty passage outside and anyway the CPO didn't look too bad, staring dreamily out of the window. Going home to see his wife and kids, they assumed talking quietly amongst themselves smoking their navy-issue cigarettes.

The bosun changed at Taunton and three times after that. He arrived in Weedon in the early evening as the wintry sun dropped over the canal. Maggie was not waiting for him. He had arrived unannounced and uncertain of the way to proceed. After signing-in at a guest house he walked to the Market Hotel, drank a pint of bitter and, thus fortified, called her number.

'Bosun! Why didn't you tell me you were coming!'

They dined at a small table in the dining room close to the large round table in the window where during the warm summer evenings the crew of the flotilla had dined and laughed. The memory nudged gently and unobtrusively at the bosun and Mrs Meredith but they too were wrapped up in private conversation to be sidetracked by reminiscences particularly as the bosun was making an awful mess of his carefully prepared speech, stuttering and stammering to such an extent that Mrs

Meredith eventually put him out of his misery by reaching across the table and placing her hand in his and saying with shining eyes 'Of course I will. I thought you'd never ask.'

'You're not going to leave us, Maggie?' said Mr Browning anxiously next morning when Mrs Meredith arrived with the bosun to convey the news of their engagement.

'Not unless you want me to,' said Mrs Meredith demurely.

'Good heavens, no!' said Mr Browning rising from his desk to shake the bosun's hand. 'Congratulations, bosun, well done. I'm delighted.'

'Thank you, sir. I wouldn't dream of trying to take Maggie from Weedon Narrowboats, I know how much she enjoys her work here. Plymouth is no place for a woman, any roads, not these days. I shall just make it my business to travel back here as often as I can, until the war's over and I get my release.'

'Well now,' said Mr Browning. 'I've got a better idea. How would you like to work for us?'

'Work for you, sir?' said the bosun.

'We're stretched to breaking point here, with all our new contracts. Our yard manager can't cope. We've got barges arriving late, or with the wrong loads, and constantly breaking down. What we need is a fleet manager to travel the canal, trouble-shooting, sorting things out, maintaining the reputation of Weedon Narrowboats as the best operator in the region.'

'Fleet manager?' said the bosun, eyes widening.

'You'd have your own barge, of course, a small high-powered one, to get you around smartly.'

'My own barge?' said the bosun, eyes widening further.

'What do you say, bosun?'

The bosun suddenly looked downcast.

'They'll never let me out, sir, not while the war's on.'

'Oh yes, they will. What with all those minesweeper parts we're producing,' said Mr Browning pointing out of the window at the yard, 'and the transport contracts we've got, the ministry has already said we can apply for service personnel.'

'Wouldn't that be marvellous?' said Mrs Meredith clapping her hands.

'Unfortunately you wouldn't have much in the way of home life,' said Mr Browning to the bosun sitting back in his chair and examining the ceiling, 'because you'd be on the canal seven days a week, twenty-four hours a day, with no leave, except on compassionate grounds.'

'No leave?' said the bosun startled.

Mrs Meredith leaned over and said into the bosun's ear, 'I've warned you about him before, my darling. When he stares at the ceiling, he's joking.'

'Of course I'm joking,' said Mr Browning. 'You'd be your own boss, bosun. We'd be honoured at Weedon Narrowboats to have a person of your calibre and experience working for the company. What do you say?'

'I would say,' said the bosun grinning in turn at Mr Browning and his attractive warm-hearted fiancée, 'that Christmas has come early this year.'

Stoke Mandeville Hospital

Nurse Trims missed Sub-Lieutenant Lindsey very much and endured a sequence of dull replacements in his room, a Grenadier Guards officer who slept with a hairnet on his head and by day received visits from languid females who stubbed their cigarettes onto the linoleum floor, a hearty Dragoon captain with wandering hands, and a paymaster lieutenant with bullet wounds in his chest who called his mother "mumsy".

More than once she found herself absent-mindedly opening the bedside cabinet to check the level of whisky in the bottle which was no longer there, and looking out at the clump of trees in the rough grass between the two lawns where Lindsey used to sit surrounded by pieces of paper anchored to the ground by stones from the herbaceous border.

Until one morning she entered the sunlit room to find that the paymaster lieutenant had been replaced by an American air force pilot with a bruised jaw, cheerful smile and bandaged head. In a further uncanny resemblance to Lindsey his right leg was elevated in a sling.

'Good morning,' she said brightly, checking inside the sling. The plaster cast was around the patient's knee.

'My parachute dropped me into a quarry, ma'am,' explained the pilot.

'Under your tongue, please,' she said popping a thermometer into his mouth.

'The last patient with your kind of injuries kept a bottle of whisky in there,' she said indicating the bedside cabinet whilst taking his pulse.

'I'd be glad to follow his example, ma'am,' mumbled the pilot.

Nurse Trims removed the thermometer from his mouth and recorded the temperature and pulse readings on the chart at the foot of the bed.

'Do you happen to have a girlfriend awaiting execution in the Tower of London?' she said.

'Not that I can recall, ma'am,' grinned the pilot.

'Well then,' said Nurse Trims with the cutest smile the pilot had encountered either side of the Atlantic, 'I'm sure we'll get along fine.'

British Embassy. Washington

Lindsey crawled along the floor of his apartment searching for his front collar stud. He was late for the reception. His starched white collar was attached satisfactorily at the back but, as men accustomed to the formality of naval, military or civilian evening dress know to their discomfort, without that small pesky object in the buttonhole at the front one might as well abandon attempts at getting dressed and instead wrap oneself in a silk dressing gown, reach for the whisky decanter and spend the evening at home listening to gramophone records and writing notes of apology for non-appearance.

The consequences of non-appearance at the British Embassy's fabled Christmas Ball were too dreadful for Lindsey to contemplate however. As assistant naval attaché he was expected to be in the entrance hall of the embassy behind the ambassador and naval attaché ready to accompany guests into the reception rooms and introduce them to other guests with words of flattering grace.

'Dammit,' swore Lindsey giving up the search. He checked his watch. There might just be time to get to Macy's department store. He wrapped a scarf around the incomplete collar, clambered into a coat, raced to the elevator and stood outside the building in falling snow waving at taxicabs.

'I need a front collar stud, please. Half a dozen, just in case,' panted Lindsey arriving in Macy's gentlemen's clothing department.

'Of course, sir,' said the aged but immaculately-dressed assistant disappearing into the depths of the stockroom.

Lindsey anxiously examined his watch while he waited. After five minutes Lindsey spoke to the other aged assistant behind the counter.

'As a matter of fact, I'm in something of a rush.'

'Mr Finklestein will be back shortly, sir,' said the other assistant mechanically.

A few minutes later Mr Finklestein re-appeared shaking his head.

'It's never happened before, sir. It seems we're completely sold out.'

Lindsey raced down the escalator into the snow storm and took a taxicab to Gimbels department store.

'Gee, are you British?' said the sales lady behind the counter in gentlemen's clothing.

'Yes, and very late . . .' said Lindsey checking this watch.

'You look just like James Stewart.'

'Really? Well, if you could possibly . . .'

'Mary-Lou, don't you think this gentleman looks just like James Stewart?' said the sales lady to her assistant.

Racing back down the elevator holding a box of collar studs wrapped in candy-striped paper with a Rudolph the Red Nosed Reindeer gift card attached, Lindsey caught a taxicab back to his apartment, fixed his collar, completed his wardrobe, brushed his hair and protected from the snow cascading from the sky by his cap and boat cloak waited impatiently for a taxicab and arrived at the embassy an hour beyond the scheduled reception time to find the entrance hall empty and the sound of music drifting down the marble staircase from the ballroom.

Inside the ballroom his path was blocked by Polly Wertheimmer swaying slightly on account of her father having left her a considerable fortune and the largest wine cellar in America.

'Edward, where have you been?' she said taking Lindsey's arm.

'Buying collar studs.'

'My glass is empty,' said Polly.

'Then we'd better fill it.'

Lindsey stood on his toes and scanned the crowd for a steward and instead found himself staring across the ballroom at an exquisitely beautiful girl in a long white gown with a tiara on her head.

'What's the matter, Edward?' said Polly.

'Who's that?' cried Lindsey.

'I can't see.'

'Over there,' said Lindsey lifting Polly who was not very heavy.

'That's April Tree. Isn't she lovely? But it's so sad,' said Polly.

'Tell me,' said Lindsey urgently.

'All I know is she was working on munitions boats in England and there was an arrogant young naval officer with an injured leg in charge, who for some reason she fell in love with. He was absolutely beastly and ignored her, you know the type. He wouldn't even talk to her when they danced, can you imagine that! She was so hurt by his attitude that she nearly resigned. Then one day it turned out the boats were being used by German agents and April, poor girl, was accused of being involved, and the two other girls on the boats, a pair of lesbian bitches, who were the real criminals, lied at the trial and April was found guilty and sentenced to death. Just imagine . . . I'm sorry, April's story always makes me feel so desperately miserable,' said Polly starting to cry.

'Here,' said Lindsey giving Polly his handkerchief.

'Just imagine, alone in a damp cell waiting to be hanged. The horrid naval officer didn't lift a finger to help her, didn't bother to visit her or write, nobody helped, they just let her shiver alone in prison. What a swine, that man! He had a walking stick apparently, because of his leg. That's another thing, every time she tried to help him with his injury he just ignored her. In the end the only person who did anything for April was a police detective. At the last minute, when the hangman was literally preparing to place a hood over April's head . . ,' wept Polly.

'Go on, for heaven's sake!' urged Lindsey.

'Apparently the police detective realised something was wrong and, at the last minute, managed to get April released. Her father was so angry about it all he decided to leave England. To pay for his family's passage to the States he sold a manuscript passed down from his great grandfather, who'd been a violinist in Vienna, and the manuscript turned out to contain several priceless lost symphonies. So they're rich now, and live in New York where he spends his time at the Metropolitan Opera, and would you believe it,' wept Polly, 'despite everything April still loves the awful naval officer, and came here tonight because she heard a rumour he'd been posted to the embassy, and when he wasn't here she told my friend Amelia her heart was so broken she would become a nun. Edward! Where are you going, Edward?' Polly called out.

Lindsey marched blindly though the throng of dancers on the floor to the other side of the ballroom where the girl in the long white gown and tiara was standing alone staring out of the window at the snowflakes drifting down from the sky.

He paused as he approached, collecting himself. How could he explain what happened? Claiming to have been the person who saved her might sound ridiculous under the circumstances. Blurting out that he had not tried to communicate with her, or write to her in prison, to avoid raising her hopes of rescue in such an apparently hopeless situation, thereby hurting her more, would probably sound contrived. She might even slap his face. If she did, he must accept the blow without flinching.

'April?' he said gently.

She swung round, the hem of her dress swishing in a swirl of lace and silk.

'Skipper?' she said, hazel eyes opening wide.

They stared at each other.

Lindsey cleared his throat.

'For the record, I couldn't visit you in prison because I was in hospital,' said Lindsey.

Serenaded by music from the orchestra on the balcony, music which neither of them heard because of the emotions spinning in their heads, they continued to look at each other.

'Also, for the record, it wasn't just the police detective who rescued you, I was involved too,' said Lindsey.

By coincidence the orchestra was playing the same selection of Cole Porter melodies they had danced to at Weedon Barracks months ago though the fact didn't register in their brains on account of the continuation of the spinning sensations.

'Nor has there been a single moment in a single day since we first met that I haven't wanted to be near you,' said Lindsey.

April's lustrous eyes travelled down to the two gold rings on his sleeves.

'You've been promoted?'

'Yes.'

'No walking stick, your leg's healed?'

'Yes.'

'So may we dance again?'

Nestling into his arms on the dance floor April said, 'As I don't have to support your weight any more, do you mind if I do something I've always wanted to?'

'Not at all.'

April drew closer and rested her head on Lindsey's shoulder with a look of such rapturous contentment that it caught the attention of Mrs Worthington-Platt, a prominent Washington socialite who was discussing matters of inconsequence with the British naval attaché on the perimeter of the ballroom.

'I doubt me that those two will be separated this night,' observed Mrs Worthington-Platt surveying the couple wistfully.

'It's too bad of Lindsey,' said the naval attaché following Mrs Worthington-Platt's gaze. 'The ambassador is most insistent that junior officers and members of the embassy staff circulate amongst the guests and not drape themselves around the prettiest young lady at the dance.'

OTHER BOOKS BY JONATHAN DIACK

The following books by Jonathan Diack are available from Amazon and major booksellers

No Barking Please
Royal Podium
The Quince River Parchment
A Gentleman's Guide to Women, Commoners & Cooking
A Gentleman's Guide to Cooking
Peter the Perpendicular

The following screen play is scheduled for publication in December 2022

The Escape of MV 'Duchess' from La Cocina

For details of the books visit the publisher's website
www.oldenglishpress.co.uk

Printed in Great Britain
by Amazon